Fro
Past Life

Penny Faith

belongs to
hut 9

FLAME
Hodder & Stoughton

First published in Great Britain in 2000
by Hodder and Stoughton
First published in paperback in 2000
by Hodder and Stoughton
A division of Hodder Headline

A Flame Paperback

10 9 8 7 6 5 4 3 2 1

A CIP catalogue record for this title
is available from the British Library.

ISBN 0 340 72843 4

Printed and bound in Great Britain by
Mackays of Chatham plc, Chatham, Kent

Hodder and Stoughton
A division of Hodder Headline
338 Euston Road
London NW1 3BH

For Lucy
Thanks

With thanks for tireless support to Patrick Walsh, Carolyn Mays, Jane Hoodless, Jane Rogers, Harriet Grace, Jo Pestel. And with huge appreciation to Jackie Groom and Charlie.

Thanks to Penguin Publishers for permission to reprint an extract from *The Great Gatsby* by F Scott Fitzgerald, to Tro Essex Music Ltd on behalf of Bart Howard for permission to reprint a verse from *Fly me to the Moon* and to A. P. Watt Ltd on behalf of Michael and Anne Yeats to include three lines from *The Phases of the Moon.*

What love is, if thou wouldst be taught,
Thy heart must teach alone –
Two souls with but a single thought,
Two hearts that beat as one

Friedrich Halm
Der Sohn der Wildnis

And so we beat on, boats against the current, borne back ceaselessly into the past.

F Scott Fitzgerald
The Great Gatsby

PROLOGUE – APRIL 1922

A small hole in the road, badly negotiated by her taxi driver, woke Rachael by throwing her sideways against the window. The darkness she had left behind in the West End had given way to a lightening sky, against which the details of the trees were slowly coming into focus. After straightening herself out, Rachael decided to indulge herself in the beauty of her favourite time of day. She leaned forward.

'I'll get out here, thanks.'

The driver took the crumpled cigarette from his mouth and threw it out of the open window.

'You sure, Miss? It's a fair walk.'

'Yes, just here will do.'

The taxi trembled to a halt. He got out and opened the back passenger door for her.

'How much is that?' she asked, without moving.

'Ninepence, Miss.'

Rachael pulled open the cord on her beaded purse and took out a shilling. As she got out she handed the coin to the old man, placing it in his open palm. He put his hand in his pocket, letting his tired eyes revive on the perfect collar bone that peeked out from Rachael's silk chiffon wrap.

'That's all right,' she said and turned away.

'Thank you, Miss,' he said, getting back into his seat and driving off.

The car had dissolved into the early morning mist before the sound completely diminished, then all was still and quiet again.

Rachael left the pavement and let her satin slippers sink into the soft, damp grass. She knew she was ruining them. The suggestion of sunlight was teasing through the haze, creating a silver glow over the spring green leaves.

She took a deep breath and tried to expel the smoke, the brandy fumes and the irritatingly trivial facts she had absorbed during the night's revelries. She began to feel calmer.

A row of ash trees lined the walls of those houses whose gardens had direct access to the Heath; a natural boundary between private and public land. At the last tree Rachael would leave the Heath and cross to where her house stood on a bend in the road. She was walking directly into the rising sun and, with the mist distorting her vision, she didn't see the body hanging from the tree until she brushed away a leg thinking it was a low branch.

The feet, well and expensively shod, pointed down and tapped the bridge of Rachael's nose. She took a step back, not yet able to make the link between feet raised five foot above the ground and a human body dangling, dead. Her eyes were fixed on the shoes; highly polished, practically new, stiff brown leather brogues. She continued the journey up the leg; a brown and green herringbone tweed trouser and matching jacket complete with leather elbow patches that somehow seemed ill-fitting. The arms that hung down revealed stiff white cuffs, a brown leather strapped wristwatch and the unmistakable silver cufflinks, each enamelled with a robin redbreast.

'Robin?' She shouted louder and louder, repeating his name over and over for all sorts of reasons; because maybe he couldn't hear her, because maybe it wasn't him, until she finally dared to look up into the opaque, blue face of the man whose removal from her life had been her unrelenting daily prayer.

PART ONE

From the first crescent to the half

One – March 1921

The old man tries to take a breath. For some time it eludes him and he chases it around his throat as if attempting to catch a butterfly in a net. At last it is captured. There follows its painful journey down to his lungs that are so full of disease there is hardly space for the air. The breath creaks around the obstacle course, does what good it can, then groans its way out of the toothless mouth, now carrying the vile stench of its journey.

The young man runs his fingers through his blond hair, staring at himself in the piece of broken glass that sits on the worm-riddled chest of drawers. He adjusts the knot of his silk tie, pulls his cuffs down, and smiles at the dirty, cracked image.

'Let me make you comfortable, Father.'

He takes the few steps to his father's bed. He pulls up the blanket, smoothes out the sheets and flicks the eiderdown, releasing dust and feathers into the already overcrowded atmosphere.

'Shall I get you another pillow?'

The tired old man makes the slightest of nodding movements. He cannot waste his energy, he needs it for his breathing. His son takes a pillow from the pile of bedclothes he has lifted from the sofa and places it under his father's head. He then takes the sheets and blankets he had neatly folded and places them in the bottom drawer. It is a futile gesture, but every day he does it. Every day he attempts to bring a small sense of order and tidiness to the desperation of their existence.

'I'll see you later, then.' He places a kiss, though it disgusts him, on his father's head, sneaks one final look in the mirror and leaves the basement room.

The train from Southampton is not due until midday. Give the ladies another half an hour to gather their luggage, work out the taxi system, and travel the short journey to their hotel; he will be waiting in the foyer of the Waldorf from half past twelve.

That leaves two and a half hours. He runs his fingers over the side of his face. It's smooth, but is it smooth enough? Perhaps some time spent on his appearance would not be wasted. He walks briskly down Columbia Road to the small barber's shop.

The bell clangs as he opens the door.

'Good morning, Charles,' he says to the old man sharpening his razors on the strap.

Charlie gives him his habitual sneer of disapproval. 'What can I do for you?'

The young man seats himself in the second of the three chairs and grins at the blond, blue-eyed angel reflected in the mirror.

'What can I do for you "*Sir*"?'

'I'll give you "Sir",' mumbles Charlie.

'Did you say something, Charles?' he asks, staring at Charlie through the mirror, his frighteningly clear eyes challenging the old man's patience.

'Don't gimme that, will ya,' says Charlie. 'There's only you and me 'ere. 'Ow's the old fella?'

'Father was particularly unwell this morning, I'm sorry to say.'

Charlie throws his eyes to the heavens; his customer says nothing. It's bad enough having to endure the stink of Charlie as he breathes his unclean breath over him during the close shave; you don't have to put up with that in Jermyn Street.

Soon, soon.

Charlie gossips away merrily on matters that his customer has no interest in. Yet it is understood that Charlie has no particular need to inform him; it is merely how he works. Charlie is simply incapable of going about his business with his mouth shut; as is everyone in this grim part of London. The ambitious young man had early on equated silence, or at least the understanding of when to be silent, with a grace that cannot be learned: it's something you are born to; it is a sign of good breeding.

As Charlie applies hot towels, soft soaps and sharp blades to his face, he closes his eyes in an attempt to shut out the sounds, the nagging reminder of who he is and where he comes from.

Finally it is done. Coppers are handed over and he is gone, leaving Charlie in mid-sentence, halfway through the sorry story of yet one more old man who has died leaving no money to pay for his funeral.

He walks to the Aldwych. This has a twofold purpose: it saves him his bus fare and puts a healthy tinge in his cheeks. As he gets nearer to the West End his step brightens and quickens. His soul feels lighter, as does the air; this is where he belongs. He reaches the hotel with half an hour to spare, so he buys himself a newspaper and settles in the foyer to await the Americans.

It pleases him enormously that he is asked three times, by three different waiters, if he requires tea. This assures him that he does not look out of place; he looks, and feels, exactly like the sort of well-bred young man who could afford to take tea at the Waldorf Hotel. Fleetingly he thinks of the old man at home, struggling to swallow a thin brew from a tin mug. He needs to remember this in order to fire his ambition and sometimes to get him through the job he has undertaken, especially if the most willing candidates for his attentions are particularly physically unappealing.

Conjuring up the sounds of his father's painful breathing and the horror of his cough could often get him through the revulsion he feels in caressing torpid breasts. But it would always, always be worth the rewards. To begin with, it would be tips – pennies, tanners – in exchange for information on what was worth visiting in the city. Then, as he convinces them (sometimes this was the hardest part of his job) of his devotion, his pride in being in their company, only then will the expensive meals begin; ferocious flirting leading to serious seduction. Sometimes, at this point, guilt and shame will produce a cash payment that ends the arrangement. But if the woman is the right mixture of suitably grateful and unbearably lonely, then come the shopping trips. Tearful goodbyes accompany a long velvet box. Another watch.

He is well known in an alley off St Martin's Lane, where watches are exchanged for cash, which, after the rent is paid (and medication for Father bought) is then turned into clothing, or a good hat, or an expensive pair of shoes; whatever will ensure that he looks the complete gentleman.

A burst of activity at the hotel entrance signals him to put down his newspaper and go to work.

The first woman to approach the reception desk is not even worth considering. He knows instantly by her posture that she is not the type to fall for his charms. Besides, she is followed, several steps behind, by the dreaded spinster niece. The companion. No. These ladies have their slaves; they don't need a young man to do things for them.

Two rather silly women come in next. Their hats are large and cheap, their lipsticks too red and their luggage too plentiful. These women want a good time. His preferred choice is for a woman who doesn't realise that is what she is after.

Another taxi drops off a young couple: honeymooners. He looks the girl over. She spots him staring at her and blushes, hiding her head behind her husband's shoulder. The wicked young man puts on his best grin and notes her as a possible, should all else fail.

But then she arrives. Perfect in every way. Alone. Confident yet unsure enough. About fifty years old. Exactly the right age for a widow. Well dressed, a woman of class. A certain attractiveness yet an obvious sadness. Vulnerability. That is the key element. That's what allows him in. He watches her check in, never taking his eyes off her. She begins to move nervously. She knows she is being watched, but she has yet to look at him. The desk clerk is telling her he hopes she enjoys her stay. She could turn away from her admirer to follow the bellboy towards the lift, but she doesn't. And that's when he knows he has her. She turns towards the handsome young man and looks directly at him. He nods his head, ever so slightly, in acknowledgement and almost smiles. She puts her head down modestly, then turns and strides away from him.

As she disappears, he relaxes. He can wait another hour or so. She knows he'll be there. This is good. He loves it when it is this easy. He orders some tea, safe in the knowledge that the woman will appear in time to pay for it, and settles back in his chair.

Two

'Distracted as usual, I see.'

Rachel untwined her fingers from the pearl rope, letting it drop into her lap where it coiled like a snake retreating from danger. She looked up.

'I didn't hear you come in.' She extended her neck, offering her mouth, her cheek, a choice of places for Brendan to place his returning kiss. He chose the top of her head.

'How are you two?' he asked, placing his large hand on the hillock of her stomach.

'Good,' she smiled.

'You been buying again?'

'It's only an old necklace.'

'This time.'

'I found it in the junk shop. I looked in to see if they still had that chair.'

'And did they?' Brendan's voice called, closely followed by the sound of the gentle pop of a cork being released from a bottle of South African Merlot.

'They sold it two weeks ago.'

Brendan returned and dropped himself into the leather armchair, displacing several photocopied sheets of paper as he did so. Rachel rushed over.

'Hang on,' she said, kneeling down and feeling around underneath him in case any had got trapped.

'While you're down there—' he said.

Rachel stood up abruptly.

'Come on love,' said Brendan. He stretched out his arm and gently touched her elbow. 'It was only a joke.'

'Are you sure it wasn't a criticism?' Not waiting for a reply, Rachel busied herself sorting the papers.

'Let's pull in the reins before this gets out of proportion.' Brendan overfilled one of the wineglasses and, slopping it, handed it to Rachel. 'Sit down,' he ordered, 'and drink this.'

'Not while I'm working, thanks.'

'Well, fuck you.' Brendan emptied a glass in one then stomped his big feet up the stairs, banging doors and cupboards, turning on the bath and singing loudly.

Rachel returned to her desk. The printer had stopped its spluttering and she pulled out the collection of papers, collated them in numerical order, punched holes in them and, opening the file marked 'Karma', placed them on top of the already well stacked pile. She signed off from the Net, shut down the computer then collapsed into the chair recently vacated by Brendan, surprised that his brief stay in it had left such a warm impression. She sank into the uncomfortable reminder of his presence and closed her eyes, thinking about her husband.

Brendan.

Brendan was huge. He was tall; he was large. He took up so much space. Not just the physical space his presence required, but the sheer mass of his soul overshadowed all those around him. She curled herself up in the chair, making a small space for herself and drifted into a dreamless sleep.

When she opened her eyes the day had almost gone. Light from the kitchen shone a corridor of warmth across the twilight. She could hear the sound of sizzling, and the smell of ginger and garlic threatened to overpower the incense that burned from a small cone on the mantelpiece. Rachel smiled and got up.

'I'm sorry,' she said, placing her arms around the waist of the chef and leaning her head between his shoulder blades. 'Why do you put up with me?'

'Now there's a leading question. I'm not sure we should have that conversation right now.' Brendan shook her off and opened the cutlery drawer. 'Lay the table,' he said, 'there's a good wife.'

Rachel took two pairs of wooden chopsticks and placed them opposite each other at the kitchen table. Without looking at him she said, 'It's just that—'

'Cut the hormone crap. I've been here before, remember?'

Jonno.

Always Jonno.

'He rang.'

'Mm?' Brendan placed two stir-fry laden, heavy Moroccan pottery bowls on the table and sat down.

'Jonno. He's got an important interview. A new job.'

Brendan grimaced. 'Can just imagine.'

Rachel looked down, picked up her chopsticks, played with them, mixing her food. 'It sounds interesting. A brand new clinic. Opportunities for research.'

Brendan puffed irritation. 'He won't find any answers there.'

Rachel's ungracious thoughts accused Brendan of so successfully avoiding the questions that his son was forced to look for answers in extraordinary places.

'I wish you wouldn't—' started Rachel, but a butterfly flitted across her womb. 'Oh my God,' she said, a stack of noodle and beansprout showering onto her lap. 'He kicked.'

'Are you sure?' Brendan asked, his chopsticks frozen midway between bowl and mouth.

'I don't know,' she giggled. 'How do I know? It hasn't happened before. But that must have been it. There it is again. He's all right. Oh, thank God.'

A hot tear of relief dropped onto a sugar snap pea releasing a miniature geyser of steam. Brendan reached across the table and held tightly onto her hand.

'Of course he's all right.' Then a change in his tone because he knew his wife. 'Why would you think he wouldn't be?'

Rachel looked up at him, smiled as convincingly as she could. 'I'm going to have a baby. Of course I'm going to worry about whether he's all right.'

'Just normal healthy maternal concern?'

Rachel blinked back another tear. 'Yes,' she said.

But she couldn't be sure.

Three

'There's one theory that there aren't enough souls to go around, so they have to be shared out.' Rachel attempted to retrieve the cake slice from the slab of chocolate brownie. The side of the knife was spread with the sticky topping, so she slid it across the side of the plate and handed Brendan the mess.

The next slice came out cleaner.

'Well I hope they're doled out more efficiently than chocolate fudge brownie cake,' said Brendan. 'Or is there some significance in my mountain of crumbs and your neat slice?'

Rachel hiccuped a small laugh. 'Some of us have whole souls—'

'Are we the better people then?'

'And some of us have fractions of souls. Some think that in searching for life partners we search out the fraction that will make our soul whole.'

'And what do you think? What have your intense researches into the subject taught you?'

'I don't go with that theory at all.'

Brendan looked at her with what Rachel interpreted as a renewed curiosity.

'You surprise me.'

'Do I? Why's that?'

'I would have thought that was just the sort of theory that appealed to your romantic idealism.'

'It's to do with what you said before, the notion that a whole soul implies a better life. That's why I don't like the expression "lost soul", as if the dysfunctional portion of society were made up from the fragments. I prefer to believe that it's just in a different phase. All souls, all of us, will eventually have been all things; poets and beggars.'

'I stand corrected. You have replaced one romantic idealist notion with another that manages to surpass it.'

Brendan beamed with what Rachel hoped was a kind of pride. She hadn't seen too much of that lately and was grateful for it in a way that seconds later made her feel angry. This should be built in, not hankered after. 'Scratching for crumbs again,' she told herself.

'You're in a jolly mood today. It's nice,' she added quickly for fear of sounding patronising.

'Why wouldn't I be?' boomed the bearded giant she had married. 'I've got a beautiful, intelligent, successful wife who's going to give birth to a beautiful, intelligent boy; a comfortable home; rewarding work and—'

'And?'

Brendan gently nodded his head.

'You got the grant?'

'Yup. Josh called today. My beauty goes on a small tour of Northern Ireland's galleries starting in November.'

Rachel got up and hugged Brendan from behind, spitting kisses into his thick, long, greying hair.

'This is fantastic. Why didn't you tell me before?'

'I only heard late this afternoon. I didn't want to tell you on the phone. I wouldn't have got this response.' He hooked his arm round Rachel's waist and pulled her onto his lap. And Rachel sank her face into the softness of his beard.

She broke away suddenly.

'November?'

'Yes.'

'And you'll have to be there?'

'Of course.'

'But the baby?'

'Hey, there are thirty days in November. That's thirty to one odds on the opening being the day the baby is born. Let's not worry about that now. If the worst comes to the worst, the baby is born in Belfast. Like Father like Son. That wouldn't be too awful, would it?'

'No, no I suppose not. I really am thrilled. I know how much this means to you.'

She leant against him, but in doing so knocked his plate of uneaten cake onto the floor, smashing it and carpeting the slate tiles with crumbs, like a million chocolate souls being released into the universe. Rachel's contemplation of the sight at her feet was interrupted by the piercing of the doorbell.

Brendan eased her off.

'I'll get it. You clear up.'

Rachel waited to hear the voice of their visitor before setting on her task, but when she recognised it she wearily tore off some kitchen towel and knelt down to collect the crumbs.

A pair of purple, eight-eye DMs squashed and spread chocolate around the kitchen floor. Rachel addressed the boots.

'Leah! Sit down for God's sake. You're making it worse.'

Leah dropped onto a chair with a thud, her kilim rucksack landing next to her boots.

'And move the bag, can't you?'

The bag was lifted.

'Guess I'm in the way then,' Leah said to Rachel's face as it rose from beneath the table.

'No more than usual.'

'And I'm happy to see you too.'

'Have you eaten?' Brendan asked.

'Has she ever?' snapped back Rachel.

'I don't want to put you to any trouble.'

'Ha!'

Brendan glared at Rachel.

'It's good to see you, Leah,' he said, sitting down opposite her at the table. 'So how are you?'

'Do you mean "How am I" or do you mean "How *am* I"? If you mean "How am I", I'm hungry, strapped for cash and could do with your spare bed for a couple of days. If you mean "How *am* I", I've been clean for four weeks.'

Rachel looked at Brendan, who refused to return the compliment.

'That's great news. Well done. We're proud of you, aren't we Rachel?'

Rachel looked at her little sister; the pale face, sunken cheeks, over-kohled eyes; the matted hair ('dreads' she insisted on calling them), wrong-coloured lips and something new, a small silver ring through her left eyebrow and Rachel was torn between pity and concern, jealousy and resentment, irritation and care. But Leah always made her feel like this. It wasn't her she'd come to see anyway, it was Brendan; Brendan who never had a bad word to say to her. Leah had told him that in one of her group therapy sessions in one of her rehab centres, they had done an exercise on 'Unconditional Positive Regard'. No one else had been able to think of a single instance of it in their entire lives, and she had thought of him because he'd never interfered, never judged her, never asked why. But, as Rachel knew, this was just his way and could as easily be interpreted as disinterest.

Rachel went to the fridge and took out butter, humus, salad, cold chicken and placed it with half a ciabatta in front of Leah, who barely noticed she was so busy making Brendan roar with laughter over some anecdote involving a dog, a *Big Issue* seller and a woman in a fur coat. She decided to leave them to it.

Upstairs in the quietude of their bedroom Rachel lay on the faded eiderdown, placing a lace cushion under her head, and reached over to take one of the half-dozen crystals that decorated a small dish on the bedside table; rose quartz for clear thinking. She placed the smooth-edged, warped pyramid on her forehead, closed her eyes and breathed deeply. The blue light came quickly and she enlarged and reduced it in time to her breathing.

The face came again to her; the silvery blueness, the swollen eyes, the pendant tongue.

'Stay with it,' she told herself.

But it went, swept away by a small red feather.

Leah fell into the room.

'How are you feeling?' She threw herself onto the bed. The lights switched off, Rachel sat up.

'Yes, well, most of the time.'

'No more horrid sickness?'

'I never had that much.'

'You're lucky,' Leah said quietly but loudly enough for Rachel.

'Leah?'

Leah kept her head down and continued to play with two yellow and orange beads that prevented one of her dreads from coming unlocked.

'Leah, what are you telling me?'

Leah sat up.

'That being sick all the time is really horrible and not just if you're pregnant.'

Rachel moved closer to Leah and put an arm around her shoulder. Leah didn't respond.

'You've done really well and of course you can stay, for as long as you like.'

Leah moved away.

'You know that won't work. I literally only need a few days. I'm waiting for this guy I met in India to get back. He's got his own house in Balham, he said if I needed a room—' She looked down again. 'Of course, I know people are always saying that. Thing is, it may happen, it may not. Is that all right?'

'I appreciate your honesty. Of course it's all right. Why don't we go and see Mum and Dad for a few days? It would do us both good to get out of London.'

'With or without Brendan?'

'Without,' answered a yawning voice from somewhere outside the room.

'Then I don't want to go,' said Leah.

Rachel got off the bed. 'Whatever you want to do; it was only a suggestion. I'll go and make the bed up.'

'It's done,' said Brendan, striking the pose of a magician's assistant in the doorway. 'Do you want a bath?'

'I'd love one, thanks.' Leah skipped out of the room, placing a kiss on Brendan's chest as she did so. 'Night!'

Once the bathroom door was locked and the silence was filled with the sound of running water, Brendan said, 'If she's going to stay here, you're going to have to do something about that face.'

'What face?' asked Rachel.

'The put-upon, weary, responsible, "banging-my-head-against-a-brick-wall", older sister face you wear whenever she's around. She's doing OK; she doesn't need you to be responsible for her, so let it go, will you?' He was standing in front of her and lifted her chin with his middle finger. 'Will you?' he repeated, his grey eyes sending pleading lasers into her resistant green ones.

Rachel started to get undressed. 'Old habits blah blah . . . Actually, I've got such a lot on, I can't see me devoting too much time to her anyway.'

Brendan gave her his 'I-don't-believe-a-word-of-it' look.

'Believe what you want. It will be what it will be and then she'll go, like she always does. It's no big deal.' Rachel put away her clothes and climbed into bed, turned on the bedside lamp and reached for her reading glasses, notebook, pencil and paperback.

Brendan moved over to read the cover.

'*Life After Death and How Theosophy Unveils It.* And how does it?'

'I'll let you know,' Rachel answered, absorbing herself in the pages.

'It will—' Brendan started then changed his mind, letting the unfinished statement hang around in the air like exhaled cigarette smoke. He turned off the main light and left the room.

'Goodnight,' Rachel said to the empty space.

Four

Up until now Rachel had been unable to determine the sex of the face. It had only been in close up. But now the camera pulled back a bit and Rachel could see it was a young man, blond fringe flopping over the bulging blue eyes. Behind him there was light and mist and a vague greenery.

She was pleased with the progress. She had been beginning to worry that she would lose it; it had taken this long to reveal itself. Usually communication was established within two or three visions. And then there were those wonderful occasions when someone would come to her and immediately state their business. This didn't happen frequently enough for Rachel to consider using her gift to help others, even though she had often been pressed to.

She didn't want to live like Louise, who seemed constantly distracted by the voices in her head. Lovely Aunt Louise, who had recognised Rachel's gift when she was a child and had helped her learn not to be afraid of it. But Rachel needed to live amongst the living, although she loved the idea of Louise's world where those 'in spirit' lived comfortably with those 'on earth' and there was no difference between the two.

Rachel was acutely aware of both the limitations of her psychic abilities and the potential of her enquiring intelligence, and had managed to convince a publisher than an encyclopaedic history of spiritualism would fill a gap on the shelves between hand-bound expensive tomes containing pages and pages of painfully transcribed messages from the spirit world and the plethora of cheap paperbacks on Near Death Experiences that spilled out from the Mysticism sections onto the Self-Help Popular Psychology shelf. It also allowed her to fill the time in her extended sabbatical that was intended to cover the final part of her pregnancy and her first six months of motherhood. Due to the extremely short academic teaching year this, in reality, gave her a year out of work.

Rachel was getting nothing more from her vision. She must let him come to her now. Nor must she deviate from her daily routine; slipping into meditation just to check if he were there, in the way she was tempted by the Internet to check on her e-mails when she should be writing. She closed down as she had been taught to do, drank the glass of water on the bedside table and left the bedroom.

Leah was in her room with the door closed. Rachel smarted at how quickly the spare bedroom had become known as 'Leah's Room'. So far there were no signs of her vacating it. The phone rang and Rachel ran downstairs to get to it before the answer-phone.

'Hello. It's me.'

There was only one 'me'.

'Hi, Mum. How are you?'

'Oh, you know. You are still coming on Sunday, aren't you?'

'Of course.'

'Are you bringing Louise?'

Rachel sighed. 'You know we are.'

There was a pause in which Rachel knew her mother was deciding how to bring up the subject of Leah.

She settled on, 'How's your sister?'

Rachel laughed. 'Fine. You'll see her on Sunday.'

'So she is coming, then?'

'Yes. She's in if you want to speak to her. I'll get her.'

Her mother whispered a couple of ums and ers.

Rachel knew she was being unfair. Her mother had great difficulty with what she called 'Leah's problem'. Her father coped better; but he understood the responsibility he was carrying. He believed that his experience at the hands of his childhood persecutors was so potent, it had manifested into a gene that he had passed down to his daughter. The effects were reaching into the next generation and this was the way the world would never forget.

But it was Leah's antisocial response that both differentiated her from her father and provided the glue for their inseparable bond. Rachel and her mother felt varying degrees of exclusion from their relationship; Rachel less so for she could see how much Aza and Leah needed each other.

'Well, your father will be pleased to see her.'

'Mum! What about you?'

Her mother changed the subject. 'How's the book coming along?'

'Very well, thanks. It's a fascinating topic. I may have to persuade the publishers to run to several volumes.'

Her mother laughed nervously. 'Yes, well you know my views on it. Are you seeing Louise at all?'

Rachel knew this was her mother's way of both keeping track of her sister's movements and providing her with ammunition to attack Louise's lifestyle; Rachel and Louise accompanied each other to Spiritualist Meetings.

'I'm seeing her tomorrow.' Rachel could hear the lips tightening. 'All right then, we'll see you Sunday; about one.'

'Bye dear.'

'Mum, before you go. It went completely out of my mind. I asked Jonno to come. Hope that's all right.'

There was a short pause. Just long enough for Ella to register the level of her objection. 'Lovely dear. See you Sunday.'

The line went dead.

Rachel growled into the phone and replaced it.

The timer on the oven rang. She went to the kitchen to turn it off and poured herself another glass of water. She had set it ten minutes early in case, as had been proved, Brendan was not yet here to take her to the hospital.

She rang Brendan on his mobile. The soundtrack of roaring furnaces behind his 'hello' told her that he was still at the workshop. The usual apologies and excuses followed. They decided Rachel should get a taxi and he would meet her there. Suddenly her heart was not in it. She lost interest. But this was a protection against the anger she was really feeling; the abandonment and rejection that said to her that Brendan just simply did not care enough to watch the clock, leave enough time to finish what he was doing and come to her, be with her, look after her.

She dialled the number of the local cab company.

Five

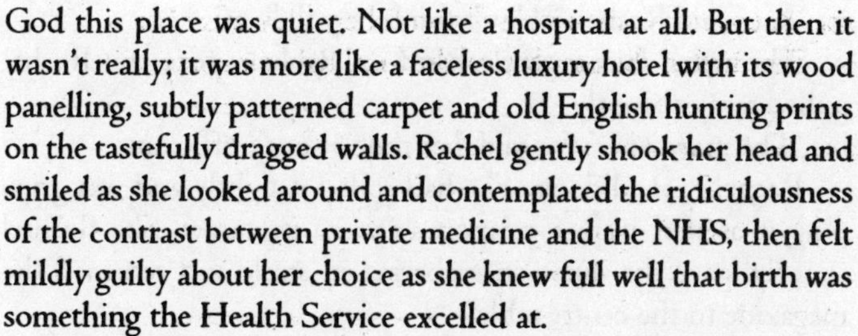

God this place was quiet. Not like a hospital at all. But then it wasn't really; it was more like a faceless luxury hotel with its wood panelling, subtly patterned carpet and old English hunting prints on the tastefully dragged walls. Rachel gently shook her head and smiled as she looked around and contemplated the ridiculousness of the contrast between private medicine and the NHS, then felt mildly guilty about her choice as she knew full well that birth was something the Health Service excelled at.

But relaxing to the albeit contrived sound of softly piped classical music, she could only be glad of her decision to put her publisher's advance towards her own comfort and her attempt to cushion herself against her fear.

She picked up a magazine; she shouldn't have been surprised that it was the latest edition – this was part of what she was paying for. Only half concentrating, she flicked through the glaring colour photographs of would-be celebrities smiling through their pain having overcome disappointments, personal tragedies or just plain public neglect, while the other half of her mind wrestled with Brendan's lateness.

'Mrs Treacy?'

Rachel looked up from the luxurious delights of a blonde's blonde living room.

'Yes,' she replied.

'You can come through now.'

Rachel looked around her, then at her watch, checked it against the wall clock and sighed. 'I was hoping my husband would be here.'

The nurse smiled sympathetically as if she had heard it all before and stood defiantly holding the door open. Rachel reluctantly rose from her chair and slowly passed in front of the nurse. Evidently they were running to a tight schedule, even though Rachel was the only one in the waiting room, and would not entertain the idea of delaying the procedure.

Rachel took one last glance behind her into the empty space.

'I expect he'll be here any minute,' the nurse said softly.

'No,' said Rachel. 'I don't think he will.'

The nurse laid a gentle hand on Rachel's forearm; Rachel pulled away abruptly.

'The magazine?' she said, her tone at once officious.

Rachel looked down. She had rolled it tightly and was gripping it as if it were a weapon awaiting its target. She flushed slightly, gave the nurse an embarrassed smile and returned the magazine to the centre table.

'Is your bladder full?' Rachel was asked as she was shown into a small cubicle.

'Yes, I think so.'

'Is it uncomfortable?'

'Yes.'

'Good. That's how we know whether it's full enough. Pop your things on the bench and put on the gown. Then I'll come and get you.'

Rachel was left alone in the changing room. As she removed her linen dress, she took several deep breaths and tried to calm the anger she was feeling towards Brendan. The most she could hope for was to soothe it into a disappointment that wouldn't use up so much energy.

As she stepped out into the corridor, a large dark figure propelled itself at her, black raincoat swishing around, dirty boots resounding even against the carpet.

'I'm not—?'

'No,' she said. 'But only just. Don't offer me any explanations, I'm not interested.'

The nurse appeared through double swing doors. She stepped back slightly at the sight of the panting, sweating, bearded man.

'You made it! I am glad. Follow me.'

Brendan enquired of Rachel with his eyes. She smiled smugly in response.

The room they were taken into was huge and dark. A second nurse in a deep blue dress greeted them.

'Is your bladder full?' she asked as Rachel climbed onto the bed.

Rachel laughed. 'Yes. Full and uncomfortable.'

The blue dress fiddled about with blankets, arranging and rearranging them around Rachel's exposed stomach. Brendan hovered in the large space between Rachel and the wall.

The door opened.

'Mr Treacy, Mrs Treacy, how nice to see you both again.'

A small pin-striped suit held its hand out to Brendan, who shook it lamely. It then leant over Rachel on the bed.

'Now how have you been keeping? Well, I hope. Good, good,' it said before Rachel could reply. 'Any problems at all; pains, cramps, fever, headaches, sickness, shortness of breath, anything like that?'

'Er – no. No. I've been fine. Really well actually.'

'That's splendid,' it replied without looking at her. 'This is going to feel cold. Thank you nurse.' The suit stepped back to allow the blue dress through, who smeared icy gel over Rachel's abdomen. Brendan and Rachel shared a small laugh, which Brendan succeeded with a tilt of the head and a sideways glance that said, 'You chose him.'

As the plastic sensor danced around sending flashes of light onto the screen, Rachel sank back, unwilling to strain her neck to see the distorted images that this small, strange man would attempt to convince her were various parts of the body of her unborn child.

She caught the odd word, phrase—

'. . . baby's fingers . . . baby's nose . . . all seems normal . . . baby's heartbeat . . .'

Brendan was asking about a photograph. The blue dress was obliging. Everyone was smiling, happy. The suit was thanking her, looking forward to seeing her again. The blue dress was helping her off the table, directing her to the toilet. Brendan hugged her and showed off the printout. It looked to Rachel like the weather forecast. Would she be able to see, to tell anything from this mass of lines and swirls? The suit had gone, taking Rachel's unspoken questions with him.

Six – December 1899

When Rachael was eight years old her father took her to her first adult party. There was double excitement for her. It was to be the first of many occasions when she would accompany him, proudly entering a room full of people with her arm safely held by the most handsome man in London. But it was also New Year's Eve. It was the first new year she had been allowed to see in, for she would also be welcoming the new century.

Usually Nanny Green bought her clothes. They would go to a dressmaker in Wimpole Street and Nanny would put in her order for the same, but slightly bigger, version of the day dresses she had always worn. There was one party dress per season. Rachael would then be measured from neck to hemline, across the shoulder, around the chest, down the arms and comments would be made about the inches she had acquired since her last visit. She would be given a glass of lemonade, a chocolate biscuit and sat in the corner with a book, whilst Nanny and the dressmaker took tea and gossiped.

But for the New Year party her father took her shopping himself. Of course, he had no idea where to go or what they were looking for, so they came back empty-handed and Rachael ended up back at Wimpole Street, but she never forgot that day. London's shops were getting ready for Christmas and the West End was glittering.

'I'd like a gold dress please, Daddy,' she said, after staring intently at a golden clockwork fairy turning round and round on the top of a small Christmas tree in a jewellery shop's window.

'Then you shall have one,' Sydney replied, squeezing her small, gloved hand.

But there were no gold dresses to be found. They did, however, find a white teddy bear with a gold bow, a gilded jewellery box, some gold ribbon, a magic wand with a gold star on top and a jar of sweets wrapped in gold paper.

Rachael turned down the offer of tea in one restaurant because the china was plain, but accepted it in another whose crockery was decorated with gold fleurs-de-lys. She refused to put milk in her tea but added hot water to turn it 'more golden', then added a 'gold sugar lump'. She excitedly pointed out the special magic people – those with gold buckles on their bags, or shiny (brass would do) handles on their umbrellas. These were the people in the know. The rest of them were sad, lonely, drab and grey because they had no gold in their lives.

One man in city clothes – pin-striped trousers and black jacket – was immediately excluded until he opened his mouth to speak and Rachael caught the unmistakable sparkle of a gold tooth.

Over tea, Sydney produced a box. Rachael was horrified that it was dark red velvet but soon cheered up when she saw the gold hook that held the lid down. Excitedly she opened it. A locket – and it was gold! Tiny diamonds spelled out her initials.

'I was going to wait till Christmas. But as it was ready today.'

'I didn't see you. When? Where?'

'Oh, you were too busy looking out for the gold people to notice what I was going.'

'It's so beautiful, Daddy.' She got up from the table and went to her father, putting her arms tightly around his neck and nestling her head on his shoulder. 'I'll wear it at the party, but not till then.'

'May the Twentieth Century be kind to you, my darling.

Wear my gift and may it always bring you contentment.'

She felt so bad that she had had to ask her father what he meant and when he had explained, it puzzled her that he had not said 'happiness'. She wore it at the party with the gold dress that the dressmaker had made for her and it had been admired by all the grown-ups and even by the only other child there, a boy called Saul ('Your father is building my father a house' he had said) with hair even blacker and curlier than her own.

Why would she settle for contentment when she had, that night, perfect happiness?

Seven

Rachel and Louise were handed the small blue hymn book and passed through into the large living room that had been converted into the tiny church. They took their usual places halfway back on the left-hand side. Rachel liked to sit against the wall, feeling some protection and believing that the wall went some way to hiding the fact that she had a notebook and pen in her hand.

The room was slow to fill up. Louise nodded her silver bun at an over-made-up woman in a flowery skirt far too young for her, then again at a young Greek girl with bad skin and cheap lipstick.

'I've not seen her before,' said Rachel.

'She was here on Wednesday when I came to healing circle. Poor kid.'

'Not very busy tonight.'

'It's the rain. You know what we're like.'

'Or the football,' said Rachel, thinking about how she had left Brendan.

'Don't think that's a big area of conflict,' laughed Louise. 'Football or the local Spiritualist Church.'

Rachel reeled slightly. A punch of stale cigarette smoke caught her with each separate breath of Louise's laugh.

'New earrings?' asked Rachel, fingering the turquoise stones set in silver nestled into Louise's sagging earlobes.

'Present from America.'

'Hasn't he given up on you yet?'

'I only keep it going to annoy your mother.'

Rachel laughed. 'Well good for you. I only hope I—'

'When you're my age? It's all right darling. This is your Aunt Louise. You can say what you like to me.'

There was a pause.

'Flowers look as crappy as ever,' Rachel said. They had been speaking in hushed tones, but Rachel's voice began to creep up to its normal pitch. 'Always the same cheap, service station-bought chrysanthemums. Doesn't matter which churches you go to, there they are – insultingly yellow and nasty. If I were in Spirit I'd send a message down saying, "Change the bloody flowers."'

'Are you all right?' asked Louise. 'It's not like you to be like this.'

'I had the scan yesterday.'

'And?'

'Everything's fine.'

'That's wonderful news, darling.' Louise took Rachel's hand.

'But I don't believe them.'

Before Louise could answer, the lights on the small altar area turned on.

A lanky, hollow-faced man welcomed the congregation and announced a change from the usual hymns. He produced a bulky cassette player and placed it on a low table.

'This is a special request from our guest medium, Roger Whelan.'

He pressed a button and the loud silence filled the room. The music started. Rachel emitted an involuntary snort; Louise stabbed her with her elbow.

'Abba?' she whispered, giggling. But looking around her the audience was entranced and even started humming along. 'Well I suppose it makes a change from "There is no death."'

Louise stabbed her again.

'I Believe in Angels' came to its end and Roger Whelan

stepped out from a side door onto the small platform. Rachel was always amazed at the ordinariness of the male mediums. They were uniformly middle-aged, middle-class, middle-management types in grey suits and navy ties who you wouldn't be surprised to see driving Ford Mondeos up and down the A1 as they sold their souls on the Industrial Estates of Middle England; and when they opened their mouths to speak the sound was as uninspired as the image.

And yet, and yet there *was* something special and different about him and, as Roger began his welcoming address, Rachel once again became seduced by the philosophies, the attitudes and the passion of the conviction of a belief in Spiritualism. And Roger was good. He wasn't offering answers; he was telling his listeners that he had no proof of reincarnation, that no one on Earth or Spirit had shown him sufficient evidence; a question mark would forever remain. He talked movingly of the used-up body to be discarded like a worn-out overcoat; of entering Spirit as akin to a butterfly who had spent its previous existence munching drearily on a cabbage leaf and was now free to fly and experience the sights and smells of the whole garden.

Rachel scribbled furiously and at one point looked up to find the comfortingly ordinary face of Roger staring right at her as she wrote. She put down her pen and he continued without a pause.

The lights were dimmed again as Roger prepared himself for the clairvoyancing.

'Please speak loudly and clearly. Spirit respond to the vibrations. And remember your "nos" are just as important as your "yeses".'

He began slowly to pace up and down. His speed increased and he nodded his head. He turned to his audience and stared around the room.

'May I come to you?' He held his arm out towards the girl/woman in the flowery skirt.

She beamed her assent.

'OK. I'm tall, taller than me, and broad. I have a red, rugged face. My hands, I work with my hands. They are raw. I am feeling a pain in my chest. I am being given the name John. John. Does that mean anything to you?'

The woman leaned forward slightly.

'Ye-es.'

'You must be sure. Wait, there's more. I'm getting steam. And I'm being handed an envelope. There's a secret in this envelope.'

'Yes.' Her voice was sure now.

'Someone knows. I think that's what the steam meant. Someone has, perhaps symbolically, steamed open your life and discovered your secrets.'

'Yes.'

'And John is giving me this message for you. He says it is all right to trust. Do you understand that?'

'I do. Thank you.'

'John is telling me that this is very hard for you.'

'It is.' She had produced a greying handkerchief from her bag and was clutching it fiercely as she dabbed her eyes.

'And now there is a woman. Small but powerful. She is standing in front of John and shadows him despite his size. Do you know who this is?'

'Yes.' The voice allowed itself a small laugh.

'I can hear him laughing, because he is telling me in Life she always disagreed with him. But now she is reinforcing his message. The person who has discovered your secret will not cause you any harm. There is only Love there for you. Love and Trust. Please accept it. That is all I have for you.'

'Thank you, thank you. God bless.'

'Thank you.'

Rachel glanced over at the woman. Black mascara-ed tears trickled out over her cheeks and her thin pink lips drooled slightly. Stillness and silence were smashed by the awful sound of her blowing her nose.

The next message was for a young man whose brother had recently died. Roger had to keep asking him not to volunteer so much information, so eager was he to let the messages suit his circumstance.

Then there was a muddle of confused characters. No one seemed able to claim knowledge of any of them. Eventually it transpired that one woman could, but was as hesitant to speak out as she had been reluctant to attend in the first place. It was only when Roger confronted her with her reticence that she came clean and accepted his message.

'He is good,' Rachel whispered to Louise, who smiled in return.

'May I come to you – the young lady in the denim jacket?'

Rachel looked up and instinctively lowered her notebook.

'Yes?'

'There is a young man. An attractive young man. He died prematurely. You know him.' It wasn't a question. Then Roger appeared to whiten. 'I can feel something around my neck—'

Rachel straightened. He had her full attention.

'—and a pain in my heart. He is angry. He's telling me you have hurt him. I'm sorry,' he looked at Rachel, his colour was back – he was out of his trance. 'Sometimes they're not very kind to us.' He gave a small, unconvincing laugh. 'Now he's telling you it's not too late. You still have the chance to make things better. Does any of this mean anything to you?' Before Rachel could answer he added, 'Could he be your son?'

Rachel shook her head violently.

Roger sort of smiled. 'No, of course not. I'll try and get some more information.' He cocked his head slightly. 'Now I have a lady. She is a real lady. Very well dressed, very well spoken. She is holding hands with a young girl. A fat-faced child with wild red hair. It's not her child. Do you know who this could be?'

'No.'

'She is holding a book out to you. Does this mean anything?'

'Not so far.'

'She tells me you are going to be a mother.'

Rachel's heart leapt. The amazed smile on her face stung her eyes.

'She says you must look after him.' Roger was holding a hand against his chest. He spoke quietly. 'There is pain in his heart.'

They stared at each other until Rachel's effort in blinking back the tears became too much for her.

'It only takes Love,' he said.

'Thank you,' Rachel mumbled, grabbing for her notebook and scribbling illegible notes blotted by tears.

'Thank you. And thank you to everyone who came tonight. And if nothing came through for you, I'm sorry, but remember Spirit is always there for you.'

Rachel and Louise sat as the room emptied around them.

'He's good,' said Louise. 'One of the best I've seen. How are you?' She took Rachel's hand. 'There was some extraordinary stuff there.'

Rachel said nothing.

'Maybe you should have a one-to-one with him?' said Louise.

'I'm going to have to think about this.'

Rachel got up slowly, put her arm through her aunt's and they wandered out into the hot night rain.

Eight

'Leah!'

Silence.

'We're leaving!'

Flush of toilet. Opening and closing of door. Loud stamps down the stairs.

'What the fuck—?'

'What?'

'You know jolly well what. What have you done?'

'I was getting bored with it.'

'What? How? I can't bear to think about it. Brendan!'

Brendan appeared from the kitchen with a Marks & Spencer carrier bag and did a cartoon skid as he bumped into Leah.

'Whoah!' He put the bag down and ran his hand over Leah's smooth scalp. 'Neat.'

'Great isn't it? Look, now you can see my tattoo.' Leah turned her profile to reveal a lizard slithering out from behind her right ear.

'And what does the bathroom look like?' asked Rachel.

Both Leah and Brendan burst out laughing.

'Don't worry. I've cleaned it all up.'

'I think it looks fantastic,' said Brendan, giving her a hug.

'So do I,' said Leah. 'Do you want me to take anything to the car?'

Brendan handed her the carrier, Rachel handed her a plant and another carrier.

'I'll need the keys,' Leah said, peering through the foliage.

'It's open.'

Brendan opened the front door for her.

'How could she do that?' said Rachel as soon as Leah was down the steps.

'Because she wants the attention. She wins either way; whether you approve or disapprove, she gets what she wants.'

'Actually I'm thinking of Dad. I don't think he'd appreciate his daughter turning up looking like a camp inmate, do you?'

'I think you're being over-sensitive.'

'It's his birthday, for goodness' sake.'

'Maybe in a strange way, that's why she's done it.'

Rachel gave a bark of annoyance. 'I can't get into all that now.' She turned to the hall mirror and applied her lipstick. 'You ready?'

Brendan smiled at her. 'I love watching you do that.'

'I know. That's one of the reasons I married you.' She placed a claret-coloured deposit on his nose and picked up her handbag.

The phone rang.

'I'll get it.' Brendan moved towards the kitchen to pick up the phone. It stopped. 'Damn,' he said.

'Do 1471.'

'Doesn't matter, let's go.'

'It might have been the estate agent.'

'On a Sunday? I know she's keen to the point of irritation, but even she needs a day off.'

Leah was settled in the back of the car, humming along to the sounds coming from her earphones.

'I think she looks lovely,' said Brendan. 'And I think she's sort of content, you know.'

'Is that why she shaved her head?'

'Perhaps.'

Brendan opened the passenger door for Rachel then ambled around to the driver's side.

'That's so sweet the way he does that,' said Leah.

'I know,' answered Rachel.

Louise was waiting outside her block of flats. She attempted effusive hugs over the seats but only Leah, next to her in the back, received the full impact.

'Your hair—' she said.

Leah smiled mischievously. 'I knew *you'd* like it.'

The traffic was slow through to the West Way. Brendan swore to himself. Rachel made sympathetic sounds; Brendan was not good in traffic.

'Gorgeous day for it,' said Louise and sat back, flicking through the *Sunday Times Magazine.*

Ninety minutes later they left the M4. Suddenly there was traffic again.

'God, they're all out today,' said Brendan impatiently.

'Well, it's a perfect day for viewing the sites of ancient Britain.'

Leah stared out of the window expectantly.

'Almost there,' said Brendan, teasing her along. 'Just around this bend.'

Leah squealed when she saw it. Rachel got tears in her eyes.

'My God, he's beautiful.'

'She!'

Rachel laughed. 'You always say that.'

'Well, I've always thought it,' said Leah.

The White Horse disappeared behind a wood then reappeared again. Leah kept her nose pressed against the window. They left the horse behind, Leah watching it until the last chalk piece was no longer visible.

The car crushed the already tiny gravel stones and pulled up in front of the house. As Rachel opened the car door the front door opened. Rachel jumped out and ran into her father's open arms.

'Happy Birthday!' she said, squeezing him hard around his waist.

She let him go and looked around. 'The garden looks fantastic. I don't think I've ever seen it looking so good.'

Aza had turned his attentions to Brendan and Louise, handing out warm handshakes and conspiratorial kisses. Leah was still in the car. Aza tapped on the window; Leah wound it down.

'Hello, my darling,' he said.

Leah leant out of the window and gave him a kiss full on the lips. 'Hello, Daddy.'

'Are you coming in?'

Rachel was unloading the boot. 'Come on Leah, I need your help,' she said.

'What do you think she'll say?' Leah asked her father.

'Who? About what?'

This answer seemed to please Leah so she got out of the car and flung herself against Aza.

Ella had appeared in the door, unaware that Louise's fervent greetings and insistence on helping out in the kitchen were a ploy to keep her attention momentarily diverted from Leah's lack of hair.

Rachel followed them in and handed her mother bottles of champagne, chocolates and, of course, the plant.

'It wasn't necessary for you to bring all this, really.'

Rachel shrugged a response.

'Especially not the plant. Do we need another plant?'

Rachel laughed. 'But I promised Dad I'd find him a pale yellow hibiscus.'

'And where do you think he'll put it?'

'Well, it will either have to go in the conservatory—'

'Have you seen the conservatory lately?'

Rachel wandered through to take a look. Conservatory was not the right description anymore. Hot house, perhaps? It was excessively full, but everything in it was so healthy, so luscious, so more than green – how could you deny any plant the chance to live this life? Aza had devoted his retirement to what had previously been only a time-consuming hobby. Ella indulged him as she enjoyed the benefits of being the wife of a prize-winning amateur horticulturist, but she had never really understood Aza's passion.

'He'll find a place for it,' said Rachel, returning to the kitchen.

'Where's your sister?' asked Ella.

'Ella?' interrupted Louise.

'Yes? Is something wrong? You look awfully serious suddenly.'

'Leah's done something to her hair.'

Ella laughed. 'Is that all? Well, I'm past being shocked about what Leah does to her hair—'

'Hi Mum!'

The bowl of cherries Ella was carrying fell out of her hands and shattered.

Aza stood behind Leah, holding his finger to his lips.

Leah giggled as she crawled around on the floor, picking out blood-red cherries from their hiding places. Suddenly she came face to face with her mother underneath the table, also on her hands and knees. They stalked each other like a pair of alley cats spoiling for a fight.

'You couldn't just let him enjoy his birthday, could you?' Ella hissed.

'Mum!' Leah was shocked at the ferocity of her mother's tone and tears came to her eyes.

'I just don't understand you,' Ella spat and backed away, banging her head on the underside of the table as she lifted it up too soon.

Rachel was there to help her out.

Louise came back from the dining room to fetch the napkins. Rachel smiled at her with her eyes pointing to the heavens. Louise gently touched her arm.

'How long before we eat?' she asked Ella.

'Ten minutes or so. I wasn't sure if Jonno was joining us for lunch or later. Should we wait?'

'No,' said Rachel very firmly.

'But—' started Ella.

'He'll be fine. Let's just get on with it.'

Ella appeared hurt.

'There's no need to take it personally.'

Ella shot darts of annoyance to her daughter. Rachel took a deep breath and internally counted to ten, attempting to justify to herself her mother's attitude. To put it simply, Ella was all cared out, a traumatised husband, two girls born ten years apart, not without their problems, and an imagined conflict with her family gathering momentum within her: 'They need me, I don't want them to need me: I need them, they don't want me to need them.'

It was only in the small ways that Rachel could help, so she opened a drawer and removed a bottle opener.

'Get Brendan to open the wine.'

'It's all right, I can do it.'

'OK,' said Rachel's mother.

Brendan and Aza were seated in the conservatory. Rachel went in and handed them both a glass of red wine, then perched on a rattan footstool.

'How's my grandson?'

Rachel didn't answer.

A flash of concern crossed Aza's eyes. 'Is everything all right?'

'We had the scan. All seems OK,' said Rachel.

'But you don't sound convinced.'

'It's perfectly reasonable anxiety,' said Brendan. 'When Jonno was born, there wasn't any of this scanning or amnios or anything. And I spent nine months worried sick that he was healthy.'

'I'm looking forward to seeing Jonno. It's been ages.'

'I think he may be bringing a girlfriend,' said Brendan.

'What? You never told me that. Who?'

'He didn't mention her name.'

'As I recall,' said Aza, 'he rarely sticks around long enough to ask them their names.'

Brendan roared his lion laugh.

'I don't think,' said Rachel, 'in the five years I've known him that I've ever met one of his girlfriends. So this is a portentous occasion.'

'That's a dreadful word,' laughed Aza.

Rachel laughed with her father. Ella appeared at the door.

'What's so funny?'

'Nothing really.'

Ella put on her sulking face. 'Well lunch is ready if you can bear to tear yourselves away from the entertainment.'

This only made them laugh more.

Rachel was in the kitchen about to serve the chocolate mousse when the doorbell chimed. Taking the bowl in the dining room she was, as ever, momentarily disoriented by Jonno's presence. She watched him nervously hug his father. Two giants in an awkward embrace. Opposites. Jonno light, pale. Brendan, dark, black. It was no wonder his father didn't understand him; seeing them so close together it was perfectly obvious to Rachel that they inhabited different planes. Then Rachel noticed the tiny flower girl hovering in the doorway.

Jonno, seeing Rachel, removed himself with relief from his father. His face relaxed with genuine pleasure at the sight of her. Rachel felt that slight flush in her cheeks, the habitual response to her dazzling stepson.

'You look well,' she said. And he did. His hair was blonder and his eyes bluer than ever. Jonno's eyes. On a clear day you could see right into his soul.

Jonno moved away from Rachel. 'Hi Twin,' he said, winking at Leah, who giggled in reply.

'Everyone,' he said, rescuing the tiny figure at the door, 'this is Iris. Iris, everyone.' He put a protective arm around her, which was fairly difficult considering the difference in their sizes, and Iris smiled the best she could.

Aza fetched chairs. Ella fussed with food.

'How did your interview go?' Rachel asked Jonno.

Brendan's silence filled the room.

'What interview was that?' asked Aza.

Jonno looked over at his father. 'I was going to tell you—'

Brendan turned his head away.

'Perhaps this isn't the time,' said Jonno, placing his knife and fork together on his plate.

'Go ahead,' said Brendan. 'Tell us.'

Rachel closed her eyes. It was too late to stop it now. Brendan, confused about the son whose otherness he had mistaken for distance, had forever branded him 'difficult'. Disguising his confusion with apparent hurt. Neglecting a son he had never been able to comprehend. And holding the reflection of that neglect as if he were the injured party.

'I've been offered the job.'

'That's marvellous,' beamed Aza. 'What is it?'

'A new clinic. A rehab centre. Working with all kinds of addicts. I'll be able to put into practice some of the, what some may call, experimental psychotherapeutic techniques I've been developing. It's a fantastic opportunity.'

Rachel clocked the effort Ella was making in not looking at Leah.

'Where?' Aza, playing the interested father. Well, thought Rachel, at least someone was.

Jonno looked at Brendan, who refused to look at him. 'New Mexico,' he said quietly.

It was as if a cannon had been fired.

Rachel looked at Iris who, oblivious to the change in the atmosphere, sat quietly. Rachel felt a pang of envy for a young girl in love setting off on an adventure, being able to believe in a future where anything might happen. Then she saw that it wasn't Iris at all. It was her own young innocent self.

Brendan was beginning to boil. How could Rachel contain the volcano? Prevent it from erupting? Ella pre-empted her by choosing this moment to prepare the birthday cake.

'I think it sounds marvellous,' said Aza. 'I envy you. I only wish I'd had such opportunities when I was young.' There was a silence in which the reference to how Aza had spent his youth was acknowledged and suitably respected.

Then Brendan spoke. 'I can't believe you're considering this. Turning your back on your family. Have you thought this through, Jonno?'

To Rachel's amazement, Jonno laughed. He sat up straight-backed, put his head back and laughed. It wasn't something he did easily. He smiled beautifully. But rarely did Rachel see him laugh.

'Brendan,' he said. 'What do you think? That I'm possibly changing the course of who knows how many lives, without thinking about it?'

Rachel wondered who else had caught the fleeting glance at Iris and her blushing response.

'New Mexico!' boomed Brendan. 'I won't let you do this.'

'You can't stop me.'

'I am your father. And it's perfectly obvious how much weight that holds in your life.'

'And who created that situation?'

'Ah! It's what I've always thought. This is my punishment, is it?'

'I can't believe you're only concerned with how it will affect you!'

'How dare you say that. I've worried over you from the moment you were conceived. I've worried over you every day of your life.'

'I didn't ask you to do that.'

'It's what parents do!' Brendan bellowed.

Rachel imagined a hurricane sweeping through the dining room. 'Brendan?' she pleaded gently.

'Stay out of it!' he screamed back at her.

Ella appeared with the cake.

The birthday song was unenthusiastic. If Aza noticed, he

didn't acknowledge it. Ella distributed the cake.

Rachel tried to rescue the day, her self-respect, her marriage. 'Iris, have you climbed the hill? Seen the Horse?'

'Er, no. I was, we were hoping to. Weren't we?' She looked desperately over at Jonno. But Jonno appeared to have forgotten all about her.

'Brendan, why don't you take her? And I'm sure Leah would go.'

'That will give Jonno and me a chance to have a real chat,' beamed Aza.

'Come too?' Brendan almost whispered, but she needed more of an apology than this.

'No,' she whispered back, 'I'm needed here.'

Ella and Louise cleared up in the kitchen. Jonno was making a phone call. Rachel and Aza sat in the conservatory.

'Is he always like that?'

Rachel was shocked. This was unlike her father to be so direct.

'We have our fights.'

'But does he do that? Attack? Blame?'

Rachel said nothing.

'It was horrible,' said Aza. 'I had no idea.'

'You've seen him lose his temper before.' Rachel's reluctance to be disloyal was overpowered by her need to reassure her father. 'He's guilty. He lives with guilt every day of his life. And he sees the consequences of his actions in Jonno. It's not him or me he's angry with. It's himself.'

'He's not the first man to walk out on his child.'

'You know, when he left, well, not long before he left, he'd built Jonno a tree house. It's still there, what's left of it. Jonno climbed the tree and wouldn't come down. For days.'

'Poor kid.'

'Wouldn't eat or drink. Tried to waste himself away.'

'What happened?'

'You can see what happened.'

'I meant—' Aza started.

'I know,' said Rachel.

'But why should Brendan choose here, now?'

'I think it's because of Iris.'

'Nice impression he's giving. Poor girl. If I were her, you wouldn't see me for dust.'

'I think she's pregnant.'

Aza looked amazed at his daughter.

'Where did you get that from?'

'Just a hunch.'

'You don't get hunches. You're never wrong.'

Rachel leant back and placed one hand on top of another to keep her baby warm. 'I hope sometimes I am,' she said.

Nine

The journey home was painful. Rachel offered to drive and was refused and accepted several times before she took charge of the keys and control of the situation.

Louise sat behind Brendan, leaning forward to hold his head. He jerked away from her touch but not her reach, so she unobtrusively sent healing to him. Leah curled herself up on the back seat, hugging her knees and almost, but not quite, sucking her thumb. Within minutes she was asleep. What with Louise's concentration, Brendan's remorse and Rachel's driving, the return to London was long and silent.

Rachel saw Louise to the front door of her flat.

'He is worth it, my dear,' Louise whispered as she hugged her niece. 'Hang on to that.'

'You've always believed that.'

Louise tapped the side of her nose with her finger, indicating a secret she wasn't prepared to divulge. Rachel smiled wearily.

'You be all right?'

Rachel nodded and went back to the car.

'I don't want to dissect this, analyse it to within an inch of its life, flog it for all its worth. And I don't want you to hold it in store for later use. But I do want us to get over it.'

Rachel took Brendan's hand. 'Thank you for that,' she said.

*

Rachel lay in bed waiting for Brendan to finish brushing his teeth. Like everything he did, he brushed excessively, wearing out toothbrushes in days. Eventually he came in and climbed into bed.

She lay on her left side and nestled into the space he made for her against him, sliding his left arm under her to hold her ever-expanding waist.

'Where were you hiding all this skin?' he said, drawing circles over her stomach.

'Same place you hide your rage,' she answered, then wished she hadn't. But he didn't pull back. He laughed.

'Because you never know when you're going to need it,' he said, placing his lips on her shoulder.

Part of her hated him for this, part of her adored him for it; rage and passion came out of the same bag. But isn't that what the critics both praised and found difficult in his work?

He turned her around and attached his face to hers.

'Don't hate me,' he said, gliding into her. 'Please don't hate me.'

But this Brendan she could never hate. The Brendan that tried to climb right inside her, who couldn't get far enough, who wanted to be where her baby was, warm, safe. This was the compliment he paid her – that she could do that for him.

They lay facing each other, Brendan making the smallest and gentlest of movements, and Rachel danced with him, conscious of the rounding moon between them.

'Hold on,' she said, lifting herself off him then turning her back to him again. 'This way.'

He was in her again but everything had changed. Now he was lifting himself up onto one knee, the other leg stretched out, holding her firmly round the middle. Rachel also had to kneel in order not to feel uncomfortable. Then he slid his legs out in front of him and sat up, forcing Rachel to do the same so she was now sitting on him but facing away from him. He wasn't holding her anymore, his hands lay flat on the bed. She placed hers on top and grabbed on to the fingers, worried she would lose her balance, so ferociously was he driving her to rise and fall.

He couldn't sustain this position for long and took her hand to where their bodies joined in order to hold him there while he shifted again, this time as they had started, how Rachel had wanted him and how they ended.

After recognising the change in his breathing that announced he was asleep, Rachel disengaged herself from Brendan and went to get a glass of water.

As always she argued the moral stand with herself that said something was not healthy in a marriage whose physical pleasure ran on verbal abuse, whether or not she was at the receiving end of it. Yet what caused her the most alarm was her own response to him. This was collusion; she could convince no one, least of all herself that she was a victim in this. It was so out of place with the rest of her character, she almost believed it was leftover from another life. Brendan's passion, wherever it sourced itself, excited and aroused her. His petulant moods, however, did not.

She got back into bed and kissed him on the forehead. Despite having the classic artistic temperament (never mind the Irish in him), five years of being married to a man twenty years her senior had given Rachel a feeling of security and contentment that had always been her vision of 'happily ever after'.

She and Brendan had known each other before, of that she was sure. And despite his playful scorning of her beliefs, she knew that he knew it too. How else could he account for not only his attraction, but his fidelity to her? (His past having been so predictably volatile and excessive in his choice of partners – models, muses, actresses, crazies.)

When they met they were ready for each other. And that, Rachel had learned, was the single most important factor in predicting the potential success of a relationship. And the man who had forsworn marriage, after his last dip in the waters, married the girl and carried her off to his castle.

Rachel snuggled up to him. In his sleep he put an arm around her. Rachel closed her eyes.

Ten – March 1911

'They always look so proper, standing there like that.' Rachael extracted her arm from Saul's and bent over to peer at the rows of furled ferns.

'I think they look rather menacing. It's just that there's so many of them,' said Saul. 'And where do they hide?'

'What?'

'One moment the ground is flat, bare, then suddenly they appear from nowhere like a silent army waiting to attack.'

'It is extraordinarily peaceful here.'

Rachael stepped back and took her place alongside her fiancé. As she replaced her arm in his, she ran the fingers of her right hand over the pearl on the fourth finger of her left. One day, she thought, I'll forget it's there. She didn't want that day to come; she wanted to feel the daily thrill of the symbol of her persisting happiness.

'I used to come up here with my mother,' said Saul.

Rachael didn't quite know how to respond. This was the first time Saul had ever mentioned her.

'Oh. I, er didn't realise—' She took a breath and dived in. 'How old were you when she died?'

Saul was silent. Rachael felt angry with herself for asking so blunt a question. The longer the silence went on the more humiliated she felt. She wanted to cry, she wanted to run away, but Saul's grip on her arm had become tighter. Finally he spoke.

'You didn't know yours at all, did you?' he asked. 'Neither did I. In a different way, of course. But then when she did what she did—'

Rachael said nothing; she just let him speak. He relayed the horror of a sinister silence that had fallen over his childhood home – male servant's eyes averted and female ones, red and sore, pity and sorrow all over their rough faces – eventually being called into the drawing room where a fortress of formidable aunts played word tag, attempting to break the news of his mother's death.

'I love you, Saul.'

Saul turned to face her. She could feel his fingers pressing deep into her flesh as he gripped her arms. Gently he shook her, then shook her again. She tried to protest, but no sounds came. All the sounds were his. No, he was telling her. Don't, he begged her. Then the grip relaxed and he pulled her towards him, engulfing her, her head pressed uncomfortably against his neck. Now her hair was being showered with kisses and now she understood. He allowed her to pull back slightly and placed the full force of his lips against hers.

A genteel cough made Rachael draw away. A middle-aged man, accompanied by his wife and followed by a slope of children in their Sunday best, was expressing his disapproval. Rachael hid her head from him. The family passed them and the father pointed his walking stick to a bird building a nest atop a distant tree, apparently anxious for his impressionable brood to witness the glories of the natural world, not the base instincts of man.

When they had gone, Rachael looked back at Saul. He appeared to be in some kind of trance. She whispered his name. He looked at her as if he didn't know who she was. She kissed him softly on the cheek and suddenly he was with her again. He took her arm and they walked slowly on.

'But there's so many of them,' Saul said, running his fingers along the tops of the ferns. 'Where do they all hide?'

Eleven

'Gorgeous to see you!' Rachel returned her stepson's genuinely affectionate hug.

'Brendan here?' asked Jonno.

'No. Working of course. I am glad to see you.' She squeezed his arm, then led him into the kitchen.

Jonno sat at the table and smiled at Rachel. 'How is he?'

Rachel loved his smiles. No one had as many smiles as Jonno did, and this one was especially for her. 'He doesn't really worry; he just thinks he should.'

Rachel prepared the teapot, conscious of Jonno's stare.

'Tell me about Twin?' Jonno asked. 'I didn't really get the chance to speak to her the other day, what with all that stuff going on.'

It was an endless source of amusement to both Jonno and Leah that they shared a birthday, literally, causing Leah to taunt Rachel with the jibe that she was old enough to be her stepmother.

'She doesn't seem to let things affect her,' Rachel replied, joining him at the table.

Jonno leant across towards Rachel. 'Is she getting good support?'

Rachel put her head down. She was ashamed to admit that she didn't know.

'Presumably she's having follow-up appointments at the clinic?'

'Yes, I suppose so. She doesn't tell me much.'

'Is that because you won't listen?'

'I help her in the way I can.'

'Healing, you mean?' Jonno made a face. 'How does all that "communion of spirits and the ministry of angels" help?'

'I'm surprised at you being so dismissive.'

'I'm not. I'm being challenging. Stirring up a healthy debate. Come on, tell me.'

'There is a crossover, you know.'

'With what?'

'Spiritualism and Psychoanalysis.'

'Go on. No sugar thanks.' Jonno took his mug of tea.

'They're just different approaches to self-development.'

'Not sure about that.'

'You're forgetting one of the Seven Principles of Spiritualism is Personal Responsibility.'

'Ah yes. Accountability. How does it go?'

'"Compensation and Retribution hereafter for all the good and evil deeds done on earth."'

'The main difference of course, being, that in psychoanalysis it's about being accountable in this life, not your next one.'

Rachel laughed nervously. 'I have to say that this is where I sort of divert from, well, from the Seven Principles, anyway.'

'What do you mean?'

'The continuous existence of the human soul, bit. And the implication that it's not just the soul but the personality that survives. Well that clearly contradicts any notion of reincarnation. And a lot of it is, I mean it needn't be, but it's often too closely linked to Christianity.'

'As in Christianity embracing death as representing a return to Eden?' Jonno paused. 'You know,' he said, 'there's no one in the family that I can talk like this with.'

'You mean, "with whom I can talk like this".'

'Neatly deflected, Mrs Treacy.'

'Not even Iris?'

He took a sip of tea then replaced his mug on the table. Then Rachel thought he said, 'I think about you, you know.' But possibly she imagined it because he was ignoring her question and asking: 'What news on the moving front? I think you're crazy even thinking about it.'

'Really?' Rachel was genuinely surprised by his comment.

'Leaving London would be the only excuse for giving up the perfect London home – period property lovingly restored in convenient but slightly run-down area.'

Rachel laughed.

'I love this house.'

'I know you do.'

'And hate it.'

Rachel understood that perfectly. It was, she knew, the same for Brendan. Too much had happened here. There had been too much happiness, too much sadness; too much life. Jonno had seen his father walk out, his mother die, his father come back. She wanted to start again somewhere else with her new family. Make a new history.

'You're not thinking of leaving London, are you?'

'No, I don't want to.'

'You'll never do it before the baby's born. Why put yourself through it?' His eyes twinkled, flirting.

'It would help if your father and I could agree on any aspect of the move, like where we want to be, what sort of home we're looking for.'

'Here, I'll find you one.' Jonno grabbed the copy of the *Ham and High* that was lying on the table.

'And Brendan doesn't see the point in moving to a district that's served by the same local paper,' she said over her shoulder to Jonno as she refilled the teapot.

'Iris is pregnant,' he said, his face hidden from hers behind the newspaper.

'I thought so.' Rachel placed a fresh mug in front of him and pulled the paper away from him. 'Happy about it?' she asked.

'I, er, was expecting to be going away alone.'

'I see.' Rachel sat down.

'I'm, we're, trying to find a way to make it work. I probably will go, but that means leaving her here alone, pregnant.'

'Why can't she go with you?'

'Let's just say, it wasn't the point of me going.'

'Jonno—' Rachel put her hand out to him and, as he put the paper down, her eyes caught sight of something. 'What's that?' she said.

'What?'

She blinked and looked again. She could have sworn that a colour photo stood out from the rows of black-and-white pictures, but on the second glance it had gone.

Her head was bursting with pictures, memories. She put a hand to her forehead.

'Are you OK?' Jonno asked. 'You look a bit weird.'

'Just having one of my moments.'

Jonno laughed. 'My stepmother, the wicked witch. Look,' he said, 'I'd better go.'

'But—' Rachel couldn't concentrate. She needed peace and quiet. She was grateful to Jonno for going but guilty for curtailing their talk. 'We'll speak,' she said, not looking at him, her eyes closed, holding off the barrage of images.

She was only half-aware of the sound of the door closing behind him.

Rachel sat on the floor. Back straight against the wall. Deep breaths. Flash. A pond. Flash. A scream. Her hands held outwards, yoga-like. Her left hand jumped. A tickle. A finger tracing the lines.

Breathe deeply. The sound of laughter. The wind blowing curtains. A polished floor. A room with a wall of windows opposite a wall with two doors.

Louise holds her hand. Rachel stares up into a kind but sad face underneath a large hat. The garden. The sound of running water. 'There used to be a pond.'

Rachel sits on the grass with a pink iced cake and a glass of pink milk. Louise and the lady with the hat sit on a bench talking and laughing. Rachel looks at the house. The face of a small girl, younger than her, peers out from an upstairs window. 'Who's that?' she asks. But a cloud has covered the sun. The lady disappears underneath her hat, hiding her face. Louise takes Rachel on to her lap.

'Can I come again?' she wants to know.

The lady opens the front door for them and says, 'Goodbye.' Louise walks out. Rachel is scared. There's something out there she doesn't like. Louise has to drag the distressed child, down the path, through the gate. But once outside the gate she stops crying. She turns to look at the house, which is once again bathed in sunshine, a kind old lady in a large hat waving to them from the arched doorway.

Twelve

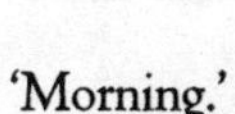

'Morning.'

'Yeah,' replied Leah, flopping onto a kitchen chair and hiding her head in her arms.

'Coffee?' asked Rachel, the cafetière in one hand and a china mug in the other.

'I will,' said Brendan, sitting down next to Leah. 'But not in that prissy thing. Where's my cup?'

He got up, went to the dishwasher, took out an oversized cup and saucer and placed it on the table. Leah looked up and giggled.

'We've got a house to see today. You coming?' Rachel asked Brendan.

'What time?'

'Eleven.'

Brendan sighed whilst he thought about it. 'Is there really any point?'

'Are we moving or aren't we? Because if we are, we need to look at as many places as possible in order to give us the best idea of what we want.'

'I'm beginning to feel that it's going to put too much pressure on us, on you. Why don't we put it all on hold till after Christmas? It will be so much easier then.'

'What are you frightened of?' Rachel snapped.

'The Samson Syndrome,' said Leah.

Rachel and Brendan spoke together. 'What?'

Leah sat up and stretched her arms in front of her. 'You know Samson? Had his hair cut off and lost his strength.'

'Yes,' said Rachel impatiently. 'So?'

'Fear of change,' said Leah. 'If things don't stay exactly as they are Brendan could lose his strength, which could be his creativity or—'

'Said the girl with no hair.'

'Guess *I'm* not scared then.'

'What crap,' said Rachel.

Brendan was roaring his laugh. 'I think it's a marvellous theory. Not heard it expressed like that before.'

'It's the bloody Oprah Culture. It makes me sick.'

Brendan was still laughing. 'OK, OK, I'll come and see the house with you – just to prove I'm not frightened of anything. What about you, Leah? What are you doing today?'

'Probably meet the gang up at the Grove. We might go up to Womad.' Leah sank back onto the table.

'But you haven't got any money,' said Rachel.

Leah raised her pierced eyebrow pleadingly at Rachel.

'Forget it,' her sister answered.

'I'll drop by the workshop—'

'Oh no you don't,' said Rachel. 'We'll go together from here. That's the only way I can be sure you'll be there.'

'Have I ever let you down?' Brendan winked at her.

'Don't think I'll answer that one.'

The letterbox rattled as the post passed through it.

'I'll get it,' said Leah, jumping up.

Rachel sat down next to Brendan. 'So. Dad's birthday never happened.'

Brendan took her hand. 'That's why you're so snappish. We've not exactly had the chance to talk about it, have we?'

'No,' said Rachel. 'You did what you always do.'

'You need to relax, honey,' Brendan said, giving her a kiss on the cheek. 'What's the rush? No one's going anywhere. We'll talk about it later. I promise.'

Rachel flinched at the word. She detested the ease with which promises were not only made, but broken. On the day she found out that she was pregnant she spoke to the two pink strips on the stick in her hand. 'I'll never lie to you,' she said. 'I'll never expect anything of you and I'll never promise you anything.'

She looked into Brendan's eyes. 'Don't promise,' she said.

Leah came back and dropped two letters in front of Rachel and three in front of Brendan. Brendan opened his, immediately spreading invitations for both private views and bank loans over the kitchen table. Rachel got up and took hers to her desk in the front room.

She had reached the point in her research where she was now forced to write. Reincarnation had been occupying her for the past couple of months. She had volumes of notes and could carry on filling folders, but there came a time when she had to stop reading and start writing. This would usually send her into a 'I-don't-know-enough-yet' type panic. There was always one more book that needed looking at, one more essay to read, one more lecture to attend, one more past life therapist to interview.

There was one thing that had been nagging at her – although she had visited several practitioners, she had yet to speak to anyone trustworthy who had actually experienced past life therapy. She had placed adverts for willing volunteers in all the relevant journals; the few that had come forward to share their experiences were all uniformly unconvincing. Ancient Egypt cropped up with alarming regularity, as did Victorian work-houses and the cotton fields of the Deep South. All the participants had an extraordinary predilection for poverty and slavery that told Rachel that however bad people's lives were now, they needed to believe they had once been even worse. She was working towards the conclusion that the only way to get the information she needed was to experience it for herself.

She thought of Roger Whelan and the 'lady' who had spoken to her through him. But she was reluctant to mix her own curiosity with her research, despite her experiences at the Spiritualist meetings. Her academic side told her to be objective, collect the facts, devise the theory, backing up the argument with the fruits of her research. But it was a specific interest in the subject that had led her to this point. She had to let go of these thoughts; she couldn't afford to sabotage her work. Yet her absolute unquestioning acceptance of the existence of Spirit occasionally biased her reading of the facts and sometimes she doubted whether this made her the right person for the job.

She needed a distraction. She would get no work done if she had doubts nagging at her.

She pulled a box marked 'Videos' from the shelf above her computer and, with her eyes closed, opened the lid. The first video her eyes rested on when she opened them would be the one she would watch. The video she fixed on was dated 8/9/98. Rachel took it out of the box and out of its case and wandered over to the television.

She knelt by the video machine, pressed all the right buttons and waited. White lines raced across the screen then settled on a weather girl. Rachel held her finger on the fast forward button and speeded through trailers and adverts, trying hard to remember what was on the tape.

At last the programme started. Paintings flashed on the screen like a slide show. A narrator with a calming soothing voice led Rachel through various paranormal phenomena.

'Yes, yes, yes,' said Rachel impatiently. So far there was nothing new. Then at last the subject of the programme revealed itself, linking to the opening images: Psychic Art. 'Ah,' said Rachel to herself. 'I'd forgotten all about this.'

She was engrossed in the programme when the oven timer rang.

'Damn,' she said, jolting back to the business of house-hunting.

She found Brendan sprawled on the sofa of the front room, discarded pages of the *Guardian* lying at his feet.

Thirteen – September 1916

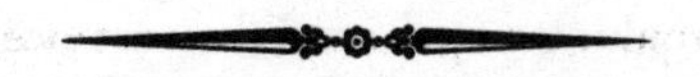

Of course she would be alone when it arrived.

She knew exactly what she was going to do, how she was going to react and what she was gong to say.

She would look pitifully at the straight-faced soldier; it was not his place to offer even the slightest sign of acknowledgement that he was aware of the contents of the telegram.

She would hold the brown envelope in her hand as her insides slowly sank into themselves until at last she would be forced to sit down. There was no real need to open it. Then a slight dread would emerge; perhaps he would only be missing. Then her life would be unbearable, for she would have to accommodate hope and fear. Perhaps he was only slightly wounded and was being lovingly tended by a beautiful, brave nurse. Did that sort of news come by telegram? She could see herself weeping as she read the inevitable letter:

'My Dear Rachael,

I never wanted to have to say this to you – please forgive me my darling. How can I write this? How can I explain to you what I have been through – you who have sat surrounded by your comforts – an armchair, a fire, four walls, with beloved Muswell at your feet, while I lay in pain and terror with only the soothing voice of Anne to remind me I was alive . . .'

No. Saul wouldn't write like that – he didn't think like that.

She would snap herself out of that one and finally open the telegram and face her future.

She could imagine fetching the letter opener, neatly slicing the envelope and carefully extracting the thin paper, searching for the important words: KILLED IN ACTION. And as she read them Muswell would look up from the rug and understand. He would drag his old bones to her side and limply wag his heavy tail, placing his chin on her lap in comfort.

Now time would stand still until she was ready; ready to grasp the reality of what had happened; ready to start to feel the grief that she knew she should, yet strangely unable to quieten the rush of adrenaline that belied it.

For this meant she was free.

Rachael got up to answer the knock of the young soldier she had watched walk up her front path.

Fourteen

Leah had been gone for nine days. Naturally, Brendan was not worried, neither did he think Rachel should be. For Brendan it was simple: had they had an argument? No. Rachel would only half concede that one, as her father's birthday was still very much in her thoughts. Was Leah unhappy? No. Rachel wondered how you would tell. Did she just disappear without telling them where she was going? No. Well, Leah had been her usual, vague self on the matters of where she was going, whom she was going with and when she would be back. Had Leah ever done this before and then turned up happy and safe, unaware of the worry she had caused? Frequently. But Leah had also turned up in the accident and emergency departments of any number of hospitals around the city, causing Rachel to go cold at the sound of a telephone ringing at an unsociable hour.

'We're not her parents,' Brendan told his wife.

'No, but while she's living here we are responsible for her.'

'Up to a point.'

Rachel refused to acknowledge the thoughts hammering to get out of her brain that would force her to face the role their parents had played. Due to their respective responses to 'Leah's problem', their parental responsibilities fell well short of even adequate. Rachel had always looked after her younger sister, albeit resentfully, and she would never not. She was continually surprised that Brendan would not accept this fundamental part of her make-up.

Rachel opened the door of Leah's bedroom. She could at least wash the sheets to make them clean and fresh for her return.

The curtains were drawn and the room smelt predominantly of stale cannabis with a trace of incense. Rachel opened the curtains and the window then looked around the room, shocked by Leah's lack of belongings.

Even in the heat she continued to wear her DMs and she had no other shoes. One or two faded T-shirts lay across a chair and some dirty knickers and tights were curled next to the bed. An incense burner, a beaten pewter dish with half a dozen assorted earrings in it, a small pile of books and the smell were the only things to show that the room had ever had an occupant.

Momentarily this alarmed Rachel. If Leah had gone somewhere with the thought of staying away, she would have taken a lot of things with her; but Leah had arrived with the ever-present rucksack, which she took everywhere, and with no other luggage.

Leah had, however, made the bed, and Rachel smiled. It was not often that she could afford a smile on Leah's behalf, she was so busy being responsible for her. Rachel pulled back the duvet to remove the cover and something fell on to the floor.

She walked around to the other side to see what it was then gasped in shock, putting both hands over her mouth and feeling an ache behind her eyes. Slowly getting herself into a sitting position on the bed, she bent down to pick up the balding, worn-out, over-loved rabbit with whom she had shared the first ten years of her life.

Hugging it to her breast, the pain behind her eyes turned to tears.

And that's how Brendan found her.

'I had no idea,' sobbed Rachel.

Brendan sat on the bed next to her and put his arms around her.

'I remember giving him to her when she was about two. No,

she must have been younger, because it was my first day at Secondary School and I felt so grown up. I didn't want the other girls to laugh at me because I still needed my rabbit, so I made this grand gesture. It was almost like a ceremony – The Handing Down of the Toy. Everyone made such a big fuss. And then Mum and Dad laughed because Leah looked at him, shrugged her shoulders and went dashing off to cuddle one of her own teddies. I was devastated. You know, considering what a big part he played in my life, I don't think I've thought of him until today.'

'Not true,' said Brendan. 'You told me that story.'

'Really?'

'Yes. Because the rabbit has some weird name. I can't remember, but—'

'Shoshi,' Rachel said quietly.

'Shoshi!' Brendan laughed. 'Where on earth did you get a name like that?'

Rachel clung onto what was left of the rabbit.

'It's so weird. I don't remember Leah having anything to do with him and here he is still in her bed.'

'So that proves that she hasn't gone far.'

'It doesn't prove that she's all right, though.'

'I think it proves a lot more than that.'

Brendan took his arms from around Rachel and stood up in front of her. Rachel gave him the rabbit, instinctively knowing that was what he wanted.

'This is so marvellous,' he said. 'Just imagine, something so special of yours to give your baby.'

'That's up to Leah, not me.'

Brendan kissed her quickly on the lips.

'She's fine.'

'Yes, I know,' replied Rachel.

'Where *did* that name come from?'

'Shoshi? I don't know. You know children. They try to say things and they come out all wrong and the parents think it's so sweet so they keep these strange sounds that their oh-so-clever children have turned into words, like they've invented a new language or something.'

'I don't suppose you'll be any different.'

'No, I won't. In fact I'm positively looking forward to it.'

'Funny,' Brendan said, 'I never had you down as a baby bore.'

'That was probably before I had a baby.' She looked at him. 'You are happy about it, aren't you?'

He knelt in front of her and looked her in the eyes.

'No,' he said, 'I'm not.'

He kept his face straight for such a long time that a panic began to flirt with Rachel's insides. Finally his face relaxed. The panic retreated.

'Let's not move,' he said. 'I like it here.'

'I know you do. Just sometimes it's a little hard.'

'It won't be hard if I make it easy.'

Rachel looked at him, amazed. 'Are you prepared to do that? I mean really, not just, "Yes of course, darling," I mean *really* really. Because it won't be easy for you. All those memories. I'll have enough to deal with, I don't want to be battling with your ghosts.'

'Perhaps you could speak to them nicely and ask them to go away.'

'I think it's you who needs to do that.'

Brendan put his hand over Rachel's. 'OK,' he said and kissed her lightly. 'This is going to be the best bit of both our lives.'

PART TWO

Rounding towards the full

Fifteen – April 1921

Matilda sleeps. She sleeps soundly, deeply, heavily, but thank God she doesn't snore. Occasionally a dreaming breath will utter a small sound but mostly she is silent, and for this Robin is grateful. His nights with Father are restless, punctuated by ghastly noises, so occasionally he will allow himself a respite and the opportunity to wallow in clean crisp cotton sheets, sunlight peering through the gaps of thick velvet curtains hanging over vast windows and the gentle clink of breakfast trays bearing silver teapots and china cups. Of course, his presence is not always desired for a whole night, but this is Matilda's last night in London and she has requested his time for the usual payment.

There is little about Matilda that he won't tolerate. His first instincts about her had been right. She is perfect; she is still attractive, her flesh still firm, her purse ever open, her spirit generous and her time available. But, however much he enjoys a woman's company, he cannot afford to ever let her feel it is anything other than a business arrangement. And Matilda has never given the slightest hint that she thinks otherwise.

But there is one thing that niggles at him; a thought that, if he isn't careful, will worry and worry itself into a passion of distaste. The one thing that he really can't tolerate is her name.

She is so unlike a Matilda, who in his head is a frumpy peasant woman with blond plaits and red cheeks. Where this image comes from he has no idea, but there it is, firm and fast as a memory. The woman, who lies beautifully rested, comfortable in her luxurious surroundings, is worth more than the name Robin refuses to reconcile with its bearer.

He had told her this and she had laughed at him.

'What should I be called?' she asked, tinkling her piano laugh. 'Actually, I've always rather fancied the name Delilah. What do you think of that?' she said, running an elegant nail down his perfect nose.

Robin turned on her. 'Don't ever tease me.'

'Or I could just ask you to leave.'

How many times will he have to act out this scene with these often ridiculous women? They need him more than he needs them; there are plenty more where she came from. And in cruel moments some of them have been told this. But Matilda, despite her name, is worth hanging on to for as long as is feasible.

Matilda continues to sleep, not hearing the knock that brings the breakfast tray. Luckily, only yesterday she had bought Robin a silk dressing-gown, and this is what he puts on to answer the door. The waiter is not much older than Robin and not yet well trained enough in discretion. He barely manages to contain a conspiratorial grin and has no control over an eyebrow that shoots skyward at the sight that greets him.

'Would you like me to open the curtains for you, Sir?' the 'Sir' comes out with difficulty, is stumbled over. Robin wants to make him pay.

So the curtains are opened (still Matilda smiles in her sleep), breakfast laid out and a bath run. The young waiter carries out his instructions with an acceptable quota of awe and Robin believes he has given the boy a glimpse at a way of life, for this was how it had started for him, with the knowledge that it was possible.

The waiter, suitably tipped, leaves the room and Robin gazes at his sleeping benefactress. He slips off the gown and into the sheets, laying his head between her thighs and gently licks her awake.

*

'Where would you like to go for our farewell lunch?'

Robin is concentrating on getting the knot on his tie right. 'Your choice.' There is a coldness in his tone that implies wherever it is they go, it will not be the last time *he* will lunch there. Last days are always difficult; there is always that chance that in the final moments something will slip, an emotion will let itself out, sullying, tainting the rewards for his labours.

Over lunch at Claridge's, Matilda asks him something no one has asked him before: 'What will you do with your life?'

The question shocks him, momentarily knocks the wind out of him. And then he realises why. Beyond earning the money to live a certain lifestyle, a lifestyle that is as yet only glimpsed at, he really doesn't know what that actually entails.

'Do you think you'll marry, have children?'

Robin practically chokes on his champagne.

'I think there's a romantic part of you that believes you'd have to fall in love before you did that. You don't, you know.'

Robin is uneasy about this conversation. There should be anger and hurt in her voice, but he can detect neither.

'Take my advice,' she says. 'Forget women like me.'

'There are no women like you,' he smiles, charmingly.

'Perfect to the end. I'll not deny your talents. How long have you been doing this? Can't be more than a couple of years. But what does it get you apart from money in the bank? Where does it get you? What you really want to do is marry.'

'Do you have a daughter?'

Matilda knocks him playfully. 'Yes, you know I do, but I wouldn't let her anywhere near you. Do some homework. Find yourself an heiress. The war must have left some rich young widows. You can't lose. Marry into that and you're set up for life.'

Robin listens to her words. She unnerves him with her coolness, her ability to remain detached; no wonder they get on so well. But uppermost in his thoughts is Father. Surely he cannot survive for much longer, then he will be free. Until then he must continue to work. But there is something else; young women terrify him. They are not his first choice.

'It's got to be easier. Look at you. You're certainly the best-looking, best-dressed man in this restaurant.'

Robin looks around him. Yes, yes, of course he is. People stare at him wherever he goes. And it isn't just the impossible blondness of his hair or the blueness of his eyes.

'I've seen how young women look at you. I guarantee that this time next year you will be married. In fact, when I see you next year, I expect to be introduced to your wife.' She bores into his eyes, challenging him.

A rush of excitement creates a fantasy in which he lives happily, opulently ever after; the house, the servants, the clothes, the parties, the blank face of the woman who will provide all this, *and* Matilda! This is a life he could live. Yet pursuing a woman for the aim of marriage requires altogether different skills. And these he will have to learn.

'All right,' he says.

'That's my boy,' she smiles, slipping a long velvet box into his hand.

Another watch.

Sixteen – April 1921

'What do you know about her?' Rachael asked.

'Not very much.'

'Aren't you concerned?'

'About what?' Sydney Cohn assumed that look of wry amusement that infuriated his daughter.

'Don't be difficult, Daddy. Middle-aged widower marries younger woman that no one knows anything about.'

'Ah, you think she might be after his money?' *The Times* admitted defeat in the battle with Rachael's attention. He folded the paper and removed his reading glasses.

'What are you thinking about? That I may marry a young girl and leave her my non-existent fortune, or are you hoping that you might marry an older, rich man?'

'You're being awful today. I refuse to answer.'

Sydney laughed.

'And don't laugh at me.'

'All the information I have is that Dulcie is thirty-five, writes poetry and has a sick mother in Pinner.'

'Hampstead's a long way from Pinner.'

'She's not that sick.'

Rachael stood up.

'I'm going for a walk. I can't talk to you.'

Sydney picked up his reading glasses. Rachael didn't move.

'I thought you were going out.'

Rachael sat down.

'I've changed my mind. It looks like rain.'

Sydney patted the space next to him on the leather Chesterfield.

'Come and sit with me.'

Rachael funeral-marched past the fireplace and deliberately sat with a gap between them.

'It will be all right,' her father said. 'This is the right thing to do. I can't bear the thought of you in that huge house alone.'

Sydney put his arm out to his daughter and she relented and fell into its comfort; closing her eyes and breathing in her father's slow, melodic tones, the vaguest hint of an East European accent sing-songing its way through his words.

'For five years I've said nothing because you needed time. But you are so obstinate, so stubborn—'

Rachael sat up, 'But—'

'No, please, let me speak.' Rachael sank down again. 'It's time now, time for you to leave all of that behind and Isaac coming back from New York and needing somewhere to live—'

'Showing off to his young bride.'

'If it was good enough for you, why isn't it good enough for her?'

Rachael pouted. 'It's a conspiracy,' she said, tapping her heel fiercely against her father's foot.

Sydney laughed. The mantelpiece clock struck six.

'Are you changing?' he asked.

'Daddy! What do you think?'

'I don't know, do I? I can't keep up with constantly changing fashions. For all I know, brown tweed skirts and pink silk blouses are what everyone is wearing for dinner these days.'

'No. I brought a dress. I'll go and get ready.'

Rachael got up and walked towards the door.

'And be nice to Dulcie, won't you?' Sydney called after her.

*

One hour later Rachael re-entered the drawing room. She tiptoed over to the sleeping Sydney and marked his forehead in red lipstick. The doorbell rang.

'Daddy, you'd better get changed. They're here.'

Sydney opened his eyes and smiled.

'I'll take them into the study while you sneak upstairs.'

'Sneak! Why would I have to sneak?'

'Because it's rude not to be ready to receive your guests.'

Sydney got up, laughing. 'But that's not the Silverman way, is it? I can recall many an occasion where dinner was kept waiting while Dorothea finished her toilette.'

'That's because she needed an extra long time to do it,' said Rachael.

There was a gentle, gloved knock on the door, then it opened.

'Mr and Mrs Lemon have arrived.'

Rachael took charge.

'Thank you, Davis. Show them into the study.'

Davis retreated.

'Now go and get ready.'

Before he could answer she pushed her father out of the room, turned him to face the stairs and went into the study.

Isaac Lemon grabbed Rachael and held her in a constricting hug. Rachael could see nothing but the black of his dinner jacket.

'Chotchkeleh! How are you? Let me look at you. You look wonderful!' he boomed, finally releasing her.

Rachael looked up into his face. The sadness that she had always associated with him had been replaced by a radiant calm that took ten years off him. He looked younger than when she had last seen him, seven years ago.

Over his shoulder, Rachael caught sight of the glowing blonde of neatly bunned hair framing an extraordinarily sensible face. Rachael smiled and stepped back from Isaac. Isaac turned.

'Rachael, I want you to meet Dulcie. Here she is, my little shiksah.'

Rachael giggled and held out her hand to Dulcie, who took it and held it tightly between both of hers.

'I am so happy to meet you. And we are so grateful to you. We want you to spend as much time as you can with us. I've left all my friends in New York, so I may be counting on you for company. I hope you don't mind.'

'Company?' Isaac's huge voice asked. 'You've got me.'

'I mean young female company.' Dulcie winked at her. Rachael thoroughly approved of the action that was so wonderfully out of place with the neat hair, barely painted face and smart, but plain, dress. She smiled back with unforced pleasure.

'Of course. I'd be delighted.'

And when Sydney entered the room he found the two women holding hands, grinning at each other.

Seventeen

'Leah! Where are you?'

'Shepherd's Bush.'

'Can you be a little more specific?'

'I've been . . . staying with . . . a friend.'

Rachel ran through all the possible scenarios, before answering.

'Why haven't you called? We worry about you.'

'There's no need.'

'Leah. There's every need,' Rachel said, although she knew she shouldn't have.

'I'm fine.'

'You always say that.'

'Maybe one day you'll believe me.'

There was something surer, more confident in Leah's voice that almost tempted to Rachel into believing her, this time.

'Leah?'

'What?'

'Have you met someone?'

There was a silence, then Leah giggled. 'Sort of,' she said.

'Oh, OK. I *am* interested, you know.'

'I bet you are.' Leah giggled again.

'Are you coming back here or are you now living in Shepherd's Bush?'

'I'll be back. But I want to ask a favour.'

'Sure.'

'Come over here?'

Rachel was slightly taken aback by this request. She missed a breath, then took two in quick succession to recover herself. Leah had more than raised interest, she had aroused suspicion. 'OK,' Rachel answered slowly. 'Can I bring you anything?'

'When can you come? Can you come now?'

'Yes, yes, I think so. Give me the address.' Rachel searched for a clean scrap of paper. Considering the amount of paper her work generated, it was ridiculously difficult to find any. She found a corner where she could squeeze the words on a sheet covered in once-important phone numbers; she had no idea who any of these people were.

'See you soon then,' Leah giggled *again*.

'And what's so funny?' Rachel was trying to sound cross, but Leah's obvious happiness was beginning to infect her.

'Byeee!' Leah said and put down the phone.

As she looked up the road in the A–Z, Rachel puzzled, as she often did, on her total inability to pick anything up from Leah. It was nearly two weeks since they had last heard from, or seen, her and in that time Rachel had on several occasions tried to concentrate her thoughts on Leah to see if she could at least get a glow that would tell her Leah was safe. But all she ever got was a tangle of confusion in which Leah was impossible to reach.

It was not as if Leah didn't believe – the usual reason it was difficult to connect with someone. Having grown up in the shadow of The White Horse, it was impossible to remain immune to the suggestion of the inexplicable. But they had both used The Horse differently. For a long time Rachel had been scared of it, not understanding that she was feeling its power. Leah had loved it from the moment she became aware of it; on one occasion alarming the family by borrowing the window cleaner's ladder to climb the roof, from where you could almost see it. It was Leah's fascination that gradually brought Rachel round; she would insist on climbing it daily and inevitably it was Rachel who accompanied her.

'Tell me about the dragon again,' she would demand of her elder sister, settling herself somewhere around the Horse's ear, her chubby fingers breaking into the lunch box to get at Ella's thoughtfully provided strawberry jam sandwiches.

And Rachel, who was seeing and feeling things that had nothing to do with knights on horses slaying dragons, would crossly retell the tale, whilst thinking, 'This isn't what it's about.'

'Wow!' Leah would say, letting jam ooze out of the bread and fall to the ground like clots of dragon's blood.

It was evident that Leah's interest lay in the tangible – she wanted to know, she needed the stories – whereas Rachel would lie on the hill, letting in images and sounds for which no explanation was required. It touched Rachel deeply that Leah actually thought that she believed but it seemed she had a scientific mind after all. And maybe that was why Rachel could never get through to her.

The address Leah had given Rachel was in a short cul-de-sac of large Victorian houses off the High Road. There was nowhere to park and Rachel had to drive around for a while, eventually finding a parking meter. The sky, which had been blue with a bright burning sun as Rachel was parking had suddenly turned dark grey and released a fierce shower, soaking Rachel during the short walk to the house. By the time she rang the doorbell the sun was out again.

The door was opened by a short, round, pock faced man of around fifty. She tried to place his face.

'You must be Rachel,' he said with an accent from which Rachel placed his privileged education and low status establishment career. 'Do come in.'

Rachel went in. As she passed close to him her hands felt dry and her stomach contracted slightly. It was all she needed to confirm she didn't trust him.

From the outside the house looked as neglected as the others in the street; paint peeling off the stonework, shutters tight across dirty windows. But inside, bare polished floorboards and white walls crammed with framed prints told an altogether different story.

'I'm Trevor Rushcliffe,' he said, holding out his hand.

She was not surprised that his grip was ineffectual, his eyes empty. 'Pleased to meet you,' she lied.

'Leah knew you would be.'

Her guard went up. Instant hostility. This wasn't simply protection of Leah; he was a nasty unlikable man. To remove herself, Rachel took a close look at the drawings on the wall of the hall.

'Do you mind?' she asked.

'Please,' he said.

Her eyes scanned the walls. Then it came to her – where she had seen him before. The programme on Psychic Art. She tried to remember what he'd said but could only recall him being arrogant. 'And you did all of these?' she asked.

'Yes,' he said, standing back and letting her study them.

Each picture was completely different. They were of varying ability and diverse styles. Yet what made them so remarkable was the way the paint seemed to float above the surface, making the pictures appear to move. Rachel could only describe them as painted on puddles.

'Come with me,' he said and she followed him into the large, bright living room where a hundred or so more pictures covered the walls from floor to ceiling.

'This is incredible,' she said. 'Tell me. What do you know about these artists?'

Trevor Rushcliffe smiled, a distorted, grotesque movement of his mouth. 'Very tactfully put, my dear. Leah said I'd like you.'

A shiver chased down Rachel's spine. 'Where is she?'

'She's just making tea, she'll be with us shortly. Do sit down.'

He directed her towards a sleek, modern armchair, surprisingly comfortable.

'Tell me about the first time,' Rachel asked him, trying to be as professional as possible. It was the only way to overcome the discomfort she felt.

Trevor looked beyond her as if his childhood were being replayed somewhere in the space between her left shoulder and the window.

'I can't remember the first time it happened, only when I started to become aware that this wasn't something that happened to everybody. I always drew well, but maybe I was always drawing other people's drawings.'

'Dead people's drawings.'

'Not only.' He fell into an armchair opposite Rachel. 'I can't do it on demand. It happens in the moments before I fall asleep. It starts with a smell, or a sound, something that doesn't belong in my home. A crushing weight on my heart leaves me short of breath and then an unbelievable release, after which I feel nothing. My sense of touch disappears while my other senses become sharper. I see colours within colours, smell the pollen on a bee, hear the clash of clouds rolling over each other—'

Rachel became aware that she need not be in the room; Trevor had no sense of her presence whatsoever.

'—In this state I go to my studio. I am, as we know it, unconscious as I paint—'

As he talked, Rachel studied him. It seemed incongruous, unfair even, that this ugly, nasty man was the conduit for such beauty. Looking round the room her eyes caught sight of a faint pencil drawing, surrounded by wine-coloured mount and a thin gold frame. Trevor had come to the end of his part of his narrative and broke out of his half-trance in time to see Rachel squinting at the picture on the other side of the room.

'Come and see,' he said.

As she got closer Rachel could see it was an amateurish attempt at a house. A cold wind blew over her. She knew the house.

'When did you do this?'

'Let me see,' he said, taking the picture off the wall. 'They're all dated on the back. Ah yes, May 1921.' He put it back.

The wind froze her spine. 'No, I mean when did *you* do it?'

He smiled patiently. 'I'm sorry, my dear, that's all I can tell you.' He returned to his seat.

Rachel stayed staring at the picture. She became aware of Trevor's voice.

'Occasionally,' he was saying, 'I remember it in a dream. If, when I wake in the morning back in my bed, the dream is still there, I'll jot it down on a piece of paper and put it with the picture. If that happened, then the paper will be inside the frame.'

Rachel dared not ask.

Leah came in with a tray of tea.

'Have you shown her mine?' she asked him, kneeling down to pour the jasmine tea into tiny cups.

'Ah, no.' Trevor went to a draughtsman's chest and removed a pile of papers. They were covered in a thick heavy charcoal. Rachel came back to the armchair and Trevor handed her the pile.

She took them and the tea together, looking for the first time at Leah. 'How are you?' she said. 'You look good.' But the combination of her hair growing back and the fixed grin did not fool Rachel; Leah may have looked better than she had in a long time, but something wasn't right.

Rachel looked through the pictures. At first the subject matter was indiscernible but as she looked closer she could make out the White Horse, their parents' home, the garden, Leah's bedroom. 'You did these?' she asked Leah.

'No,' said Trevor. 'I did.'

'Oh,' said Rachel.

Trevor and Leah both began to speak at once. Leah giggled then allowed Trevor to talk.

'I have one of these for every night that Leah has been staying here.'

Rachel wanted to know how long that had been, how they'd met, what on earth was going on between these two.

Leah couldn't wait for Trevor to tell the tale his way, so she interrupted him. 'Trevor was showing his work at The Mind, Body and Spirit exhibition.'

'My pictures are sometimes for sale,' he said without apology.

'Show her the picture,' Leah told him.

Trevor reached down behind his chair to where a few framed pictures were resting.

'I did this about a week before the exhibition.' He handed it to Rachel.

'It's Jonno,' she gasped.

'I know, isn't that amazing?' said Leah, practically on the edge of her seat with the memory of the excitement she had felt on first seeing it.

The picture was drawn in the same heavy charcoal as the other 'Leah' pictures, yet within the bold lines and smudged edges was the unmistakable image of her stepson. She didn't like this, she didn't like this at all.

Leah was prattling on: 'So when I saw it and told him who it was, well Trevor and I got talking about all sorts of things and I told him all about you and your work and those things that happen to you and after a while Trevor told me that he believed it was me that gave him the drawing. Isn't that amazing? I mean, I'm not really into any of this stuff, not like you—'

'Why were you there?' Rachel asked her.

'You remember – I was helping Brie on her crystals stall.'

'Oh, right. Go on.'

Leah continued. 'Then Trevor told me he had done another picture in this style so I came back with him. Show her the other one.'

Trevor handed Rachel a framed picture of a lizard covered in hair.

'Isn't that bizarre?' screeched Leah.

Rachel looked at Trevor.

'These are for sale,' he said. There was something cruel and desperate in his tone, which Rachel flinched at.

'May I speak to my sister alone?' she asked him.

Trevor looked shocked, but only for an instant. 'If you'll excuse me,' he said, rising and leaving the room, as if it had been his idea.

'Leah? What is going on with you two?'

'He's kind to me. I have my own room. I make tea, and sometimes cook for him. He likes having me here. I inspire him,' she said proudly. 'You've seen the pictures.'

'What else do you do for him?'

Leah burst into tears.

Rachel would not be kind. 'Why haven't you phoned? What is going on?'

'He said if there were any outside influences it could jeopardise the work. You know, like radio interference.'

Rachel felt a fury rise in her. 'But it was all right to phone today.'

Leah looked at her as if this hadn't occurred to her, hadn't thought to ask why. Rachel recognised Leah's lifelong resentment of those who planted doubt, and knew they were now locked in a battle.

'I'm sorry, Leah, this feels a little like exploitation to me.'

'Of course you'd say that.'

'Why would I? I wouldn't just say it for the sake of it. The man may have an extraordinary gift, I can't deny that, but I don't trust his motives. And I don't like you being here. I suppose you've told him all about us?'

Leah was sobbing now. 'So?'

Rachel got up and paced the room. 'This doesn't feel right. It feels like blackmail or something. I'm going to have to buy those pictures off him like a ransom for your release.'

Leah stopped crying. 'I think perhaps you're over-reacting slightly.'

Rachel suddenly caught sight of the sketch of the house and

stopped still. 'All right,' she said and sat down. 'Will you come home with me?'

'He's been kind.'

'I'm sure he has. Will you come home with me?'

'I thought you'd be pleased. I thought I was doing something to help you.'

Rachel looked over at the sketch again. 'You did. You have. Now go and get your things together.'

'You always do this!' Leah suddenly screamed at her, then sat down obstinately in the armchair vacated by Trevor, a five-year-old's sulk on her face.

Rachel realised that she was going to have to leave without her. She knew also that any more resistance would firm Leah's stand, the purple boots trenching themselves deeper in the life she had with Trevor.

'Leah, Leah, Leah,' she sighed.

'What?' spat the cross face.

'Do you think he'll sell me the drawing of the house?'

Eighteen

'£75,' Rachel repeated.

'You're fucking crazy. That could have bought a hell of a lot of nappies.'

'Come on. Things aren't that tight.'

'No,' Brendan admitted. 'But they will be if you carry on like this.'

'Like what? Never mind Leah. I had to buy this picture.'

Brendan picked it up and studied it. 'It's crap,' he said. '£75 worth of crap.'

'You're missing the point.'

'No, you are,' he said, banging the picture down on the table.

'Careful!' Rachel said, leaning over to grab it.

'This has gone too far,' he said, lowering his tone.

'On the contrary,' snapped Rachel, taking up the picture and walking towards the door. 'It's only just begun.'

She went upstairs to the bedroom, breathing deeply as she climbed the stairs, noticing for the first time in her pregnancy that it had been an effort. And still eight weeks to go. So this is what there was to look forward to, a creeping debilitation. So far she was still fairly small, her bump neat and round, very little fluid retention, no swollen ankles. Lucky, they called her. She wasn't lucky – she was fit; spending the first eighteen years of her life climbing that steep hill at least twice a week to be with The Horse had paid off in terms of her health.

She arranged the cushions on her bed so that her back was well supported, lifted her knees and placed the picture on her thighs, like a book rest, and took a long look at it. She turned it over and began to pick at the masking tape holding the frame together, then paused to ponder the black felt-tip lettering: May 1921.

She dug her nails into the tape. Finding the right edge the tape came off, quickly and easily, taking the hardboard backing with it. She lay her hand flat, letting the back drop onto it, then lifted the glass and the frame away from the drawing. The paper was haphazardly stuck to the inside of the mount with two small pieces of tape and yes, there were two pieces of paper between the drawing and its backing. She put all the pieces of the picture down next to her, carefully unfolded the paper and read:

'There are some who see it as an unnecessary indulgence on my father's part, after all the house he built for Saul and I as a wedding present was ample generosity for one lifetime. But, Father was right; it was too big, too grand for a woman on her own, a widow.'

The handwriting was small and neat, only the disproportionate space taken up by the tails of the 'y's hinting at a creativity; the carefully calligraphed brown ink lettering seemed completely anachronistic against the cheap, lined paper roughly torn from a spiral-bound notebook. Rachel assumed that this was not Trevor's handwriting but a continuation of his brief possession by the spirit of the occupier of the house.

'This house is perfect. I miss the old mansion in the same way I miss my husband; only when overcome by an extreme of unwelcome nostalgia.'

That was all on the first sheet. On the second sheet the writing was less formal, certainly less neat.

'Dulcie, bless her, in her exasperating mission to find me something to do, took me down to the East End where she and other Ladies provide meals and shelter for destitute women. I am ashamed to admit it but I have fallen in love. When I told Dulcie, she laughed and said everyone felt like that about Shoshi. Who could resist the charms of a five-year-old with such copper-coloured curls

hiding such round brown eyes? She seemed to take to me, following me around. I tried to speak with her mother, a frightened woman, younger than me, hiding her face from the world. Dulcie does not realise it but that child has stirred an attachment in me that I cannot reject.'

'Shoshi?' Hot tears stabbed at the back of Rachel's eyes. She put the piece of paper down, unaware that she was creasing it with the pressure of her thumb and finger. She wanted to scream, she wanted to tell Brendan that she was right, she knew she was right, and she would have paid five times £75 to have this happen. She looked back at the paper; there was nothing more. Nothing.

A name, thought Rachel. What is her name? The framed drawing had shown no signature. Now she realised it had been hidden by the mount, for as she picked up the paper with the house on it, a scribble was apparent in the bottom right-hand corner. It was very faint. She held it directly under the lamp and finally made out the name, *R Silverman.*

She lay back on the bed, trying to make sense of the information. That was too much to attempt so she settled for ordering it, collating the facts and working out where to go from here. She knew what Louise would say. What the hell, she'd ring her anyway.

She picked up the phone. No dialling tone. She pressed down and released several rimes. Then a voice said, 'Hello?'

'Louise?'

'Rachel?'

'I just picked up the phone to call you.'

'I must have beaten you to it. How are you?'

'Something extraordinary has happened.'

'How's the baby?'

The baby. How's the baby? No change. Rachel, feeling well most of the time. But learning to live with the nagging doubt that hopped between her heart and her womb, that everything was far from fine. Refusing to face it. There would be time enough for all that. After all, what could she do about it now?

'I heard some sad news today,' went on Louise.

'What?'

'Hannah died. You remember Hannah? My old school friend. Haven't seen her for years—'

Hannah.

'Sad life she had, I think. Living alone in that house. She never married.'

Hannah's house.

'Do you remember? I took you there once or twice when you were little. You cried the first time. She thought you were frightened by her sun hat.'

Hannah. A kind old lady in a large hat.

'She was very fond of you.'

An electric charge ran from her eyes to the drawing lying next to her on the bed. Hope. 'What was her surname?'

'Sterling. Hannah Sterling.'

Rachel swallowed her disappointment. Perhaps it was just a coincidence after all.

'What's happening to the house?'

'I really don't know. You've been very quiet and asked some very odd questions. Why do you want to know?'

And when Rachel told her, Louise berated her for even entertaining the notion of coincidence, which in her world simply did not exist. 'A concept invented by those whose minds were too small to embrace the unexplainable – otherwise known as sceptics.'

'It was a lovely house, wasn't it?'

'Yes,' said Louise. 'It was.'

Rachel hadn't taken her eyes off the drawing. The baby kicked. She liked to think he was kicking her into action. 'I wonder—' she said.

Nineteen – May 1921

Rachael was waiting at the gate as the removal van quivered to a halt outside the house. She was more excited than a child awaiting Father Christmas. Her new-found friendship with Dulcie had removed any vestige of resentment about having to give up her former home to her. She had spent all morning needlessly sweeping, polishing and mopping the brand new house in anticipation of the arrival of her belongings.

An old man and his son, wearing thinning, tobacco-coloured coats, climbed out of the van.

'Morning, Madam,' the old man said, raising his tweed cap to reveal a completely bald head.

Rachael smiled in reply. She couldn't stop smiling. The old man simply raised one of his unnaturally thick eyebrows and signalled to his similarly afflicted son to open the back.

In her head, and even on paper, Rachael had arranged and rearranged the furniture a hundred times, but to Fred Gimble & Son, she was the most obstructive of clients, ensuring a full day's work out of both of them.

Should the desk go in the window of the lounge? She could close the partitioning doors and have a nice cosy study to write letters in. The General Post Office had conveniently placed a post box right outside her front door. From this vantage point she could get to know her neighbours, if only to the point of how many times a week and when they took trips to the post box. Or should she take one of the upstairs rooms to write without distraction? This previously internal dilemma was imparted to Fred Gimble & Son, their opinions sought, the desk situated in two or three different positions until finally a decision was reached. And this was not the only piece of furniture to suffer indignities concerning its fate.

When Dulcie arrived at four o'clock expecting Rachael to be organised enough to offer her tea, Fred Gimble & Son were assembling Rachael's bed in the small back bedroom with the off-centre fireplace.

'Surely you're going to sleep in the front room?' Dulcie enquired.

Fred Gimble took off his cap, and swept the back of his hand over his brow.

'I thought I would too,' said Rachael. 'But now I'm actually here . . . I do love this room, don't you?'

'Yes,' said Dulcie, 'but it's small. Have you room for your wardrobe and dressing table?'

'No,' interjected Fred Gimble. 'Definitely not.'

'There you are then,' said Dulcie. 'It's settled.' Then, employing her best head girl voice, she ordered, 'Dismantle it and take it to the large bedroom at the front.' She took Rachael's arm and led her out of the room and down the stairs. 'Let them get on with it,' she said, as & Son blew a kiss in thanks to the disembodied voice.

There were two tea chests labelled 'Kitchen' blocking the entrance to the small scullery.

'I don't suppose you've lit the stove?' asked Dulcie, practical as ever.

'Um, no. But the coal should have been delivered. I'll check.' Rachael climbed over the tea chests and went out of the back door. The coal was housed in a brick shed next to the garage; it had a door to the street for the coal to be emptied into and a door to the garden for her to collect it. The shed was empty.

'Damn,' she said. 'Bad news,' she called out to Dulcie.

'I'll telephone Isaac and ask him to get some sent over. Is the phone connected?'

Rachael came back into the kitchen. 'Of course the phone is. It's one of the little details that Daddy was quite insistent on getting right.'

'All right. I'll see what I can do.' Dulcie disappeared into the hall and Rachael started to unwrap the kitchen equipment from its newspaper protection. In one crate she found the kettle, a set of pans, a selection of knives, half a dozen mixing bowls, some tea towels, but little else. The second one had packets of tea, jars of marmalade and assorted jams all nestled comfortably in copious paper. There was more packaging than contents. She found homes for everything she had unpacked, then took them all out and rearranged them.

She put the food in the larder, laughing at how pathetic her few jars and packets looked on the empty shelves, but all the time feeling an excitement about her newly reduced living space. Living in the mansion on West Heath Road, she rarely went into the kitchen; days would go by without her doing so. The week's menus had been discussed with Cook in the drawing room. Even after Saul's death . . . Rachael stopped what she was doing. She was amazed at her capacity to still feel the pain of that first year. The pain that everyone around her assumed was the pain of grief, but only she knew was the pain of guilt and shame.

'That's all organised then.' Dulcie's voice brought Rachael back to herself. 'You all right?' Dulcie asked, putting a hand on Rachael's arm.

Rachael responded by allowing a small tear to run down the side of her nose.

'Hey,' said Dulcie, putting her arms round Rachael.

Rachael pulled away and wiped her nose with her finger. 'I'm all right.'

'This is such a great house.'

'Yes,' said Rachael looking around her at boxes and crates. She smiled at Fred Gimble appearing hesitantly at the door.

'Excuse me, Madam. Where would you like the sideboard?'

'That's an easy one,' answered Rachael. 'Only one place that could possibly go.' She led Fred Gimble into the dining room and pointed to the wall between the two doors. 'There,' she said decisively, immediately feeling better.

Twenty

Rachel sat up in bed. She was feeling cold. The sheets were damp and creased beneath her. Putting her hand to her chest, she could make dry channels with her fingers through the sweat. She looked over to Brendan who lay with his back to her, oblivious to her terrors. The blood pumping around her body seemed alarmingly close to the surface of her skin; she was aware of every pulse.

She got out of bed and straightened the sheet she had been lying on. It was visibly damp, but she didn't want to wake Brendan and change the sheets, so she took a towel from the bathroom to lay on the bed. She changed her T-shirt, all the while taking deep breaths and trying to get back a little bit of whatever it was that had caused such a reaction.

In the bathroom, she splashed cold water on her face, looked up into the mirror over the sink, then reached for the white towel that hung from a mahogany ring next to it. Patting her face dry, she slowly revealed her mirror image to herself and was shocked at what she saw.

Rachel had never been one for showing her emotions; whatever she was feeling inside, her face remained resolutely expressionless. This was frequently mistaken for unhappiness, boredom or superiority. Although there were times when she may have been feeling a small amount of one of these, they were none of them her predominant state.

But that face that peered back at her was as visibly distressed as the blue/gold woodwork that framed it.

Rachel leant towards the mirror, touching noses with her reflection. Small patches of breath clouded the glass as she examined her eyes. One of the joys of the whites of her eyes being palest blue was that she remained unblemished. Whites of eyes were often stained; dirty with over-exposure, displaying soaked-up pollutants like lime tree leaves. Rachel's eyes were smooth and clean, the irises competing with darkness against her pupils. There was no shading in Rachel's eyes; this added to her apparent lack of expression, as her mood was only evident in how she much crinkled the skin around them.

Her heart beat was now nearly normal. She stayed staring at herself until she was satisfied that the terror she had seen somewhere in her eyes had abated. But as it retreated, the images from her nightmare became clearer.

Blood, there had been blood, but controlled. That's it, blood and muscle pumping. A heart, it was a heart. Surgeon-gloved hands moved around it amongst flashes of silver – scalpels, clamps. The heart was divided, sliced in two and the hands went inside and pulled out a . . . Rachel closed her eyes against the image but it would not go away. The tiniest, blood-and-slime-soaked baby jumped out like a frog disturbed from a pond. Voices cheered, an audience clapped, cries of 'It's a boy!' deafened her. But the frog baby born out of the heart would not be caught. She remembered her own voice screaming, 'Cut the cord. What about the cord?' But she could neither see herself nor discern what part she played in this. As a needle threaded with black tapestry wool sewed large clumsy stitches across the heart, it was turning into a mouth and the stifled cries of 'Rachael, Rachael' reverberated in her ears until she woke.

As she got back into bed, Brendan stirred. He turned over and mumbled in his half-sleep, 'You all right?'

'Mmmm,' she replied.

He put an arm across her, 'Baby nightmare?'

'Yes,' she said.

'Tell me about it tomorrow,' he yawned, removing his arm and turning his back on her again.

Rachel reached for the notebook she kept next to her bed and scribbled, furiously recording the dreadful images and her own responses. She was well practised at this. As a child, her favourite times had been overnight stays with Aunt Louise. In the morning over bread, cut and toasted from a freshly baked loaf and spread with thick, home-made marmalade, Louise would ask her about her dreams, encouraging her not only to remember as many details as possible but constantly prompting her with, 'And how did it make you feel?' So Rachel learned to feel comforted by the unknown.

But there had been no comfort in the dream of the frog baby. She had felt nothing but extremes of fear, frustration, helplessness. She'd had other baby nightmares – giving birth on a bus then getting off without it, not being able to identify her baby amongst hundreds lying in plastic cots in the hospital nursery, giving birth to a fully formed, fully clothed adult who said 'Thanks, bye' and left her – there were hundreds of variations of anxiety dreams. But this was no anxiety dream, this was something else.

She tried to settle herself and get back to sleep. It was hopeless, so was anything else she attempted to distract her from her thoughts. So she lay there watching the red dots on the clock flash as the numbers changed and the night crept towards morning.

Twenty-One

'Hello. Yes, I'm enquiring about the house in Wildwood Road.'

'It's gone under offer, I'm afraid.'

'Oh. I know this sounds odd, but I really would like to look at it.'

'Exchange is this week. Even if you came in with a higher offer I don't think you'd be able to beat them to the exchange.'

'Ah, no. You don't understand, I mean I haven't made myself clear. I have no interest in buying the house. I just want to look at it.'

There was a short silence at the other end of the phone.

Then: 'Do you mind if I ask why you want to see the house?'

'I'm writing a book. It's for my research.'

'Oh, I see. Well, we have the keys here. I don't see any real reason why not.'

The agent was waiting for Rachel at the front door. 'Hi, I'm Shelly,' she said.

A fat, not unattractive face smiled at Rachel through a blonde feather cut that her hairdresser should never have advised her to have. Short arms held the door open.

A kind but sad face underneath a large hat.

Rachel half smiled at her, trying to think of something to say.

Shelly was perhaps quite new to the job. She looked to Rachel like a girl that would have difficulty settling and had probably tried several careers (definitely a travel rep at some point). Rachel got the impression that she thought selling houses was an easy option. Shelly was a troubled soul, maybe couldn't find a boyfriend while all her friends could and had. She looked like a girl who was waiting to get married.

'Thanks so much,' Rachel said.

Shelly, who seemed to be trying to make Rachel feel bad about this unproductive use of her time, melted slightly at Rachel's obvious sincerity. 'That's OK,' she said. 'I wasn't very busy today.' She unlocked the door. 'To be quite honest, I was glad to get out of the office. There's no rush, take as long as you like.

'What's your book about?' Shelly asked following Rachel into the kitchen.

Rachel faltered slightly before answering; she didn't really want to get into this. 'I'm researching into Spiritualism.'

As she had expected, Shelly said nothing for a moment. It generally was a conversation stopper. But Shelly then appeared deep in thought, her forehead crinkling with indecision. She surprised Rachel with her question. 'So why did you want to see the house?'

Rachel laughed. It was a fair question. What would one have to do with the other? But something in the way Shelly had asked it told Rachel that there was not as improbable a link to Shelly as there may have been to some people.

'It's complicated,' she said.

'I go to Spiritualist Church,' said Shelly.

Rachel tried to appear surprised. 'Really? Which one?'

'In Wimbledon. I only go when I visit my Mum. We go together. That's where she lives.'

'I've not been to that one.'

'It's . . . good,' Shelly said.

Rachel smiled. 'Yes,' she said. 'It is.'

'I thought you said you hadn't been.'

'No. I meant, you know, generally, it's good.'

'Oh.' Shelly giggled with embarrassment. 'Yes. Look, shall I leave you to it? I've not had lunch. I'll just nip out and get something. I'll see you later.'

'Thanks,' Rachel called after a self-conscious Shelly trying her best to make a quick exit.

Rachel waited a few moments to allow the dust to settle on Shelly's departure, then took a few deep breaths and tried to focus her mind. She opened her handbag and removed the two sheets of paper that had come out of the framed drawing and re-read them several times, trying to allow images, sounds, smells in. Nothing was coming from the kitchen. She went back into the hall and opened the first door she came to. She found herself in a perfectly symmetrical room. The room had two doors onto the hall that faced two huge windows either side of the doors that opened out into the garden. A fireplace faced a flat wall.

Rachel could picture a square oak table in the centre of the room and an oak, glass-doored sideboard resting between the doors. This may have been where meals were taken but she felt sure it was also where letters and diaries were written.

She perched on the wide sill of the left-hand window and glanced out into the garden and got a strong sense of water. But if there ever had been a pond, it had been filled in and grassed over.

Sitting on the grass drinking pink milk.

She turned her attention back to the room.

The walls started to flash colour. Immediately Rachel's eyes began to sting, a sure sign she was getting somewhere. It was a creamy yellow and, when the sun shone on it, the room basked in a golden glow. The oak sideboard had decorative copper plating at the corners, blinding her as the sun reflected off them. Then Rachel was back in the empty, white-washed room.

A sudden coldness brought the idea that there may be a connection between this house and the face of the hanged boy that had been coming to her. If the thought had come into her head then, there very probably was a link. She thought back to a time when she was unable to identify those thoughts that released themselves from her unconscious which would have a psychic pay-off, and the infuriation combined with pleasure when they did.

She left the room and climbed the stairs.

At the top of the first flight she immediately turned to her left and entered a room on the right side of a staircase that led up to the attic.

'Here,' she said.

The room was completely bare. The carpet was dark green and the walls white. She thoroughly approved. Throughout the house the walls had been painted white. The small fireplace was off centre of the left-hand wall, which made Rachel smile. She felt immediately comfortable in the bare, bright room; Rachel loved it when she felt like that. It wasn't quite a *déjà vu*, it wasn't so specific. But a warming calm would fall over her, like sunshine being poured from a jug and parts of her would awaken, come alive – awareness, perception, belief. It was like falling in love, when everything seemed possible and nothing was too ridiculous to accept.

A short, shrill scream coming from the garden turned her towards the window.

The face of a small girl, younger than her, peers out from an upstairs window.

'Who's that?'

She searched the trees for the bird that'd made the sound, but could see nothing. Rachel felt a huge defeat come over her, shortly followed by a giant frustration, like writer's block. She felt full to bursting with thoughts and ideas, yet was totally unable to gain access to them, articulate them. Her mind seemed distracted but she did not know by what; yet her eyes were still stinging, so she knew she was close to something.

The baby kicked, then turned and kicked again; a sudden burst of fervent activity. This calmed Rachel down, containing her feelings. She knew that this was when she worked at her best, when she had a reminder of who she was. It wasn't enough to pick up images, messages. Louise had always taught her that there was a reason that those messages came to her. It was vital for her to remember this.

She heard the scream again and the baby kicked as if in response to it. She now realised that it was not an actual sound. It was inside her head. She closed her eyes and waited for it to come again. But the sounds she heard were of water, the gentle trickle of a fountain. Then there was a muffled sound, a woman's voice beginning to form into words; she couldn't make out the words but she could detect panic. Then, clear as anything, as if the anxious stranger were standing next to her in the room, she heard her call out, 'Shoshi!'

Silence. Nothing. No water, no cries. Rachel shivered. Her baby curled itself up and pressed against her.

Shoshi.

Was it just before Christmas? Christmas Eve perhaps. It wouldn't have meant anything to her – Christmas was a cold and grey event in her life. Her father refused to have a tree in the house. And there was no present-giving tradition. If any presents were to be exchanged, then it must be done quietly, without fuss and no family member should feel obligated to either give or accept a present.

Louise comes to her as she plays in her bath.

Louise. Lovely Aunt Louise. Kind, soft, generous, warm. Arms ever open to her niece. Sharing, teaching, opening up the universe for her. Loving her without bounds. Louise. Focused, grounding. Beautiful. Soul mate. It was unimaginable not having her in her life.

She waves a crumpled parcel badly wrapped in thin, soft, red paper. Rachel squeals with anticipation, yet already knowing, in that way she has, what is inside it.

'Bunny,' she shouts out, jumping up and down in the bath.

Louise puts an arm out to steady her, afraid that she might slip, at the same time laughing at the wet black curls stuck to the chubby cheeks. 'You amaze me,' she tells her niece, whose dark eyes widen at the compliment.

'Open it!' the little girl shrieks.

'Me?' answers Louise.

'Yes,' Rachel says.

Louise slowly tears the paper, revealing a copper colour. Two ears fall out, followed by black glass eyes, a rubber nose, then acres of gorgeous soft fur.

'She mustn't get wet.'

'What shall we call her?'

'Shoshi!'

Louise laughs. 'What a lovely name.'

'But she mustn't get wet.'

'No,' Louise says. 'We won't let her get wet.'

Whose voice had she heard? The question pressed down on her, restricting her breathing.

Was it her own? Her three-year-old self calling to her over the years?

She needed to leave the house, get out, so she scribbled a note to Shelly on an old envelope found in her handbag and left.

Outside, she stood looking at the house. This was crazy; she was running away. Not facing her fears. Rachel often got powerful, insistent feelings about places, things, but generally they applied to people around her, the people close to her. Everything she had felt about this house, the drawing, the notes, she was sure was completely personal to her. And now it seemed this had begun when she was only a child. It had begun when she, for whatever reason, had given a name to Louise's Christmas present.

She went to sit in her car. The day was lightless, threatening heavy showers, cold, windy. A slither of white sunlight broke through the clouds and briefly lit up a tree on the Heath, across the road from where she was parked. And there he was. All of him, not just the face. He swung from the tree, tweed trousers flapping in the wind over brown brogues. Her baby woke, kicking her furiously. She had never felt it like this. She blinked hard. He was gone. The kicks subsided but she felt sore, wounded. For the first time in her pregnancy she felt resentful, angry, tired.

She wanted it to be over.

It was time [illegible] she was pulled. And then he was [illegible] man, not just the face. He swung from the tree, [illegible] happily in the wind [illegible] her mommy. [illegible] She thanked him. He was gone. The kicks [illegible] She wondered, for the first [illegible]

She wanted it to be over.

[illegible]

Twenty-Two

She was surprised, but relieved, to find Brendan home.

'Jesus, you look terrible,' he said. 'Sit down, I'll make you a cup of tea. Do you want to lie down?'

'No, no. I'll be all right.'

'You really look bad, you know. I think you should lie down.'

'Maybe. In a bit. How come you're home? What are you wearing?' Brendan only had two looks. Work clothes and best clothes. His work clothes were overalls over trousers he had worn for thirty years. His lucky trousers, he called them. Their original shape, colour and fabric was indiscernible, they were just this mass of grey fibres held together by Brendan's frame. But he held fast on to the belief that they held the key to his creativity. T-shirts and overalls came and went, but the trousers stayed.

Brendan's best clothes consisted of black. Black anything. Black jeans, black cords, black boots, black shirts, black ties, black waistcoats, black jumpers, black jackets. But today Brendan was wearing something new, which looked suspiciously like jogging pants. And they were blue.

'These?' he asked, pulling them out from the side pockets.

'Yes, those.' Rachel started to laugh. 'Oh God, you're not going all sporty on me, are you? Bit late for a mid-life crisis, isn't it?'

'These are my "cleaning out the basement" clothes.'

'Cleaning out the basement?'

'Yes. I thought it would make a nice playroom.'

'Is that what you've been doing?' she asked wearily.

'Not yet,' Brendan replied. 'I'd only just got changed. I'll go and make you that tea.'

Rachel guessed that if Brendan went shopping for special clothes and was looking after her, making her cups of tea, then the clearing out of the basement may well turn into one of those jobs that would never get done.

Rachel looked around the room, breathing in its calm. She'd spent a lot of time, effort and money getting it right, trying to achieve that effortless comfort. Mismatched furnishings, a confusion of origins. Battles with Brendan who'd never had an ordered home in his life. 'Contrived', he called it. She'd loved making their home and making it baby safe would destroy all her work. Having a separate space totally devoted to her son and his toys seemed like a very desirable proposition. She must encourage Brendan in his efforts.

Brendan appeared with a cup of tranquility. 'Where have you been?' he asked, placing the cup in front of her and sitting opposite her.

Rachel pondered whether to tell him what had happened or not. She wasn't even sure what there was to tell except that it had been something of huge significance. She settled on, 'Out and about. It's getting to me now. I've not got the energy I had.'

'You're in your "three months weary", don't forget. Just take it easy. Slow down.'

'Mmmm,' she said, breathing in the fumes of camomile, fennel and orange peel. She looked up at him. 'It's so funny seeing you dressed like that.'

Brendan jumped up suddenly. 'Oh, leave it alone will you. What bloody difference?'

Rachel didn't have the energy to respond. 'I think I will go and lie down,' she said.

She stood and went upstairs, taking her tea with her. As she lay on the bed, she felt a new kind of fear. She was afraid to close her eyes, fall asleep, or even meditate. She was afraid of what was going to come to her, afraid of her dreams, and this had never happened to her before.

[illegible] her eyes fall asleep or [illegible], she was afraid of what was going to come to her [illegible] of her dreams, and that had never happened to her before.

[illegible]

[illegible]

[illegible]

[illegible]

Twenty-Three – May 1921

Robin wakes suddenly from a rare deep sleep. Something has changed. He sits up and turns on the small light that lives on the table next to his makeshift bed. The smell is worse than ever.

'Father?' He leaps across the small space between their beds. The old man is still and pale. Robin puts his head on his father's chest and hears a faint gurgling. A breath disguised as a rattle breaks the silence and his disappointment makes Robin realise how often he had hoped it was over.

Robin sits on the edge of the bed and looks at the imminent corpse, a bare flicker of a light hovering in its eyes. He looks around the room. A shadow lingers. It was the approach of death that woke him.

His father tries to speak. It bears no resemblance to any sound Robin has heard before. He shakes his head to indicate that he hasn't understood. The sound comes again; a gentle, drawn-out roar. Following the arduous movement of his lips, Robin believes his father might be saying, 'Thank you.'

Footsteps thunder down the outside stairs. Curses batter against the door. Robin puts down the photograph album and goes in dread to let his father in.

The boy stands well clear, as he has learned to do. His father, weighed down with alcohol and grief, falls into their home, greeting his son with a clip round the ear.

'What have you got to say for yourself?' The words float out on a stench of whisky and sick. He stumbles and somehow manages to fall onto the decrepit sofa. His curses degenerate into mumbles.

Robin lifts his father's legs onto the sofa and removes his shoes.

'Get out of here and leave me alone,' his father roars. 'I don't want you.'

He has heard this so many times before, the words no longer have any meaning. He gets the moth-eaten eiderdown from the bed and places it over the crumpled figure, the mutterings having turned to snores. The child loosens his father's collar, places a kiss on the sweating head and climbs on to the empty bed that, more often than not, he has all to himself.

'Am I doing well, Mother?' he whispers as his lids fall over his eyes.

The sound of the battle raging in his father's lungs is so loud, Robin has to put his hands over his ears to block it out.

He winces as the old man's eyes blink alternate fear and pleading. The shadow darkens over him.

The dark and dirty room is lit by a single ray of dusty sunshine from its one window. A beautiful but tired woman twirls round and round, raising and lowering her arms which hold a gloriously rich, deep red fabric, the colour of fine wine, shot with a silver that reflects tiny sparks of light. She laughs and sings and captures her little angel in its folds.

'One day,' she says. 'One day, my darling.' Then she swoops the child up and holds him close, tangling him, binding themselves together; mother, child and cloth, in a hopeless dream of eternal comfort.

Robin stands over his father. He can't bear to see him fight. The shadow is fast descending.

He gently removes one of the pillows from behind the old man.

White tiled walls. Barred windows. Miles of stone floors. Doors swing an occasional squeak, the time between them getting longer. Like a music-box slowing down. Like waiting for Mother's next breath.

He can't take his eyes off her. He must remember her like this for ever. Smooth, unblemished skin. No longer troubled. Eyes understanding, accepting, yet bursting with love and concern.

'Look after him,' she tries to say, her words being only different-shaped breaths.

The little boy nods his head, a thick blond fringe flops over his blue eyes. His mother slowly lifts a hand to his head, brushes the hair away. Now he can see her clearly. He leans over the bed. She, or the sheets, or the hospital, smells of dust and carbolic soap and there is only the faintest hint of her lavender water.

'Help him not to suffer. Promise me?'

He holds her hand up against his cheek so she can feel his tears.

'I promise,' he answers.

Robin turns his head away so that he can see neither the fear nor the gratitude in his father's eyes.

He eases the pillow down and presses firmly on each side of the thin face. Violent breaths cut off by soft feathers.

An angry shadow darts around him. Robin lifts the pillow. A thick, dark green slime oozes out from the side of the slightly parted lips.

. . . Mother . . . a hopeless dream of eternal comfort . . . 'Promise me?'

'I kept my promise,' he tells the shadow, which dances its approval.

Robin, dazed, sleepwalks to the wardrobe and removes a parcel tied with a silk ribbon, wrapped in brown paper soft from years of careful opening. Inside is a neatly folded length of burgundy taffeta. He holds it up, letting it unfold, then puts it around his shoulders, enveloping himself in fulfilment.

'All alone now,' he says, pulling up a chair and sitting next to what's left of his father.

But there is no one to hear him. Even the shadow of death has gone.

Twenty-Four

Rachel held the door open for the woman as she pushed her buggy through. She gave Rachel a knowing smile in thanks. Rachel was still not quite used to the conspiracy of motherhood that set her apart from the rest of womankind; she was only just getting used to her pregnancy ensuring seats being given up for her, doors held open and, of course, that awful sympathetic knowing smile from those a little further down the line.

She watched the back of the woman disappearing down the street, buggy precariously balanced with bags, toys, blankets, coats and reaffirmed her vow to the minimalist approach to baby care.

'Rachel!' Louise's voice called out across the crowded café.

Rachel negotiated her way through the maze of tables and kissed her aunt on the cheek. She had sat at a table for four.

'Are we expecting anyone?' Rachel asked.

'Yes,' answered Louise. 'I hope you don't mind.'

'Well,' said Rachel, noticing vibrancy in Louise's eyes, 'it depends who it is.'

Louise smiled enigmatically.

'Is it someone I know?' Rachel asked.

'Know of,' answered Louise.

'I'm intrigued,' Rachel said, fingering the menu, turning it around like a steering wheel. 'So, who is it?'

'Roger.'

Rachel dropped the menu on the table as the back of her eyes stung. 'Roger Whelan? The medium?'

'Yes,' said Louise, a gentle blush climbing the tiny mounds of her wrinkled face.

'You're not—? He's not—?'

Louise raised an eyebrow and half smiled.

'What? When? How?' Rachel wanted to laugh out loud. 'But this is extraordinary.'

'Not so extraordinary,' said Louise. 'He's a little younger than me. But no different than the age gap between you and Brendan, a little less if anything. Close your mouth, love, people are staring.'

Rachel did as she was told, not taking her eyes off her aunt. 'But—. Oh. Well, this is . . . great.' She really didn't know what to say at all. She put her head down and studied the menu, not being able to make sense of it. 'What are you having?' she asked.

'Lasagne, I think,' answered Louise slowly.

'You don't see too much of that these days, do you?' Rachel said dreamily.

'What dear?'

'Lasagne.'

Louise laughed and put her hand across the table to touch Rachel's. 'I'm very happy,' she said.

Rachel looked up at her. 'I can see that. Could I have a glass of water, please?' she asked a busy waitress bustling by, who nodded impatiently in return. She was feeling calmer now that the first shock had died down. 'So, tell me about it.'

'I thought you'd never ask.'

In the ten remaining minutes they had to themselves, Louise told and Rachel listened to how this seemingly bizarre, but obviously perfect relationship had blossomed. Rachel's smile got wider and wider while Louise talked about her and Roger's mutual psychic abilities, the endless synchronicities, and the place where they most essentially connected, their innate belief in the fundamentals of Spiritualism. Rachel wiped a small tear away from the corner of her right eye.

'Don't do that,' laughed Louise.

A grey figure cast a shadow over their table. Louise jumped up. 'Roger!' They kissed each other on both cheeks and Rachel saw how much Roger was in need of Louise's warmth to melt his cold reserve.

'My niece, Rachel Treacy, Roger Whelan.' They shook hands. Rachel looked into his grey eyes, desperate for a glimpse of what Louise saw.

'I remember you from the meeting,' he said as he sat down.

Rachel smiled. 'I got a lot from your speech and from your message.'

'But not quite enough, I gather,' he said.

Rachel felt suddenly uncomfortable, as if a social occasion had turned, without permission, into a business meeting. She decided to change the subject, but Roger did it for her.

'Have you ordered, yet?'

The waitress came; food and drink was ordered. Eventually, inevitably, the conversation turned to the thing that bound the three of them together.

'One of my most profound moments,' Roger explained, 'perhaps the epiphanal moment, was when my mother was dying.'

Rachel looked at Louise, who smiled and sat back in her chair; she had obviously heard this before.

'Oh, yes,' Rachel said without thinking.

Roger looked at her as if that were not enough of an invitation to continue. Rachel felt herself sufficiently reprimanded and said, 'What happened?'

'I was walking through Richmond Park. It was almost exactly fifteen years ago. The trees were glorious.'

'I love autumn,' said Rachel.

'Then I think you will really appreciate what I'm going to say.'

'Go on.' Rachel wondered how Louise handled his apparent need for constant reassurance that he was interesting.

'I thought about my mother and her approaching passing, then thought about the leaves and how they change colour, giving such a wonderful display just before they die. That almost self-conscious drawing attention to themselves.'

Rachel's interest was renewed; these were things she had felt herself.

'And suddenly,' Roger continued, 'I accepted the idea of the everlasting spirit. For what is death but a wonderful affirmation of life? The leaves come back year after year, fresh, green and new. They never really die. As with spirit.'

'And your mother?'

'My mother died the next day. And for a whole week, before her body went to the ground, like the leaves, her family and friends gathered and she was praised, glorified and remembered with love. Her final grand display.'

'That's lovely,' said Rachel. 'You must have got a lot of comfort from that.'

'I still do,' said Roger.

There was an awkward silence, which Roger attempted to break.

'I've, er, had some visions.'

'Oh yes,' said Rachel, turning to signal the waitress for the bill.

Louise leaned over. 'Listen dear. This is important.'

Rachel turned back, a small shiver creeping down her back. 'Do you think this is the right time to discuss this?' she asked him, forcefully, directly, threateningly.

Roger and Louise exchanged glances.

'Because I don't think it is.'

'Has something happened, dear?'

'I appreciate what you're doing and I would like to know, hear what you've got to say. I do need help, advice. But this is too important for after-dinner talk.'

Roger became officious. 'Perhaps you'd like to come and see me?'

'What would I be seeing you as? A friend? A client? I think we should be clear about this.'

Louise broke in, protesting. Rachel had always come to her before. But now there was Roger with his superior gifts. They wanted to help.

Rachel was affronted. She was thrown. Apart from Louise, her dealings with Spiritualists were purely on a professional basis. She was confused; she didn't want this man to take Louise's place.

Roger shed his professional skin, showing the first signs of warmth and humanity. 'Any time you want to discuss anything with me, please. I'll be there.'

Rachel relaxed and smiled gratefully. 'I'll call you,' she said.

Louise laughed. 'You once told me those were the three worst words in the English language.'

'That was before Brendan. That was before a lot of things.'

They gathered their belongings and said their goodbyes in the street, Rachel going one way and Louise and Roger the other. Rachel watched them; they made an unusual couple, Louise so small, so colourful and full of life yet so old and Roger, so tall, so straight, so grey and so young. She wondered how much they could actually do for each other.

[illegible]

[illegible]

[illegible]

[illegible]

[illegible]

[illegible] the wine [illegible]

[illegible]

[illegible]

[illegible] a lot on your mind.'

Rachel tore a piece of bread and dipped it in the [illegible] dish of [illegible]

Twenty-Five

'This is so nice.' Rachel briefly closed her eyes and let the gentle chatter, candle glows and gorgeous smells wash over her. She felt Brendan take her hand across the table. By the time she opened her eyes again, her hand was being led around his beard until her fingers touched his mouth.

'Happy Birthday,' he said, barely touching her skin with his lips, but enough to send a small electric shock down to her stomach.

'My last childless birthday.' She took her hand away from her husband, picked up her glass of red wine and took a large sip. Sitting back in her chair, she let the wine warm her.

'I can't wait for the opening.'

Rachel had forgotten. 'I can't believe it's come around so quickly.' She sighed and looked away. 'It's not the best time for it, is it?'

Brendan brought a tinge of anger to his reply. 'Not for you perhaps. But I've been waiting for this opportunity for some time.'

'I know you have. I'm sorry. I *am* excited about it, you know I am.'

'But, as usual, you have a lot on your mind.'

Rachel tore a piece of bread and dipped it in the small dish of olive oil between them. She watched the oil drip slowly back into the bowl. 'Brendan,' she said, 'please don't. Not tonight. I'm there for you. That's what we do for each other – try to do for each other,' she added, remembering how often he had let her down. 'You know I'm so proud of you, your work, this exhibition. So no recriminations. OK?'

Brendan picked up his wineglass and emptied it into his mouth. He replaced it on the table, gently licked his lips and smiled. 'Good wine, nice choice.'

'I'll take that as a "yes" then, shall I?'

Brendan was still smiling.

'That was so funny Iris sending that card.'

'Why?'

'Well, Jonno has never sent me a birthday card in his life. I think it's so sweet.'

'Don't be so patronising.' Brendan's bear hands ripped at his bread.

'I am not being patronising. I'm touched by her efforts to join the family.'

'What was that thing from Leah?'

A spark of annoyance fortunately failed to ignite in Rachel. 'Something Trevor did, I assume.' She shivered. 'I just wish she'd come home.'

'She will.'

But Rachel's imagination had started on its journey to irrationality. 'What, I mean, how do you think it works with them, to get something so specifically personal to me? How does she convey stuff to him? Oh God, it doesn't bear thinking about.'

'He's psychic, remember. He probably just picks things up.'

'No, no. He's only psychic in his sleep.'

Brendan laughed. Rachel glared. 'I just can't bear him,' she said.

Brendan was still laughing.

'I don't know why you refuse to take this seriously.'

'Simply because it's so ridiculous. That's why.'

'Look, I want her home with us, before we go away. If not then, then certainly before the baby's born.'

'It's her life.'

'So we should let her do whatever she wants with it?'

'Yes.'

'You mean like you do with Jonno?'

Brendan replied by taking the wine bottle and refilling their glasses. 'I thought we weren't doing that tonight,' he said.

Rachel chewed her lip then relaxed. 'No, we're not.' She snapped into a different role. 'When's Jonno back?'

Suddenly Rachel became consumed by fear. The anxieties, the dreams, the visions, the terrors all came back. She had hoped the warmth of the restaurant, the wine, the atmosphere, the occasion would all combine to bury her dread, but here it was back and worse than ever.

'Brendan?' she asked quietly.

He saw the change, heard the different voice and paled slightly. 'What is it?'

'It won't be impossible to love my baby, will it?'

Brendan stared at her. He was perfectly still; he had frozen the moment in time. Looking at her as if he were hearing her for the first time. As if he'd not really understood until now. He was finally convinced of her fear, that there was something very real to be concerned about even though she was unable to tell him what that thing was. She was relieved and reassured that for all their petty bickering, this man was in her life for the very best reason that there was; what Louise had always hinted at and what Rachel now accepted.

He was there because he was supposed to be.

'I want to go to the house,' she said.

Twenty-Six – June 1921

The best thing to do would be to burn it. Drench the place with gasoline and light a match. Then it'll be gone; everything would be destroyed. Robin comes alive for a second, picturing the thrill of his old life in flames, but the hollow deadness resurfaces when he imagines the aftermath, black and ashes. You can never completely annihilate; there will always be something left to remind you of what was.

But he has no enthusiasm, no passion for action. He simply packs a suitcase with the best of his clothes and accessories, reviving slightly at the touch of silk, the shine of silver, the smell of worsted, and walks out of the flat.

He stands on the pavement uncharacteristically indecisive. How will he get to Islington? Normally he would have walked, but not today with a heavy suitcase in tow. Even carrying it as far as the bus stop seems impossible. And no taxis ever happen to be just passing by this forgotten street. For a second he panics. But the sight of a front door opening across the street and four filthy children spilling out of it, followed by shouts, screams and the sound of thrown china smashing against walls, remind Robin of what he is doing and why. He picks up his suitcase and walks as fast as his burden will allow towards the bus stop that will take him to his new home.

He has located cheap rooms in a small, terraced street of

Georgian houses off the City Road. They are far from ideal but at least it isn't the East End and they are clean, dry and his. The landlady lives on the premises, a grotesque, retired Music Hall dancer, full of chatter and stinking of gin. Robin hopes to be able to avoid her, but even in his detached state he is aware of the necessity of charming her; there may be occasions when he won't be able to pay his rent, with cash.

Robin needn't have worried; Florrie Grix is one step ahead of him. For his arrival she has pinked her lips only slightly more carefully than usual and has applied a hideous auburn to what is left of her hair. A nauseous perfume mingles with the booze and sweat that can never be washed away. At the sight of her, Robin's panic returns. He almost wants to tell her there's been a change of plan and he won't be taking the rooms after all, but ultimately there is something comforting in the flowered wallpaper, the fringed lampshades, the stupid fox terrier barking at her heels and the offer of tea and toast, once he's 'settled himself'.

She gives him the key to his room and excuses herself 'to put the kettle on', not moving out of the way so that Robin is forced to squeeze past her, holding his stomach in (and his breath) to avoid contact with the feather-trimmed house coat that 'accidentally' falls open, to reveal a torn peach lace slip.

Robin climbs the two flights of stairs. His bedroom is at the back and he has extravagantly taken on the front room as well. Florrie Grix is thrilled with the arrangement, believing that only a true gentleman requires two rooms to live in. Now actually being here, getting used to it as his home, Robin has no idea what he is going to do in the front room, but the rooms are so cheap he could only conclude that at sometime he must have believed it was a good idea.

The bedroom is sparse, thankfully free of the frills and pinks that decorate Florrie's own quarters. The iron bed seems comfortable enough, it is generously made up with blankets, pillows and an eiderdown. There is a single wardrobe, small chest of drawers with the inevitable jug and bowl, and a bedside table.

Above the fireplace hangs a poster from the halls and, above the bed, a crucifix that Robin rips from its nail and throws in the drawer of the bedside table.

All this activity wearies him. A small flame, that part of Robin that is always there, wants to unpack, settle, think about the rest of his life but, for the moment at least, exhaustion takes over. He opens the case but removes nothing, then crawls onto the bed, curls himself up and tries to sleep.

A knock on the door frightens him out of a dream. 'Mr Sweeting?' a ridiculous voice calls through the woodwork.

Robin sits up, disorientated. He had wanted to sleep, obviously needed to. He feels sick and angry.

'Mr Sweeting, are you all right?'

He sighs impatiently and goes to the door. Apparently he'd locked it although he can't remember doing so. As he turns the key he can already smell her. He automatically brushes his fingers through his hair and straightens up.

Florrie has on her best little girl smile, the one that has in the past melted the hearts of many a gentleman and even on one memorable occasion an actual duke. It does nothing for Robin.

'Your tea?' she asks demurely.

'If you don't mind, I need to rest. Perhaps later. I'll come down,' he adds in order to prevent another such intrusion.

Florrie takes the rejection as she takes all her rejections – badly.

'But I've made toast,' she says, not quite angrily but certainly hurt.

'Thank you,' says Robin. 'But later.' A great apathy literally makes his knees go weak. Florrie takes this as a sign of his sincerity and tells him to knock whenever he is 'up to it'. She turns away and goes downstairs, a ferocious yapping greeting her as she descends.

Robin locks the door and goes back to the bed, this time wrapping himself in the eiderdown, holding it around himself as if he will never get warm. And sleeps till morning.

[illegible] half [illegible] the other side.

[illegible]

[illegible]

[illegible] milk and honey.

[illegible]

[illegible]

[illegible]

[illegible]

[illegible]

[illegible]

[illegible]

Twenty-Seven

Brendan stopped the car on the opposite side of the road from the house, half on the pavement. He turned off the engine but left the lights on. The rain continued to batter against the roof, the windscreen, the road, the Heath.

'This is—'

'Please,' said Rachel. 'Don't say it.'

'But there's nothing to see. You can't see a thing in this rain.'

Rachel turned to look at him. In the warmth and comfort of the restaurant it had all seemed so clear, so easy. Was that momentary? But Rachel knew there could be enough truth to hold on to in a passing moment. If she hadn't learnt that she would never have been able to stay with Brendan. 'It's not only about what I see,' she said slowly, as if explaining it for the first time to a child.

'What do you want me to do?' he asked.

'Stay here,' she said, 'keep the door unlocked for me. Have somewhere warm and dry for me to return to.'

Brendan leant over to her, taking her head between his two hands. He kissed her gently on the forehead.

'Thanks,' she said. But as she turned to open the car door a contraction took her by surprise. She took a deep breath. 'Whoah!' she said. 'That felt different.'

'Are you OK?'

Rachel didn't reply.

'You're not, are you? I don't think we should do this. Close the door, I'm taking you home.'

All was calm again.

'No, I'm fine.' This time she managed to get one leg out of the car. 'Oh no I'm not.'

'That's it,' said Brendan. He leant across her and closed the door.

'That was really fierce,' said Rachel, her heart beating faster. She took two deep breaths. 'Do you think it was the wine?'

Brendan was concentrating hard on driving. The wipers were useless, the window steamed up with every breath and the road was badly lit. 'I can't see a damn thing,' he said.

Rachel was biting on her hand. Two more contractions had followed in quick succession but now it seemed to have calmed down and she was left with a dull ache, like a bad period pain. She swooned slightly and felt a faint nausea.

'I shouldn't have had so much wine,' she said.

They turned away from the Heath onto North End Road and slowly climbed the hill up to the Pond. As usual there was traffic. Flicks of orange light reflected in raindrops from the street lamps distorted Rachel's vision, then red drops, white drops; colours were swirling in front of her, the sound of the rain beating louder and louder. Her womb tightened again, she wanted to let out a scream.

The car crawled through Hampstead Village. Rachel was feeling intermittently fine and as if she wanted to die.

'I know about this,' she told Brendan. 'It's fine. It's false labour. My body's preparing itself. Aaagh!'

Halfway down Haverstock Hill, Brendan pulled over. 'Give me the phone,' he said.

'I don't have it.'

'What?'

'I didn't bring it. What do we need the mobile for when we go out for dinner? It's not as if we need to phone a babysitter or anything. Oh my God!' Rachel clutched her stomach.

'We need it exactly for this.'

'Keep going, we'll be home in five minutes. We can phone from there. Not that I think there's any need toooooo.'

The rain was stronger than ever as they pulled up in front of their house. Brendan fled out of the car and went round to help Rachel out. As she got up she touched the back of her legs, then bent down to feel the seat. 'Brendan,' she said.

'What?'

'The seat's all wet.'

'Well, it's raining.'

'Er, no. That's not what I meant. I'm all wet too. I think my waters might have broken.'

Brendan looked at her in disbelief but managed to snap himself out of it in time to catch Rachel's arm as she swooned again because another contraction had torn through her. 'Um, perhaps you'd better stay in the car. I'll phone the hospital. They'll probably say come straight in. So no point in coming in the house then. You'll only have to come out again. Where's your bag? You have packed, I assume. Well, never mind. Shouldn't think we need it.'

'Brendan?'

'What?'

'You're waffling.'

'Yes. I am.'

'I'm coming in because I want to get changed. I don't want to go to hospital with wet knickers.'

'OK.'

'So . . . can . . . you . . . open . . . the . . . front . . . door . . . please.'

'Bad one?'

'FUCKING AWFUL ONE!'

Inside, Rachel climbed the stairs with difficulty while Brendan phoned the hospital. Her head was pounding now and she lay on the bed on her side, too exhausted, feeling too sick to do anything or feel anything except anger that she was so unprepared. 'I'm not ready. You're three weeks early, mate. I haven't even bought any nappies.'

She rolled over onto her back and lifted her knees up. The pains in both her head and her womb eased slightly. She tried to regulate her breathing and on her own bed in her own home she felt calmer and stronger. When Brendan came up five minutes later, he found her fast asleep.

He sat on the edge of the bed and gently brushed away the long fringe that kept flopping over her face. Much to her annoyance he called it her public schoolboy's hair cut. He laughed thinking about that and Rachel opened her eyes.

'Feeling better?' he asked.

'God, yes. That was horrible.'

'The hospital says we should go in.'

'But I'm fine now.'

'They say once the water's have broken there's a risk of infection. They want to keep an eye on you even though established labour may be some time off yet.'

Rachel giggled. 'That all sounded very technical.'

'Well, you've opted for a technical birth.'

'Little hint of criticism there?'

'You know how I feel about it.'

'You're just an old hippy,' she said, too tired to involve herself further. 'Not a good time to discuss it, hey? Let me sleep for a bit. We can go later.'

'I think—' Brendan started, then changed his mind. 'All right. I'll be downstairs if you want me.'

'Thanks.' She closed her eyes.

'Hey!'

She opened them again. 'What?'

'Happy Birthday!'

'I wish,' she said, floating away to her waiting sleep.

Twenty-Eight – June 1921

Dulcie left Rachael waiting in the hall. 'I won't be long,' she said. 'Then I'll introduce you to everyone.' Dulcie disappeared through one of the doors.

Rachael looked around her. It had obviously been a grand dwelling at one time but had been sadly neglected for many years. There was no furniture, no furnishings. The tiled floor was cracked and dirty, paint peeled off the woodwork. The staircase managed to retain some of its former magnificence, but the light that shone through the windows was curtained in dust.

Rachael could hear muffled voices from all over the house. Someone was playing the piano, badly. Hearing footsteps on the stairs, she looked up to see a small figure running towards her. Sunlight from the stained-glass window on the landing shrouded the child in a multicoloured aura, giving a metallic glow to her wild tightly curled locks. The girl slowed down when she saw Rachael and came to a complete standstill a couple of feet away from her.

Rachael bent down to smile at the girl, who brushed a bronze curl away from her eye and stepped backwards, unsure of the stranger.

'Hello, I'm Rachael.'

The child remained silent but coyly placed her thumb in her mouth, indicating that perseverance would reap a response.

'That's a pretty dress,' Rachael went on, fingering the fraying lace that hung off the hem of the pale pink, floral fabric. She looked down and saw a toe peeping through the laddered lisle of grey stockings and the worn leather of very old boots.

'Mummy made it.' The voice was unsure, not completely at ease in forming sentences, yet accented in a familiar way that touched and surprised Rachael.

'What a clever mummy you've got.'

'Shoshi? Shoshi! There you are.' A tiny woman lost inside shapeless and faded green linen appeared out of one of the doors. She looked at Rachael and instinctively pressed the child's head against her. 'I don't know you,' she said.

Rachael held her hand out towards the woman, 'Rachael Silverman,' she said. 'I'm a friend of Mrs Lemon.'

Shoshi giggled. Rachael smiled at her. 'It *is* a funny name, isn't it?'

Shoshi giggled louder. 'Do you think my name's funny?'

'I thought your name was Shoshi, not Funny.'

Shoshi was delighted and, despite her mother's attempts to restrain her, moved closer to Rachael.

'Dulcie Lemon is my very special friend,' Rachael said, crouching down to be on Shoshi's level. 'She asked me to come here especially to meet you.'

Two round brown eyes widened. This was too much for Shoshi's mother, who pulled her away sharply. Shoshi squealed her resistance.

Rachael stood up and was about to speak but the tiny woman moved her head away sharply, almost as if she expected to be hit. Slowly she turned her head back towards Rachael and a recognition of something shared passed between them.

'Do you live here?' Rachael asked.

The woman didn't answer, but put her head down. Rachael looked at Shoshi, who put a finger to her lips to indicate a secret. At that moment Dulcie appeared.

If Shoshi's mother had been nervous of Rachael she seemed terrified of Dulcie.

'Mrs Lemon! Mrs Lemon!' Shoshi jumped up and down.

'Hello, Yiskah,' said Dulcie.

Yiskah turned her back on Dulcie and grabbed Shoshi by the arm to stop her jumping. Shoshi lost her balance. Yiskah pulled her away.

'Shoshi!' she said sternly, dragging the crying child away from them. Rachael stood watching helplessly. Dulcie remained calm.

When they had disappeared through one of the doors Rachael asked, 'What was all that about?'

'Yiskah's a very proud woman.'

'Do you not get on with her?'

'I think she feels that I know too much.'

'What do you mean?'

There was a pause before Dulcie replied. 'It's hard for her to accept charity.'

'I can understand that,' said Rachael.

Dulcie brightened. 'Come,' she said. 'I'll show you where we serve lunch. There's only three of us here today, apart from the residential staff, that is. Isn't it a wonderful building? We're so lucky to be able to use it. There's only about half a dozen women and children living here, but on any day we can get up to fifty to feed.'

Dulcie chattered away conspicuously avoiding anything that might bring in the subject of Yiskah. Rachael followed her, only half listening. The strange couple, mother and daughter, had touched her deeply. She walked with Dulcie through doors to larger rooms, not taking anything in, her mind on other things.

PART THREE

The crumbling of the moon

Twenty-Nine – June 1921

As she chatters, Robin can't take his eyes off her teeth. They are the least attractive part of a face that is already straining in that department. But she has been the only woman out of the day's arrivals to be open to the possibility of him, and for this reason he is seated opposite her taking tea, while she talks in her aggressive, clipped South African accent about the boat journey and the plans for her visit, all the while with a piece of cress lying like a blanket over her distorted top left incisor.

This is the most effort it has felt in a while. Robin knows he is good enough at his job not to show this. He is blessed with the face of an angel and whatever he is feeling inside remains invisible on his clear complexion and impenetrable in his radiant eyes.

As if reading his thoughts, a chubby hand lightly runs an over-gemmed finger along his jacket sleeve, teasingly stopping short of his flesh. 'What a lovely looking boy you are, Robin.'

Robin employs his skill of blushing on demand. This is greeted with a gurgle of delight. 'This trip is going to be more fun than I could ever have imagined,' she sings.

Robin hates her, and himself. Stepping back from the scene he observes an overweight, middle-aged woman being embarrassingly girlie with a youth young enough to be her grandchild. A boy out of place and out of time who is ridiculously overdressed in clothes he has no right to wear, desperately trying to fit into a world that has no space for him, the he can only enter through lies and deceit.

'I assume you have a dinner suit,' she is asking him. She correctly interprets his distracted silence as a no. 'That's too bad,' she taunts. 'I've got seats for the ballet tomorrow. Ah well. I suppose we'll have to go shopping then.'

The lure of Savile Row is no contest for Robin's conscience. He buries his bitterness beneath bolts of black barathea.

Robin sits cross-legged, circling his new patent shoes, feeling the bones in his ankle click, fighting off the boredom of cacophonic sounds as his companion glows with the affectation of experiencing the *avant-garde.* Every so often she turns to him, reveals her ugly teeth, by way of smiling, gradually manoeuvring herself so that she can't help but brush against him every time she breathes. He rests her ermine-trimmed velvet cloak across his lap and is shocked and repelled to find her hand searching for his. Under the cloak she takes his hand, then places both hers and his against his groin. A small sigh of annoyance indicates he has let her down by not being hard.

Fortunately at this point the third act comes to a close and she is forced to remove her hand in order to applaud. She claps loudly and eagerly, looking around her as she does so, as if her enthusiasm demonstrates her understanding of what was, in Robin's mind, a frightful evening's entertainment.

He places the cloak on her shoulders, being careful to leave his hands touching her for the required amount of extra time that promises what is to come. He is already dreading it.

'It's a nice night,' says Robin. 'Let's walk.' Before she can protest, Robin puts his arm through hers and leads her away through the crowds.

Robin is, as ever, amazed by the capacity of these women to flaunt him. To him there is something shameful in the relationship; that's part of what he thrives on, what makes it an appealing profession. He sets himself up as something other, something unusual, something dangerous even, yet most women and fat, unattractive Sophie in particular, refuse to acknowledge this. All around him he is aware of young men accompanying older women. With his trained eye he can tell which ones genuinely were 'nephews', the title the more discreet of them generally utilise, when forced into an introduction.

But Sophie is blatant in her need. She has nothing to hide behind. Robin understands that she has very little chance of receiving the amount of attention he is giving her, unless she were paying for it. And this bores him. They wander down Regent Street, the remains of a glorious sunset still spattered around a sky that is not quite yet dark, Sophie shamefully uninhibited about what she expects of him on their return to her hotel. There is no challenge, no excitement.

She is admiring the silverware in Garrard's window. He steps back, disengaging himself from her clutches. A drunken party falls out of the Café Royal; a dozen or so men and women, not much older than Robin. A couple of the men don't look that different from him, are just as well dressed, just as good-looking. But they tease each other in accents it has taken Robin years to acquire, call each other names that tell of a camaraderie born in dormitories. The girls are pretty, confident and carefree. They bustle around the pavement in a swirl of feather, diamante and chiffon, expensive perfumes mixing with booze and smoke.

Robin catches the eye of a small, dark-haired girl, who holds his gaze then laughs loudly and rudely at him. A couple of the boys look over at him, register Sophie, laugh again and then they all move on down towards Piccadilly Circus.

Sophie retakes Robin's arm, oblivious to what has occurred inside him. But he has been reminded of a hunger that no amount of fucking this fat horrible woman will sate.

*

Sophie lies sobbing and bleeding, unable to speak the venomous words of abuse she so needs to in order to preserve what little is left of her dignity. Robin sits in the dark in a chair, watching the grotesque figure writhe, her fat lips swelling.

Robin is breathing fast and deeply. The urge to hit her more and more keeps rising up like a nausea.

She moans, but even this is too painful for her. 'Get out,' she mumbles, the words getting trapped inside her swollen mouth.

Robin doesn't move.

'Get out,' she says, 'before I call the police.'

Robin stands up and saunters towards the door. He opens it, then closes it again. 'But you haven't paid me,' he says.

He walks over to where her handbag lies on the bedside table, opens it, finds a five-pound note and a few coins. She watches carefully, not wanting to reveal the level of her fear. But as far as Robin is concerned, it's too late for that.

'Is this all you've got?' He waves the money at her. She doesn't answer. 'It's a lot less than I deserve, but I'll take it anyway.' He pockets the note then picks up the telephone, all the time not taking his eyes off Sophie. 'Hello? Yes, this is room 320. I wonder if it were possible for you to send a doctor.'

Sophie cries out in protest, Robin flashes her a look that silences her.

'Yes, that's right. Mrs van der Reiss has had a nasty accident. Thank you. Goodbye.' He replaces the receiver.

Sophie flinches and tries to move away from him, but he looms over her.

'I suppose I ought to thank *you* too,' he sneers, tenderly removing the pearls from her neck and spinning the necklace around his index fingers.

'Get . . . out . . . now.'

He is about to pocket the pearls, but thinks twice about it and goes to drop them into her lap. She anticipates his action and moves her hand to catch the necklace and for a couple of seconds they are joined together through this semi-precious umbilical cord. The image only repulses Robin more. He lets the pearls drop where they slide along her satin stomach, finally settling in the hollow between her thigh and the bedspread.

Once again he goes to the door and opens it. 'It's been a pleasure,' he says, before stepping out into the corridor and closing the door behind him.

He isn't sure of where he wants to go or what he wants to do. He only knows that what has happened has done nothing to lessen the pain.

Thirty

She opened one eye. Then the other. Rachel made out the shape of a dark figure sitting in a chair reading. 'Brendan?' she whispered.

The shape put down his book and leant towards her. 'Hello,' he said.

The radiance from her husband's eyes lit up the room.

'How is he?'

Brendan got up from his chair and sat on the bed. He pushed her hair from her face. 'Sleeping,' he replied.

Rachel smiled. She turned to look at the travel clock sitting with a water jug and plastic cup next to the reading lamp. 'Three o'clock. Is that morning or afternoon?'

'Afternoon,' said Brendan, moving closer to her.

'How long have I been asleep?'

'About five hours.'

Rachel sat up. 'Five hours! What about the baby? Doesn't he need to feed?'

'They're going to let him sleep. He'll wake when he's hungry.'

Rachel looked around the room. 'Where is he?'

'Safe.'

'I want to see him. I can't remember what he looks like.'

'He looks kind of wrinkled and tiny, with bulgy eyes and a kissing mouth.'

'I'm bound to recognise him then.' Rachel took Brendan's hand. 'How was I?'

Brendan pulled back his hand and showed her three nail marks dug deep into his palm. 'Bit like that really.'

Rachel giggled. 'Did I do that? Well, however much that hurt, I can assure you it was nothing compared to what I was going through.'

'I'm going to set a time limit on this. Otherwise you'll be pulling that one on me at every available opportunity. OK? So, no more references to the pain of childbirth after—'

'He's left home?'

Brendan laughed and moved even closer, folding his big arms around her. 'How are you feeling?' he asked.

'Now that I'm awake – not that good actually.'

'So go back to sleep. Catch it while you can.'

'What day is it?'

'Still Saturday.'

'Who have you told?'

'Everyone.'

'Really?'

'Of course! Why not?'

'So where are all my flowers then?'

A short sharp knock on the door was immediately followed by the entry of two nurses both carrying plant arrangements.

Brendan smiled. 'Haven't lost your knack then.'

Rachel thanked the nurses and foraged around in the foliage for the cards.

'Mum and . . . Louise. Of course.' Rachel was a little disturbed to note that Louise had signed the card from herself and Roger. 'Brendan?'

'Mmm?'

'Can they bring him here? Then while he's sleeping we can look at him and decide on his name once and for all.'

'Finbar.'

'Aaron.'

'Conn.'

'Ethan.'

'Diarmuid.'

'Oh, Bert, Bertie, Benjamin, bugger . . . Just go and get him, will you?'

Brendan went chuckling out of the room.

Rachel tried to get out of bed but her legs were too weak to hold her up. Then she remembered the epidural. Surely it would have worn off by now? Perhaps she was still over-tired. But she was only vaguely aware of a mild discomfort. As soon as she pinpointed it, naturally it started to get worse; a creeping soreness that seemed to be taking up the space vacated by her son. There it was growing inside her, as he had done, stretching its legs and kicking her insides. She reached over to press the bell for the nurse.

The door opened, but it wasn't a woman in uniform, it was Brendan and something had changed.

'What is it?'

'I'm not sure.' He walked slowly over to the bed. 'He was having some breathing difficulties, so they've taken him to—'

'Where?' Rachel ignored the weakness in her legs and jumped out of bed, grabbing for the dressing-gown draped over the back of the chair.

Brendan reached for her arm as it appeared through the sleeve. 'It's all right.'

'How can it be all right?'

He spoke slowly, telling himself as much as her. 'Because whatever it is that needs dealing with can be dealt with here.' Now he had both her arms, holding them tightly then suddenly pulling her to him, buying her in his chest. 'He looked so . . . so—'

Rachel knew. She knew exactly what he looked like. She pulled away from him and stared up into Brendan's dimming eyes. 'So blue?' she said.

Thirty-One – July 1921

The familiar disappointment spread through Rachael as if someone had turned on a tap. Should she honestly have expected him to be any different? He talked at her; she barely listened. She'd heard it all before.

'Do you remember when you were a little girl? It started with the mouse with a broken leg. Who ever heard of such a thing? Birds that had fallen out of nests, dirty hungry urchins in need of more than your old clothes. Then the biggest nursing job of all, your poor sad husband. And now, who? A frightened mother and her child whose only charm, I gather, is that she has curly hair and big brown eyes. Really, Rachael! Is this any more to you than the acting out of one of your beloved orphan stories?'

'You're being unfair.'

'Am I? These daily trips to the East End must be exhausting.'

'Well, it won't be for much longer.'

'I'm very pleased to hear it.' Sydney attempted to spread hard butter on a cold triangle of toast.

'I've asked them to come and stay with me.'

The toast crumbled under the increased pressure. 'You've done what?'

'I said—'

'I heard what you said.' Sydney put down his knife and removed his reading glasses. He should have known better than to believe he could receive his daughter at breakfast and catch up with world affairs.

'That's what I came here to discuss with you.'

'Discuss or dictate?'

Rachael put her head down. 'Well, I've already asked Yiskah to think about it. Dulcie knows.' Rachael made a face.

'Ha!' said Sydney. 'The sensible Dulcie. She doesn't approve either, does she?'

'Not exactly. But then they don't like each other, so it doesn't count.'

'Let's see if I can guess her objections.'

Rachael leant back in her chair and, picking up a knife, began to trace patterns over the tablecloth with its point. She wouldn't look at her father.

'One: what will Yiskah do?'

Rachael thought about responding, then decided to let him finish.

'What will her role be in your house? Are you employing her? Renting a room out? No, obviously not that. This is an act of charity. And the child. Is she school age? Damn it, Rachael! Look at me when I'm talking to you.'

Rachael looked up. She was crying. 'I just want to help. Why do any of those things matter?'

Sydney calmed his voice. 'Surely they matter to Yiskah.'

'I don't want her to, but she has offered to work for me.'

'Good. She has pride.'

'If I wanted a servant, I'd get one.'

'Rachael you are missing the point, I think'

It was always like this with him. Every time she felt like she was making an adult decision, he would find a way to reverse it. She looked over at the well-loved, familiar face. His green translucent eyes were, as ever, simultaneously fierce and inviting. She knew that she couldn't win; she never did.

Sydney recognised the moment of surrender (he was just as used to this as she was) and instantly became kinder. 'Are you sure you know what you're doing?'

'There's something about them. I wish I knew what it was. But I have to help them. I have to have them in my life.'

A puzzled frown distorted Sydney's smooth brow.

'Oh, I can't explain,' she added.

'You're not going all mystic on me, are you? Has Dulcie been taking you to lectures again?'

'I honestly don't know what it is.'

Her seriousness alarmed Sydney. He tried to alter the subject. 'Has she told you anything about Shoshi's father?'

Rachael put the thumb she had been resting her chin on, in her mouth. 'No.' Then with a sigh she banged her hands on the table and stood up. 'I should have known I wouldn't get your approval. I'm going home.'

Sydney held his arms out to her. Her tears came again. He stood up and held her while she cried.

'Sometimes—' she said.

'I know,' he replied.

'It's not that—'

'I know. I miss her too.'

'I wish—'

'Me too.'

'I'm only trying to—'

'It's all right. I understand.'

She pulled away from him, blew her nose and wiped her eyes on the handkerchief he gave her. She held the crumpled cotton in her hand, rolling it around like a ball in her palm. 'I'll get it back to you,' she said.

Sydney laughed. 'Just put it with the others,' he said.

[illegible]

They were [illegible] about their [illegible] I knew, [illegible]

But I have to tell them. [illegible] like

[illegible] smooth [illegible]

Oh, [illegible]

[illegible] going [illegible] the Dillon [illegible]

party [illegible]

[illegible]

He [illegible]

[illegible]

[illegible]

[illegible] Now. [illegible]

[illegible]

[illegible]

[illegible]

[illegible]

[illegible]

[illegible]

[illegible]

[illegible]

[illegible]

[illegible]

She pulled away from him, blew her nose and wiped her eyes [illegible]

[illegible] He said [illegible]

[illegible] When [illegible]

[illegible]

Thirty-Two

'All babies are born with a hole in their heart but in the majority of cases it closes up when they take their first breath.'

Rachel watched the doctor's lips move and tried to take in what he was saying.

'Now we've had the X-rays we know what we are dealing with.'

Brendan was looking at her. She knew what he wanted to ask.

'Is . . . is . . . ?'

The doctor assumed a patient expression.

'Is his life in danger?'

There. He'd said it.

The doctor paused. 'Ultimately, but not imminently.'

There was only a speck of comfort.

'We can help him breathe and feed and function as normally as possible until we are ready to operate. The operation is rarely performed before three months old. And certainly not in a premature baby; although three weeks early doesn't strictly qualify as premature, but there will be a need to keep a close eye on him.' He paused for a reaction but got none. 'And there is the added risk of the lungs being damaged as a result of the heart condition, so we like to operate as soon as we can. This can be an enormously successful procedure.'

Any comfort was hindered by the words 'can be'. 'I'd like to be with him now,' Rachel said solemnly.

'Of course.' The doctor looked down at his file. Rachel noted the ink stain on his fingers. Doctors and fountain pens. Why did they always go together?

'Have you decided on a name yet?'

Rachel and Brendan spoke together: 'Theo.'

All she wanted to do was hold him. But where? How? It seemed so wrong that those tubes helping him to breathe could really be doing him more good than being held close to his mother. She was the machine that had fed him, allowed him to grow, let him breathe but, now he was no longer a part of her body, how could he not still need her? She wanted to take the tiny sleeping figure, disentangle him, put him back where he came from. It was her job, her mission. She didn't want to be made obsolete by the advances in medical interference. A tube, a drip, a monitor – they were no replacement for a mother.

She looked at her husband, her baby's father. 'He's not going to make it,' she said.

And Brendan turned from her and walked away.

Thirty-Three – August 1921

'Here, try this.'

Yiskah hung her head even lower. Rachael lay the dress down on the bed where she was sure Yiskah could see it. 'I don't wear it anymore.'

Yiskah raised her eyes slightly to look at Rachael's dusky, green wool cast-off. 'Why not?' she asked.

Rachael tried to think of a suitable reply. 'I just don't,' she said. She was trying to be tactful. Yiskah's world was certainly not one in which clothes were discarded because the hemline was no longer the fashionable length, and she knew that Yiskah's pride required an answer that would allow her to accept the gift. Rachael opened the doors of her wardrobe wide. 'Look how many dresses I have,' she said. 'How could I ever possibly wear them all? It's your mission to help me get wear out of as many of my clothes as possible.' She thought she saw the beginnings of a smile on Yiskah's face.

'Thank you,' a small voice said, and Rachael released a small sigh of relief; she was getting somewhere at last.

'Do you always keep your head covered?'

Yiskah tucked an unseen hair into the scarf tied tightly around her head. 'It shows humility,' she said. 'There must be something between you and God.'

'I thought—' Rachael started, but stopped because she'd been doing so well with Yiskah and didn't want to frighten her. Yet Yiskah was a curiosity to Rachael; they shared the same religion but lived by completely different laws within it. Rachael realised how little she really knew and was surprised by how much she wanted to find out. 'Is your head not shaved?' she asked.

If it were possible, Yiskah disappeared even further into her shapeless sack. But out of it came a revelation, a confession, the first sign that she believed Rachael to be someone she could trust. 'I'm not married.'

Rachael sank down onto the bed, patted her hand next to her and Yiskah lowered herself slowly into the space indicated. But still she would not look at Rachael.

'My father threw me out. Said I brought shame upon his home, the family, on Jews everywhere.'

'Shoshi's father? Who was he?'

But this was too much. This she could not answer. But she was still prepared to talk. 'My mother helped me. Secretly. If my father had known he would have thrown her out too.'

Rachael thought about comforting her, putting an arm around her, but there was a wall around Yiskah a thousand miles strong, only surmountable by her daughter.

'Family is everything,' Yiskah said, finally looking into Rachael's eyes. Now it was Rachael's turn to be uncommunicative, lock her experience away. She was beginning to understand what had drawn her to this strange couple.

'Let's go and find Shoshi.'

Yiskah followed Rachael out of the room and down the stairs. As they entered the lounge, a small figure bounced up to them.

'Can I count the fish, again?'

'Yes please. I need to know if any are missing. While you do that I'll make tea.'

Shoshi took her mother's hand and led her through the open French windows, out into the garden. Rachael was constantly touched by Shoshi's little gestures; her innate understanding that her mother needed protection.

In the kitchen, waiting for the kettle to boil, Rachael watched them out of the window. Shoshi was kneeling over on the wall of the raised fish pond, her nose practically touching the water. Yiskah stood back slightly, forever unsure, forever wary. A squirrel broke a branch that wasn't strong enough for it and both fell to the ground. The crack followed by the small thud frightened Yiskah to the point of tears. Shoshi, however, giggled with delight and ran into the house to tell Rachael about the incident.

Rachael listened patiently as the little girl tried to turn what had happened into coherent sentences, at the same time keeping an eye on Yiskah in the garden, who seemed as nervous as ever.

'Let's go to Mummy,' said Rachael.

As Shoshi ran out ahead of her, Rachael sighed and whispered to herself, over and over, 'Yes, I am doing the right thing. This is the right thing to be doing,' before following them outside with a tray of tea.

Thirty-Four

Rachel reached out for the telephone, knocking over cards as she did so. 'Damn, damn, damn. Oh, for fuck's sake.' All of them had fallen now, like a domino display. 'Yes?' she snapped into the receiver.

'Is that Rachel?' a small voice asked.

'Yes. Who's that?'

'It's Iris.'

'Iris! How nice to hear from you.'

There was a pause. Rachel was getting quite used to this now. No one seemed sure whether to congratulate her or offer sympathy.

'When can I come and see you and the baby?'

Rachel filled with warmth. 'Whenever you like. I don't know how long I'll be here. I don't know, I just don't know.' Her voice began to falter. If she didn't talk about him, she didn't cry.

Iris was not thrown. 'I'll come this afternoon then. If that's all right?'

'Of course it's all right. I'd be thrilled to see you.' Then she remembered. 'Are you OK?'

'I'm fine. Bit sick, bit tired, but fine, you know.'

Rachel did not know. She thought constantly about how she had felt during her pregnancy. Was there anything that could have prepared her for this? Any sign? Any particular feeling, pain?

How much or rather how little weight she'd put on? What had made this happen? What she'd eaten? The books she'd read? The air she'd breathed?

She said goodbye to Iris and lay back on the bed.

Her dreams had got worse since the baby's birth. Louise had tried some healing then insensitively offered Roger's services. Any good that Louise might have done vanished, dissolved into Rachel's disapproval. It wasn't fair to disapprove. Louise was obviously content, more content than Rachel could ever remember. But there was something about Roger's Spiritualism that was limited. She wished she could work out what it was that made her feel like this. She berated herself for her snobbery. Spiritualism knew no bounds, that was the point, but Roger seemed so small in his outlook. She could never open herself up to him helping her if this was how she felt.

But it wasn't just that. Faced now with a real life crisis, a trauma, a difficulty (it was hard for her to find the right word for what was happening), if she was finding it as hard as she was to believe that an operation could save him, then Spiritualism didn't stand a chance.

She drifted off into a restless sleep.

She turned suddenly, awoken violently by a weight against her foot.

'God, I'm sorry,' Iris flustered.

'No, it's OK,' said Rachel sitting up.

'I didn't want to wake you.'

'No, it's fine. I'm pleased you did.'

'OK.' The small figure sat on the bed. She seemed tinier than ever. 'Where is he? I'm dying to see him.'

'He's in the Special Care Unit. We'll go soon.'

'Here.' Iris handed Rachel a small parcel, coyly wrapped in a blue paper with ghastly cute babies with red cheeks all over it. 'Sorry about the paper. It's all I could find.'

Rachel took the gift and played with it, checking its weight, listening for sounds. Iris laughed. 'Open it!'

Rachel freed from its wrapper a soft star made from white towelling and sprinkled with glitter. It had gold braid around it and a thin gold thread at one of its tips. She held it by its thread and twirled it.

'"A star danced and under that was I born."'

Rachel smiled. 'It's perfect. Thank you.' She leant over and gave Iris a small kiss on her cheek.

'I can't imagine what this feels like for you—' Iris stopped.

Something about their brief, shared state as mothers-to-be allowed Rachel to attempt to tell her. 'It's a bit like stepping into an alternative world where everything you thought you knew, everything you'd learned, everything that you'd planned for, no longer applies.' Her eyes welled up. 'I've gone back to "Go". Started again.'

'I had a car accident once.'

Rachel looked curiously at Iris.

'About five years ago, when I was eighteen. It was the summer and my boyfriend had just passed his driving test.' Iris started to crinkle the discarded wrapping paper. 'The sun was shining, the roof was down on the car. His dad had bought him this old MG which was really stupid but, oh never mind. It was a perfect day. Everything felt wonderful. Music was blaring and life disappeared, you know, worrying about A level results and things.' She blushed and put her head down.

'I know,' Rachel said.

Iris smiled, encouraged. 'I felt so happy. I can't remember ever having felt that happy before. But—'

'Ah,' said Rachel. 'The "but".'

'But then a woman in a mini shot across a junction without even stopping to look. Jeff slammed on the brakes and I'll never forget the look on her face as her car spun around, like in slow motion.'

She paused.

'Was she all right?' Rachel eventually asked.

'Oh, yes. Hardly hurt at all. Neither were we. But, but the thing is, you see. Ever since then I can't, I can't . . . It's like I can't trust that things will ever be good. Do you know what I mean?'

Rachel nodded.

'Of course they are. I mean like Jonno, and the baby. Our baby, I mean. Oh, I'm sorry I didn't mean—'

'It's all right.'

'But I can't get back to the feeling that I had on that day.' She picked up the star and fiddled with it. 'I'm not sure why I'm telling you this.'

'I think you mean, if this happened to you, you wouldn't be so shocked. Because somewhere, you're expecting it.'

'Oh, God. Is that awful?'

'No, it's not awful. But sometimes if you imagine the worst, you believe you can stop it from happening.'

'Did you—'

'I imagined all sorts of awful scenarios. But funnily enough, not this one.' Rachel looked at Iris, who had her head down, not looking at her. Rachel saw that she was still in that sports car on a hot summer's day trying to work out why a set of decisions made by a woman she had never met, to leave her home at a certain time, take a certain route, travel at a certain speed, should have such a devastating, far-reaching effect on someone else's life.

'You just don't know what's around the corner,' said Iris, sniffing back a couple of stray tears.

'No,' said Rachel. 'But that's supposed to be the good bit.'

'I think that's wonderful that you can say that.'

Rachel was touched. Her comment had been a natural response, one of those things you just say, an inanity, a cliché. Did she actually believe that? Even now? 'There's something else, isn't there?' she asked, suddenly aware of a growing discomfort in Iris.

Iris looked at Rachel. 'I hardly know you—'

'Jonno?'

Iris barely nodded.

'It was because of him I met Brendan, you know.'

'No,' said Iris. 'I didn't know.'

'Jonno was a student at the university where I lecture. We all ended up at the same party one night.'

Iris looked at her curiously. 'Jonno never told me any of this. I feel embarrassed asking you because I feel I should know, but what do you teach?'

'Comparative Religions.'

Iris raised her eyebrows. 'Wow!'

Rachel laughed. 'It's not that impressive. I'm on a year off. I'm supposed to be compiling an encyclopaedia of Spiritualism, After Life Beliefs, that sort of thing. But I've had to put that on hold, at least until Theo's better.'

Iris appeared not to know what to say.

'About Jonno—?' Rachel prompted.

Iris sighed. 'Do you . . . I mean, how do you find him?'

Rachel was shocked by the question.

'I worry about him,' Iris said. 'It's like he's not always here, you know?'

'I think,' said Rachel, choosing her words carefully, 'that Jonno is a strange and extraordinary person. Brilliantly clever, fiercely ambitious—'

'And a little sad?'

'Not quite whole' would have been the way Rachel would have described him, but she would never have said that to the mother of his child.

'Everything is all right between you?'

'He's back from New Mexico in about a month. Then we'll see. It's been hard keeping it going by phone, e-mail, you know. I've only been out there once. It seems nice. Actually,' she said, feeling confident now with Rachel, 'I do find it hard imagining what our life will be like together there.'

'If you both want it to work, you'll find a way.' There she goes again. Platitudes. But it seemed to satisfy Iris.

'Can I see Theo now?'

'Of course.' Rachel got up off the bed. 'Are you sure?'

'It's OK. I've seen babies in incubators before.'

'Since you were pregnant?'

'Er, no. But I want to see Theo. My – what is he? My boyfriend's half-brother. Not sure what that makes me. But he's family. Part of my family now.' She ran a hand over her stomach, hidden beneath a velvet tent.

Rachel stood up, holding Iris' hand, and led her out of the room.

Thirty-Five – August 1921

The young couple whom Robin has been observing seat themselves on a bench. Fortunately there is another vacant one fairly close by; Robin sits himself down on it and continues to watch. Hyde Park is as busy as it has ever been on a sunny Sunday afternoon and his vantage point is frequently impaired by groups, families, other couples, as they wander between him and them, giving their activities the appearance of a flicker book with several pages missing.

He first noticed them wandering along Bayswater Road, entering the Park at Lancaster Gate. What struck him most keenly was how well they seemed to fit together. They are like two opposites that make up a whole. Where he is dark, she is fair; where he is tall, she is short, where he is large, she is slim. But she is the perfect height to carry his arm comfortably across her shoulders, her waist fitting neatly into his roundness. Their clothes are matched in faultless coordination. Tones of brown and beige, blond and white, blending beautifully.

Individually neither is particularly attractive, yet together they are radiant.

They sit close on the bench. He takes from his pocket a small paper bag and, opening it, offers it to her. She removes a peppermint and puts it in his mouth. He then does the same and puts one in her mouth. They smile at each other and their lips touch, not quite forcefully enough for a kiss but certainly enough for Robin to smell the mint on their breath and feel the electric shock of their skin meeting.

As he watches them he thinks about love, for surely this is what he is witnessing. Love! It is so unappealing. The thought of popping peppermints into someone's mouth fills him with dread and terror.

For a brief instant, a quick flash, he wants it. But then it's gone, as swiftly as the disappointed sparrows hovering around him, searching for breadcrumbs.

The couple get up. He decides to leave them be and let them dissolve amongst the Sunday strollers. Turning to face the other direction, Robin watches a shape appear out of the crowd. It is almost familiar, but not quite. He keeps staring. Surely—? The rate that his heart is beating tells him what his eyes can't quite believe. It *is* her. But she looks different. Her clothes are bordering on the fashionable. She walks with another woman, beautifully dressed, naturally elegant and extremely attractive. And a small, curly-haired child makes figures of eight running around and between them. He makes an immediate assumption, a bit of him feeling wounded that Yiskah appears to have done well in finding herself a job.

They are still fifty yards or so away and Robin has to make a decision. The dark-haired woman, however, makes it for him. He can't take his eyes off her. He watches them as they walk. Every so often a few words are exchanged. Robin sees that Yiskah is still as he remembered her, shy, quiet, unwilling to be a part of what is going on around her. But then he recalls not only the pleasure of her submission, but the anger and frustration that drove him to force himself on her in the first place.

He gets up from the bench and stands in their path.

Rachael spots him first. She wonders if she knows him, has met him somewhere, a party perhaps? He obviously knows either her or her companion and by the sight of him (a quick summing up from his clothes and looks) it seems unlikely that it's Yiskah. As they get closer, Rachael realises that she doesn't know him, has never seen him before. Yet he is standing in the centre of the path, staring, almost smiling as if waiting to be reconciled with a long-lost friend.

Yiskah's eyes are, as ever, firmly on the ground.

Rachael nudges her. 'Yiskah? You don't know that man, do you?'

Yiskah looks up then turns her head in the direction Rachael is indicating. Rachael watches the colour disappear from Yiskah's face as she repeats the question. But now the man is coming towards them. Shoshi, intuitively terrified, hides behind her mother. Rachael keeps her eyes on Yiskah. She now knows what fear looks like, for it constrains Yiskah like a straitjacket.

But the young man addresses Rachael. He introduces himself and holds out his hand, offers gracious thanks for having made a friend of Yiskah, asks for her name, then bends down to try to charm the child.

Still Yiskah does not move.

Robin smiles his best smile, the special one; the one he keeps in reserve for emergencies. It isn't to be wasted on a woman who is already halfway towards integrating him into her life, for however short a time. This one is for those who have no idea, yet, that they want to know him.

He can tell it works. A faint blush tints the woman's cheeks, momentarily staining her otherwise perfectly pale complexion. Robin feels a rush of pleasure, quite unlike anything he can remember. He stares directly into her eyes as he holds out his hand and pronounces his name.

'A pleasure to meet you. My name is Robin Sweeting. I'm an old friend of Yiskah.' He knows that Yiskah will not look at him, acknowledge him nor have the guts to run away. 'We've not seen each other for a while, have we Yiskah? And you are?' he says, returning his gaze to the dark, almond-shaped eyes.

'Rachael Silverman,' she replies.

He is still holding her right hand and, as he lets go, he steals a glance at her left and feels a slight sting at the back of his eyes at the sight of her ring-free fingers.

'Mrs,' she adds.

Robin, so skilled at spotting potential, foresees the house, the servants, the clothes, the parties. And standing in front of him, the no-longer-blank face of the woman who will provide all this. Matilda's knowing smile flashes before him.

It's time for a diversion; time to make use of the child.

'Hello,' he says, peering around Yiskah to face the little girl. They play peek-a-boo, Robin popping out from different sides to search out her face, her expression increasing with pleasure at each turn. He looks back at Rachael. 'Your daughter is obviously very fond of her governess.'

He watches a delightful laugh spill out of Rachael's perfect mouth.

'I'm afraid you've got it wrong,' she says.

Robin looks from Rachael back to the child then to Yiskah, shrivelling in front of his eyes. His feet feel suddenly cold. He is losing himself in a terrifying thought. It is Yiskah who shares the copper-coloured hair. He looks at the child and thinks he sees his own eyes staring back at him. And the cheekbones, the colour of her skin. Her age. But Rachael's voice brings him back.

'Yiskah is not my governess. She's my friend.'

And the unthinkable vanishes.

There is something disturbing about Robin that brings back an unwelcome memory of Saul. But as soon as Rachael recognises it, it disappears, leaving her staring into the eyes of an extraordinarily beautiful face. The more she looks at it, the more she finds it intriguing. It reminds her of staring for hours at an enormous painting in the Louvre; an eighteenth-century portrayal of Roman decadence. There was more than one indulging figure that had a look of this young man. That's it. The being out of place. She immediately spots the phoney about him, but is overwhelmed by an inexplicable attraction. She has already forgotten that he reminds her of her husband.

He is making the most enormous fuss of Shoshi. Rachael is quite touched by his efforts and then she realises why he is doing it.

'Your daughter is obviously very fond of her governess,' he says.

Rachael can't help laughing. Surely now, governesses are only used by the royal family. It only confirms for Rachael that he is not the person he wishes to appear.

'I'm afraid you've got it wrong,' she says, smiling affectionately at his error.

But then fire flares out from Yiskah towards Rachael. Robin has not noticed, he is staring intently at Shoshi. Yiskah's pleading eyes intimate a history that Rachael can't even begin to guess at. But Rachael knows that Yiskah demands protection; it is part of the reason she has agreed to come and live with her in the first place. Security and anonymity are what she requires. In order to protect Yiskah, Rachael thinks she might have to lie. She has a horror of lying, being only too readily able to recall what it feels like to be at the receiving end. Somehow she manages to avoid it. Withholding information is a poor defence against the accusation of a lie, but in the face of Yiskah's distress it is her only option.

It works. In fact her response has an extraordinary effect on Robin. He breathes out almost audibly, not short of a sigh of relief, and a smile, far more genuine than the one he had greeted them with, stretches across his face and lights up his already shining eyes. Rachael cannot help but beam back, such is the force of the change in him. He seems relaxed now and offers to walk with them.

Rachael is acutely aware of Yiskah's discomfort. She has not moved a muscle, apart from her glares. She is firmly rooted to the spot and, on hearing Robin's request, she puts her hand onto Rachael's arm and digs icy, bitten nails into her flesh. Rachael flinches with pain and gently takes Yiskah's hand.

'I'm afraid that won't be possible,' she tells Robin and feels herself the disappointment that he displays.

A part of her is drawn to him; his presence stirring a long-buried need. It's what has been missing from all her countless suppers with an endless parade of her father's misguided idea of 'nice Jewish boys'. She hasn't been short of male company during the last couple of years of her widowhood – her looks and pride would never allow that – but no one has had this immediate physical effect on her. She thinks of all those bumbling attempts at goodnight kisses that have left her helpless with laughter once inside the safety of her home. If she hadn't laughed she would have cried with frustration and despair.

But here is Yiskah, to whom Rachael had been drawn equally powerfully, experiencing a distress that she is unquestionably obliged to acknowledge. And it seems the only way through is to remove themselves not just from Robin's presence, but from any reminder of his existence.

Miraculously he appears to be sensitive to the situation. He excuses himself, wishes them well and gives an extra special goodbye to Shoshi.

As they move away from him Rachael can see Yiskah's body come to life again and in no time, without looking back, she is following Shoshi in the direction of a shrubbery and explaining to her why they are not allowed to pick the flowers.

Rachael, however, does look back. He is still there where they left him. He puts his hand into an inside pocket and pulls out a silver card case. He removes a card, takes a pen from another pocket and scribbles on the back of it. Then he walks to the nearest bench and places the card on its arm. He tilts his head slightly towards her in a parting gesture and saunters on his way towards Kensington.

She stands still for a couple of minutes. Yiskah and Shoshi are well occupied. She checks the other direction. Robin is nowhere to be seen. She walks quickly to the bench and looks at the card. Name in raised black script on the front and handwritten on the back in small neat letters: *Selfridges. Main entrance. Two o'clock. Tuesday.* She stands holding it, fanning it so that it hits against the bench arm while she thinks about what to do. There is only one thing she can do. She wouldn't have gone this far if she wasn't prepared to take the card, welcome something back into her life that has been missing for too long. She looks about her again then opens her bag and slips the card into it, frightening herself with the noise of clasping it shut. Then back slowly towards a waving and shouting Shoshi.

A blond, tweed-clad figure leaning against the side of a tree, one hand in his trouser pocket, the other holding a lit cigarette, whispers as she walks by, 'Knew you would.'

When she turns to look, there's no one there.

Thirty-Six

The tiny thumb scratched around the small mouth, trying to find the opening, then put it in but removed it quickly. Two thin fingers went in next. This seemed slightly more satisfying and was followed by the whole hand, now fisted. He grimaced as his gums hit his knuckles and audibly whined, but didn't cry. Then his fingers found what they were looking for, a miniature tube that ran from behind his ear, up his left nostril. He tugged at it slowly, carefully, weakening the tape that held it to the side of his nose.

His whine was louder now, but still not effective enough as a cry. He pulled his knees up to his chest with the effort, his dainty feet and insubstantial legs losing themselves inside his pale green towelling baby-grow.

Rachel put a finger out to intercept the hand trying to pull on the tube. Fingers grabbed onto it, holding it tightly. The whining subsided and he opened his eyes to look at her.

Rachel stared hard. She didn't know what she was looking for in his eyes. What was there to see anyway? He was only five weeks old. His eyes, like his hair, were dark. He had a perfectly round face, a football face – his little mouth and little chin nestling comfortably between his pinchable hamster cheeks.

'I wish you needed me more,' she whispered, taking her other hand that wasn't being held by him and running it slowly over his clean, empty cheek – the one that wasn't blemished by a tube.

'Forgive me?' she asked, then removed her finger and went back to her room.

Brendan was waiting for her.

'There you are,' he said. 'Look what I found.'

'My God, it's beautiful.'

'Here, I'll show you.' Holding the tin aeroplane, he started to wind its propeller. When it was fully wound he placed it on the table at the foot of her bed.

Rachel watched, enchanted. It took a few seconds before she recognised the tune. She laughed with delight. 'That is adorable.'

Brendan was humming along.

'"Fly me to the moon,
And let me play among the stars.
Let me see what spring is like
On Jupiter and Mars."'

'"In other words,"' he put his hand out to Rachel, '"hold my hand."' She took it. He pulled her to him. '"In other words, Darling, kiss me."' He kissed her on the mouth then, in a dancing hug, began to spin her around the room.

Rachel let him, enjoying the closeness, losing herself in the place she loved the most. 'I love you,' she said, not being able to remember the last time she had wanted to tell him. What she loved him for at that moment was what she often resented him for. This was the dichotomy of their relationship – what she mostly needed refuge from was him and yet he provided for her the place where she felt the safest. Nothing was ever going to be easy, yet it was always going to be worth the effort.

'You do remember, don't you?' asked Brendan.

'What?'

'This tune?'

Rachel screwed her face up. 'Remind me,' she said in a small, ashamed voice.

'I don't believe you!'

'What?'

'Alasdair's party. The guy on the piano.'

'Ye-es?'

'Come on. You're just teasing me.'

'No, I'm not. You mean he played this?'

'This is what was playing when I first spoke to you.'

'When *you* first spoke to *me*?' Rachel was laughing now. 'I don't think that was what happened.'

'What do you mean?'

'I think it was me who spoke to you.'

'Same difference.'

'I think not. Jonno introduced us and you completely ignored me. I had to seek you out later.'

'I thought you were Jonno's girlfriend.'

'So, why would you ignore me?'

Brendan stopped dancing. A small, dark cloud hovered over his eyes. 'He used to accuse me of being jealous. And in this case I had every reason to be.'

Rachel smiled, flirting. 'You certainly did.'

'What are you saying?'

Rachel was fleetingly confused until 'here-we-go-again' set in. She'd gone too far. She was tired; she couldn't even remember how to handle it. She had neither the energy to placate nor challenge him. So she left his arms and poured herself a glass of water.

'That could have been a lovely moment,' she said, settling herself on the bed.

'But as usual I ruined it.'

'Please, Brendan. Not now. You know. I know. The end.' She turned away from him and picked up the aeroplane. The tune was playing eerily slowly by now. Rachel ran its wheels over her palm before rewinding it then sat looking at it, concentrating hard on not allowing the tears to leave her eyes.

As she stared hard at the toy the song got quieter and quieter only to be replaced by a roaring engine.

The wind created by the propellers blows her hair away from her face. She turns her head slightly to divert the terrible noise. She looks up. The plane is flying low blocking the light, casting its shadow over the sun soaked hill. She watches the shadow glide over the Horse then down to Dragon's Hill where it seems to be struggling against the wind, then rises smoothly again before diminishing into the horizon.

'I'm sorry,' she says. 'But I know I could never love you. Not how you love me. I'm so sorry.'

Rachel blinked. Brendan. Hospital room. Theo. She put her hand against her forehead and closed her eyes. When she opened them her husband was staring at her.

'What just happened?' he asked.

'Did I say something?'

'That was weird.' Brendan spoke slowly, backing away from her slightly as he did so.

'I did say something didn't I?'

'Sort of.'

'What do you mean?'

'Um, look I don't want to freak you out or anything. But – that didn't sound like you.'

Rachel took a deep breath. 'OK. Um. What do I do? OK. Breathe deeply. Phone Louise. Write it down.' She reached for her notebook. 'What did I say?'

'That you could never love me how I love you.'

'Wow!' She wrote it down. 'Brendan?'

'What?'

'If that wasn't me, then I wasn't talking to you. OK?'

Brendan nodded as if this made perfect sense to him. 'OK. But at least you said you were sorry.'

Rachel tried to smile, tried to force out a reassuring laugh. 'I was sorry.' She wrote it down. 'Good. I'm glad I was sorry.'

'This might sound crashingly obvious, but if it wasn't me then was it you?'

'Hmm. Difficult one. I think I'd better call Louise.'

Rachel wished the shivers would stop dancing up and down her spine.

There was only the answer phone at Louise's. Rachel wasn't sure what to say. She didn't want to alarm her. She was very careful about phoning anyone at the moment. Any of her friends or family that heard her voice on the phone would automatically assume that she was ringing with bad news. The sighs of relief that 'everything was fine at the moment' ran like a soundtrack to Rachel's life. She decided against leaving a message.

'Are you all right?' Brendan asked as she put the phone down.

'A bit disoriented.'

'Maybe you should have a sleep, or a rest anyway.'

'Theo will need a bottle shortly.'

'OK. I'll wake you. I'll go be with him. Ten minutes. I think you need it.' He ran a finger lightly down her pale cheek.

'Thanks.'

Raising an eyebrow, Brendan left the room.

Rachel lay on the bed. But the aeroplane was still roaring in her head. Should she go with it or try to make it go away? Going with it seemed the easier option, so she closed her eyes and sank back. Back to the sunny day, back to the hill, back to her picnic with her beautiful blond companion with the frighteningly clear blue eyes, whom she now knew she could never love.

'I know, I know. I think I'd better call Leanne.'

Rachel wished the [illegible] would [illegible] up and [illegible] [illegible].

There was only the answerphone at Leanne's. Rachel wasn't sure what to say. She didn't want to alarm her. [illegible] [illegible] phoned [illegible] at the moment [illegible] friend or family that heard her voice on the phone would automatically [illegible] that she was ringing with bad news. The [illegible] that everything was fine [illegible] like a [illegible] to Rachel's [illegible]. She decided against leaving a message.

'Are you all right?' [illegible] asked as she put the phone down.

'A bit [illegible].'

'Maybe you should have [illegible] [illegible].'

'They [illegible] about the [illegible].'

'I'll wake [illegible] with him. [illegible] I don't [illegible] [illegible] down [illegible] message [illegible].'

'I [illegible].'

[illegible] her [illegible] the room.

Rachel [illegible] but [illegible] she [illegible] in [illegible] with [illegible] as [illegible]. She [illegible] back [illegible] the hill [illegible] with her [illegible] who [illegible] she would never [illegible].

Thirty-Seven – August 1921

Oxford Street is bustling. Robin curses. Why are there so many people around on a Tuesday afternoon? Perhaps the sudden break in the weather, a welcome coolness after days of unbroken, stifling sunshine, has urged Londoners out of a heat-induced apathy and back onto the streets.

He is about ten minutes early. He leans against the stone wall, just next to the shining bronze plaque announcing 'Selfridge & Co.' and lights a cigarette. He amuses himself, as he always does, by looking at couples and writing their stories; tourists, day-trippers, honeymooners, old marrieds, and those he is expert at spotting, paid companions. Then the lone women who neatly divide themselves into two groups: those he has a chance with and those he doesn't. The criteria for inclusion in either group has nothing to do with appearance, it is pure instinct; a shrewd instinct that makes him so good at his job.

'Why! Mr Sweeting!' A horrid, shrill voice behind his right shoulder causes him to turn and there is Florrie's over-orange, pancaked face, a pink lipstick clashing horribly with her newly hennaed hair. He is going to have to get rid of her quickly. He can't risk a meeting between Rachael and Florrie Grix. Not with the way things have been with work lately. The city heat appears to be keeping all contenders locked in their hotel bedrooms and not willing to come out to play. He has had to indulge in some serious flirting, just in case there is no change in his fortunes. He is down to his last two watches.

'You must be meeting someone special.'

Florrie looks at him suspiciously. 'No,' she answers. Then the penny drops. 'Why do you say that?' her voice rising a half-octave.

'Well, someone surely will be getting the benefit of such an attractive hair style.'

Florrie pats her hair, pushing it up from her neck. 'No different to usual,' she says.

Robin smiles. Florrie melts. 'On the contrary,' he says.

'So, what brings you up to town, Mr Sweeting?'

'I have an appointment,' he tells her. He catches sight of Rachael descending from a taxi. She hasn't seen him yet, she has her back to him and is paying the driver. He is running out of time. He has to think fast. Rachael turns, Robin bends down, pretends to tie a shoelace.

'Mr Sweeting, what are you doing?'

'Flor-rie!' A shrill even ghastlier than his landlady's pierces the air.

Florrie turns. 'Renee, there you are. Where did you get to?'

'Oh God,' thinks Robin, 'now there's two of them.'

'There's someone I want you to meet,' she calls to Renee.

Renee joins them. Robin has to stand. He manoeuvres himself and them so that it is impossible for Rachael to find him and smiles beautifully at the pathetic couple. A neatly timed, not too surreptitious glance at his watch works its magic. Florrie and Renee excuse themselves. He watches the double vision of Florrie and Renee chirp and preen over their hairdos then finally waddle off together towards Oxford Circus, banging and bumping their shopping bags into fractious passers-by.

Then he sees that Rachael has been watching him all the time, a tense half-smile on her beautiful face. She walks over to him. He sighs with relief that Florrie did not scare Rachael away.

'Hello.'

'Hello.'

'I'm glad you came.'

Rachael laughs nervously. He will never know how much thought she has given it, how much the decision has tormented her; how the sight of him talking to those two women highlighted the chasm between their lives. But now in his presence all doubts disappear.

'Have you had lunch?' he asks.

'Yes. We—' she stops herself. She is not going to even think about Yiskah, let alone refer to her. 'Yes, I have.'

'Of course, you lunch with your daughter.'

A difficult moment. She must think quickly. Rachael hates the idea of deceit but for Yiskah's sake (and to soothe her own guilt) she has no option but to keep up the pretence. She moves her lips into the shape of a smile and slightly nods her head, hoping that she can successfully perform the role of mother. This doesn't feel like a good beginning.

'Shall we walk then?' He holds out his arm for her to take.

Rachael hesitates before taking it, lightly running a finger over the cream linen of his jacket, feeling surprised by its softness but then, as if it were the most natural thing, as if she has done it a thousand times before, slips her arm under his, letting her hand rest on the inside of his elbow. She isn't even amazed by how calm she feels.

Robin, however, is shaking inside.

'Whereabouts do you live?' he asks her.

'Hampstead, in the Garden Suburb. It's very pretty.'

'I don't know it.' He amazes himself. This is very probably the first time in his life he has admitted ignorance of anything.

'I've not been living there long. But after my husband died—'

Something in her tone makes Robin ask if it was recent.

'Oh no. He was killed in the war. But—' She stops herself from admitting how long it has taken her to get over it, for now, being here with Robin, having taken decisive action, she feels foolish, even a little angry, that she has removed herself from life for so long.

'I'm sorry,' Robin says.

'That's all right. It was a long time ago, now. Five years. Did you—?'

'I was too young.'

Rachael is shocked. She has assumed that Robin is younger than her, but if he was too young to be called up then that would make him twenty, perhaps twenty-one. She turns her face to look at him. He does look young but he also seems ageless, timeless; Rachael has a strange feeling of him never growing old and looking like this for ever. Suddenly she doesn't want to be there, it's wrong, no, more than that, it's grotesque. But as if he knows that she is about to reject him, he lets the arm that is holding hers drop, then takes her hand in his, the sureness of the action immediately disguising her fears.

They cross the road and turn into Bond Street, where it is quieter.

'Thank God it's cooler,' says Rachael.

They look up at the London summer sky; picture-book clouds hanging immobile against a pale blue backdrop, preventing the sun from providing its expected warmth. Then, returning their gaze to street level, they catch each other's eyes. And there it is; both see the same thing.

They walk and window-shop and make small talk, very quickly becoming breathless from their battles to prevent themselves from falling into each other's arms.

Robin suggests they stop at a café.

'I should go,' she says, but Robin holds her upper arm in a tight grip and Rachael is back on Hampstead Heath caught in a similar moment, but it's too quick for her to recognise it as a memory; it just feels comfortingly familiar and suddenly all right.

'No,' he says, his grasp dangerously close to being hard enough to mark her arm.

But then it comes back to her. It's her father's voice warning her, only this time she listens and agrees. 'Don't let me want to look after him,' she thinks. Then it goes again, burying itself back in the dark corner of her memory where she is too afraid to go.

Rachael clinks her spoon against the inside of her empty cup. Robin is mesmerised by the sound, a sure steady beat marking out the time before a decision is made. She can't look at him.

'Would you find me a taxi?' she says slowly, her eyes firmly on the lipstick- and tannin-stained cup.

There is a mild explosion in Robin's heart. He puts his hand out to steady her own, to make her stop that infernal row, the ghastly rhythm now reminding him that she doesn't want him, that she's said no.

'Rachael. I—'

She looks up at him at last. It's not the expected disdain. Her eyes sparkle with desire. Thank God; it is only her morality he's fighting.

'When will I see you?' he asks.

'I don't know,' she says.

He takes her hand in his. 'I will see you again.'

'Yes,' she says. 'But please don't call me.'

Robin leans back in his chair, muttering 'Yiskah,' as he does so. 'Meet me tonight.'

Rachael laughs, 'I can't.' Then: 'Well, I suppose I could.' She seems to be close to tears. 'What would we do?' She turns away. It's too painful to look at him. 'No. Not tonight.'

He still has her hand so he exerts some pressure. 'Tonight. Please. Come to my rooms. My landlady,' he grimaces as he mentions her, 'she's always out on a Tuesday. It's her gin night.'

'If you're sure—' Then, letting go of his hand, almost throwing it onto the table, she stands up. 'What am I saying? No. No. It's unthinkable.'

He is losing her. She is on her way out. He puts his hand in his pocket and flings a handful of coppers onto the table, rushing now to catch her. What is he doing? He never pays for tea unless he is on his own.

In the street she stands staring at the traffic, willing one of the cars to become a vacant taxi.

'Rachael.' He has her arm again in that hold. Strange how it doesn't hurt; strange how it feels warm and wanting; even stranger how in one small movement, the defences she has spent years building can just collapse, tumble to the ground.

He knows he has her. Now he can wait. Now there is no hurry. He sees a taxi, waves it down, opens the door for her, truly relaxed and smiling for the first time that day. She gets in, she is smiling too. She lets him kiss her lightly, not too near her mouth but close enough to indicate promise, willingness, perhaps even eagerness.

But as the taxi drives off a darkness descends over Robin. He wants the good feelings back again, the happy ones, the ones that make him entertain feelings of warmth towards a beautiful young woman; the ones that allow fantasies of a future and the ones that make him want to skip down the street feeling lighter than he has in years.

And there is only one way to get them back.

Thirty-Eight – August 1921

By the time the taxi had shaken and rattled its way along the Finchley Road into Hampstead Village, Rachael had bitten both thumb nails down to nothing and was starting on the skin around them. It was only when she tasted blood that she jolted herself out of her thoughts.

'Can you wait here for a minute?' she asked the driver.

Rachael left the door open as she ran to a flower stall and loaded her arms with stocks and antirrhinums, anemones and tulips, roses and gypsophilia. She climbed back into the taxi and laid the flowers over her lap like a blanket, picking up one at a time and smelling it, arranging them by size and colour, anything to distract her mind from Robin.

But it wasn't only Robin who occupied her thoughts. All her fears, doubts, guilt and shame manifested themselves in the form of Yiskah. To betray Yiskah, when she had offered her so much, became the single most potent argument for never seeing Robin again.

As the taxi pulled up outside her house, the front door opened and the inimitable smile of Shoshi warmed Rachael in a way the sun was failing to on this cool summer day. Shoshi ran out of the gate laughing and skipping, loading her arms with the flowers. As Rachael delighted in the child's glow an icicle pierced her, letting freezing drips trickle down her spine – there was only one other whose smile could have such an effect and Rachael had just left him in Bond Street.

Yiskah was in the garden, sitting on the stone bench engrossed in a thin green book. Rachael, whose movements were slowing down with each niggling thought, carefully arranged her flowers in several vases, watching Yiskah as she did so, wondering why, how, she could sit so still on something so uncomfortable. Suffering seemed so commonplace to her.

Since they'd met Robin in the park, neither of them had mentioned him. Rachael had to keep all her thoughts about him strictly to herself. For a day or two Yiskah had engrossed herself in fervent activity, avoiding being left alone with Rachael, presumably to evade any questions. Silver that hadn't asked to be polished shone like mirrors in moonlight and in the garden the first sign of a dying flower was cruelly beheaded, thus side-stepping a long malingering, ugly decline. Shoshi revelled in the extra attention. Yiskah needn't have worried. Rachael knew that she could not talk about him. If her feelings towards him had been different, she may well have been inclined to push for further information but as it was she was forced to hide her guilty secret, keep it locked up in a place that was difficult for even her to gain access to.

Yiskah looked up as Rachael approached the bench.

'What are you reading?' Rachael asked.

Yiskah handed her the book. She had tears in her eyes.

Rachael traced her fingers over the letters:

The Stupid Princess
a Fairy Tale Romance
by
Sarah Cohn

Fairies danced in between the gold letters. She opened it.

'My mother wrote this. I got it out to read to Shoshi. I'm glad you found it.' Rachael could never resist flicking through the pages and never ceased to warm with pleasure at her father's quirky line drawings that occasionally interrupted the text. The book was the only thing she had that her mother had given her and the handwritten inscription: *'18th September 1891 For my child, for you, forever'* the only evidence that she had ever thought about Rachael at all. For how else could a bereaved father convince a child that she was loved by a mother she never knew?

Rachael sat next to Yiskah on the hard, cold bench. She momentarily forgot about Robin and immersed herself in memory, not realising that Yiskah was leaning against her, affectionately resting her head on her shoulder.

'She died, didn't she?' asked Yiskah eventually.

Rachael looked up from the book. 'Yes. In childbirth. Well, a few days after.'

'I worry so much. About what would happen. I mean, if I – if anything happened to me.'

'You mustn't,' said Rachael. 'I mean, it won't.'

'Shoshi trusts you, you know.'

And Rachael knew what was being asked of her. 'If I'd had a child, she's the one I'd have wanted.'

'You will. You're young.'

A familiar emptiness returned. 'I *was* married for five years—'

But Yiskah was on a different track. 'And I don't think it will be long.'

Rachael looked at her in surprise. 'What do you mean?'

'I've seen the way you've been moping around the house. Shutting yourself in your room. Disappearing off at lunchtime all dressed up. You've met someone, haven't you?'

But before Rachael had time to even stop to think about an answer, Yiskah jumped up. 'Wait here,' she said and ran into the house.

Rachael closed the book and held it against her heart, troubled and confused as to why even indulging herself in childhood memories, revisiting her grief, should lead back to the afternoon's events and the disturbing but compelling presence of Robin. What was he to Yiskah?

A minute later Yiskah reappeared, clutching a wooden box. Rachael watched her as she went over to the small wrought-iron table and sat on a chair. There was so much she wanted to ask her; there was so much she didn't want to know.

'Come,' Yiskah said. 'Sit opposite me.'

Rachael did as she was told, partly because this new Yiskah intrigued her.

'Palm first,' she said. 'Then the cards.'

'You're not . . . seriously?' Rachael was trying not to laugh.

'Come on.' Rachael was impressed by Yiskah's confidence. 'Left hand.'

Rachael held her left hand out. Yiskah took it, running short fingers over the lines. For a long time she said nothing. Then she gave Rachael her hand back. 'I think I'll do the cards first. If that's all right?'

'Yes, all right.' Rachael smiled to herself. Was this all part of the performance?

Yiskah opened the box and took out a piece of black silk tied with a knot. She laid it on the table, undid the knot and fanned out a thin pack of oversized cards.

'Tarot?' said Rachael. 'Surely not?'

'No,' said Yiskah. 'Something else.'

'I didn't think—' Then Rachael remembered a word her grandfather had told her she must never say out loud. A word full of mysticism and wonder, a secret held by mysterious magicians. Sydney had tried to explain that it was only a superstition, probably engendered by the mystics themselves in order to secure their position of power. Sydney had an abhorrence of secrets and banned them. But Rachael had not been reassured.

'These are my great-grandmother's cards,' Yiskah said proudly. 'Here,' she said, handing Rachael the pack, 'shuffle them.'

'It's the same principle as tarot cards, right? I mean, I ask a question?'

'You don't need to be that specific. I can just do a general reading, if that's what you want.'

Rachael smiled. She hadn't wanted this at all, but she was enjoying seeing Yiskah being confident, doing something she was obviously so comfortable with. 'All right. That sounds good.'

'Or you can ask a question.' She gave Rachael a knowing smile that immediately made her reject the idea.

'No, no. General is fine. Where's Shoshi?'

'Dressing her new doll. She's quite happy.'

Rachael shuffled the cards, trying very hard not to think of Robin. But his face would not go away. She handed the cards back to Yiskah who made a triangle out of the top six cards, two on each side then a seventh card in the triangle's centre.

Four of the cards had dark night-blue backgrounds with silver geometric designs that reminded Rachael of the lines that linked stars creating constellations in astronomy books. The other three had strange drawings of serene faces surrounded by varying colours and shapes.

'They're taken from the Kabbalah,' Yiskah said.

Rachael instinctively flinched in memory of her grandfather, expecting, at the very least, a thunderclap at the mention of the forbidden word. But the sun continued its weak shine and the clouds still did not move.

Lightly running her finger over, but not touching, the first two cards, Yiskah appeared to be in deep thought, concentrating hard. She looked at them and up at Rachael several times before she spoke.

'You are . . . seeking fulfilment.'

'Who isn't?' thought Rachael, disappointed that Yiskah should resort to the platitudes of fairground fortune tellers.

'You must be careful to try not to let your desire to be fulfilled feed your frustrations at being unable to achieve what you want. Do you understand?'

Rachael was impressed. She had never heard Yiskah sound this assured before. Maybe she really did know what she was doing. She nodded her encouragement.

'There is a danger of becoming stuck on a wheel of disappointment. But there is a break. You will take, or already have, a bold move.' Yiskah looked at Rachael with that knowing smile again.

Then Yiskah's short fingers hovered over the fourth card. Samael, the angel of Adversity, wearing a cloak made from crystals, his silver halo appearing to be attacked by bolts of lightning.

'This isn't a bad card. There are no bad cards. He's only there as a warning. Samael blocks your way only if you have chosen the wrong path. He is there to remind you of your limitations.'

Next to Samael sat the card of Wisdom, 'a constant reminder of what is in us all.' Rachael assumed she was supposed to be reassured. She wasn't.

But then came a worried angel – red snakes, Medusa-like, crawling out of his head. Yiskah faltered. Rachael smiled. It was an old gypsy trick 'What is it?' she asked, playing along.

'Hanael. Blood.' Her voice took on a serious note. 'You must not fear to go into battle. Hanael will provide you with the weapons. You will have to take up arms against chaos and put things in order. He will help you to fight.'

Rachael let this sink in. This obviously applied to Robin. He had already shaken what little order there was in her world, and she had already accepted that whatever was going to happen was not going to happen effortlessly. 'And the last card?' A single silver line running vertically down the centre between two dots and a thin rectangle lying across its middle. It was the only one with a self-contained shape within the design. It intrigued but unnerved Rachael.

'I'll come back to that. Give me your palm.'

Rachael held out her hand again. Again let Yiskah run her fingers over the lines.

'So much blood,' whispered Yiskah.

Rachael's hand stiffened.

'This house, your home. It won't always be your home. But you will come back to it, again and again and again.'

Rachael looked up and saw Shoshi watching them from an upstairs window. Rachael smiled, waved her other hand. But Shoshi seemed not to have noticed. Rachael, confused, feeling a change in the atmosphere, looked back to Yiskah, still concentrating hard on her open palm.

'I see a baby—'

'Oh.'

'But so much blood.'

Rachael was feeling cold now. Cold and scared. She looked back up to the upstairs window. She was still there, watching them.

'A large man. He's dark. He loves you.'

Not Robin.

'This is his baby. The baby is crying. I think he's in pain.'

'I think I'd like you to stop now.'

The face at the window, gone.

'You will be happy with him, in the end.'

Rachael pulled her hand away.

'But it's all right,' said Yiskah. 'Look. The last card. You will live the true life.'

'I . . . I don't understand,' Rachael said, but she felt calmer, warmer.

Yiskah's eyes flashed. 'But it's very clear. There is love for you, but you must be careful.' There was a panic in her voice, her round eyes fixing Rachael in a questioning stare. Rachael looked down.

Yiskah wrapped up her cards and her confident, assured self back in their black silk cloak. 'You don't believe, do you?' she asked.

Rachael looked up surprised. 'No, not really.'

'Then perhaps it won't count.' Yiskah forced a smile. 'These cards have passed down through the eldest daughters of four generations,' she said proudly, 'and I can't wait to start teaching

Shoshi. She's already showing an amazing knack for it.'

A strange silence.

'She sees things.'

'Who? Shoshi? What things?'

No time to answer. A small voice calling for her mother, getting louder and closer. Yiskah giving Rachael a look that says, 'Maybe another time.'

Yiskah held the cards, back in their wooden box, tightly against her chest and backed away into the house.

Rachael stood up and walked over to the fish pond. She pulled some petals of a sweet pea and threw them onto the water. Pink, white, lilac, scattering like confetti over the dark, dank surface. 'Damn, damn, damn!'

She wanted to cry out. Or just cry. She was losing her reason.

There was nothing at all that had helped her.

Nothing about Robin. Why? Why did she feel this compulsion to have him in her life?

He was ten years younger than her. She had no idea how he earned a living. He was well dressed and well spoken, although she knew he was not of her class. He was mysterious, indefinable, enigmatic yet real and solid in a purely physical way that both frightened and excited her. It was no good even attempting to explain why she was drawn to him and it was ridiculous to think that Yiskah's cards would have helped.

She knew she could not leave it.

She knew she would see him again.

Thirty-Nine

'I want to go home.'

'Ah. You know I won't be there.'

Rachel had forgotten. She hadn't given Brendan's work a single thought. He'd only attended the first date, the opening of the small tour of his vast new piece of work. He'd only been away from Rachel and the baby for one night, just over a month ago, just before they moved hospitals. Rachel knew the sacrifice he was making. She knew it was tearing him apart to think that his work was on show in places where he would never see it, never know whether they'd got the lighting right, painted the walls the right shade or, more importantly to him, how many people were seeing it, and who they were.

Brendan loved to watch people looking at his work. He would amaze Rachel by recognising them, weeks, months even years later. It was as if he owned them. They were carrying a little bit of him in their minds; their memories storing the image of his creativity, keeping it with who knew what, to be called upon when and be triggered off how? Brendan got a huge thrill from believing this and he paid his public back by never forgetting the faces of those he had seen contemplating the results of his labours. It was as much a part of his creative process as the regular visits to scrap-yards or his famous wet and windy solitary walks on Hampstead Heath.

'I only go to the Heath when it's raining,' Brendan had told Rachel, not long after they had first met when she suggested a Sunday afternoon stroll. 'And NEVER on a Sunday,' he added, making Rachel feel inferior for enjoying such an activity. Instead, they had gone to an exhibition at the Whitechapel Gallery that she would never have visited herself and, in the light of what she saw, battling with the throngs of North London families for a carefully rationed portion of fresh air seemed like a poor second choice.

Despite how he'd made her feel, she was ultimately grateful. When she finally acknowledged that she was falling in love with him she would remember that day and recognise it as when she first allowed him to open up her world.

'I'll be all right on my own. I'll be *here* most of the day.'

'You won't be on your own.'

'What do you mean?'

'I hadn't had a chance to tell you. Last night, Leah slunk back.'

'Thank God. At last. How is she?'

The door opened. 'She's fine,' said Leah.

She didn't look fine. Rachel tried not to show her reaction to Leah's physical appearance. Her face was thin, gaunt, grey. Her hair was growing back in tufts unevenly spread over her scalp. She'd looked better at the height of her addiction, at least she'd seemed to have a sense of calm about her then. Of course she'd been calm, that's why she was taking the drugs, so as not to feel anything.

'How's my nephew, then?'

'He's doing well.' Rachel was fighting back the tears. So, it appeared, was Leah. As they fell into each other's arms they both gave up the fight.

'He will be all right, won't he?' asked Leah. 'I can't bear the thought of it.'

Rachel hugged her sister tightly. She was the only one who hadn't thought she had to put on a brave face and Rachel now realised how much she had wanted Brendan, her mother and father, Louise, anyone, to do exactly what Leah was doing. Aza had come the closest to breaking down, but Rachel felt so consumed with guilt about reintroducing suffering into his life, that she put up the barriers in order to protect him, and refused to let him see how much it was paining her.

This is what they all had done; taken the lead from her. But Leah, wonderful Leah did not. Leah, whom now Rachel could thank for never thinking of anyone else. Leah who was letting her do what she had been wanting to do with all her family. She had wanted to cry with them all.

'So, you don't mind?' Rachel asked Brendan as she wiped the tears from Leah's thin face.

'Mind?'

'About me wanting to be at home.'

'God, no. It's not been easy. I've been waiting for you to say it.'

Rachel got that pang that appeared whenever she felt criticised. 'I needed to rest. I needed to be with him until I was sure he was safe.'

Brendan's expression did not change.

'I've been away from things too long. I've forgotten—'

'Rachel?' Brendan sat on the bed. He tilted his head slightly at Leah, who smiled and left the room. It was evidently some sort of prearranged signal. Rachel stiffened. She hated conspiracies.

'I spoke with the consultant this morning.'

Rachel said nothing, her anxieties increasing. She knew from experience that very soon Brendan would confirm her doubts and she could tell herself she was right to be paranoid.

'He thinks Theo's ready to go home.'

'But the operation?'

'He's breathing well, there's little risk to his lungs now. He doesn't actually need the attention he's getting here. And they could probably use the cot,' he added. A poor attempt at humour.

Rachel was wondering why he was treating her like the patient. 'But he can't,' she said.

'Why not?' asked Brendan.

'Surely he needs—'

'No. That's the point. He doesn't.'

Rachel did not know that she had gone white with fear.

'I'll be gone for a week. They'll show you how to feed him, how to thread the tube.'

She hadn't thought of this. She wasn't prepared. 'But I'm not a nurse.'

'You'll be fine. You know the bottles aren't enough for him. He uses up all his energy breathing. And it would be constant with his little and often feeds.'

'When do we go?'

'Tomorrow. I'm sorry it's worked out like this. But at least Leah will be there.'

Rachel felt as if she had woken up out of a bad dream only to discover she was still asleep, still dreaming, only this time the dream was worse. She was suddenly distant, removed. Things had been going on that she'd had no part in. The doctor and Brendan had been conspiring. They'd been talking about her, assessing, making decisions. They'd been deliberately excluding her. Why? For what reasons?

Then it clicked. Damn them. Damn them all: the doctors, the nurses, especially that Emily. Rachel had always thought there was something about her she didn't trust. Coming in here every day pretending to be her friend, asking questions and talking about what? Theo and his progress? No. It was all about her, Rachel, how she was feeling, how she was coping. It all seemed very innocent, but now she understood. Now she understood why Brendan had changed the subject so abruptly when Ella had commented on how little time Rachel was spending with Theo. It was only because she believed that it was the nurses and doctors who could help him. Why else was he here? They knew what they were doing. They were trained, for goodness' sake.

She started to shake with anger. 'I do love him, you know.'

'Rachel—'

'No. Too late. The damage has been done. Go on, fuck off

to Ireland. But better hurry back, your son needs you. He can't survive on Mother Love alone.'

'Rachel. Come on. I know it's been hard for you.'

'No it hasn't.'

'WELL, IT SHOULD HAVE BEEN!'

Rachel was totally confused and feeling a little betrayed.

'Look, I'm sorry I shouted.'

'Oh, God,' she sobbed, the tears in full flow now. 'I didn't know I should have been doing anything different.'

Brendan went to her and put his arms around her. 'You can't do what you don't feel.'

He held her for a couple of minutes. 'But you told me, you said, "He's not going to make it."'

Rachel moved away from him. 'That's what all this is about?'

'No. Not only. A bit. You forget. I believe that you believe these things.'

'Does everyone here think I'm a terrible mother?'

'No, Rachel. It's not that. This is a hospital that specialises in these cases. I think they've seen all this before.'

'All what?' she was calmer now.

'Mothers, parents, finding it hard to, you know, bond, start a relationship with their babies, frightened of loving them, in case, you know. Oh, Rachel don't make this any harder. You're an intelligent woman. You know exactly what's going on.'

She refused to be beaten. 'This sounds like one of those cases where someone who thinks they're all right is suddenly made to feel like they have a problem that they had no idea that they had.'

'I don't believe you had no idea.'

'Brendan! I've never had a baby before. I don't know what to do.'

They stood staring at each other across the bed, the moment only broken by a knock on the door and Louise's radiant face peering round.

'All right to come in?'

Brendan sighed and turned away from his wife. 'Yes, of course, Louise. Come in.'

Louise came in, followed by Leah.

'I was just telling Rachel the good news,' said Brendan. 'They are letting Theo home to wait for the operation.'

'Is that what you look like when you've had good news?' Louise asked Rachel, putting a light kiss on the hard, cross face. 'I'm thrilled.'

'We all are,' Rachel said sternly. 'But what if—?'

'Don't worry. They give us what they rather alarmingly call an Emergency Card. So if there are any problems we don't have to go via casualty. He'll always be seen straight away. At any hospital.'

Rachel looked terrified. Louise took her hand.

'I'm just going for coffee. Leah?'

'Oh, right. Yes. Coming.' She turned back to Rachel. 'I'll see you later,' she said and followed Brendan out of the room.

Rachel smiled. 'That's one of the nicest things she's ever said to me.'

Louise laughed. 'Come dear. It's not that bad.'

'Have you spoken to her? Found out what happened to the ghastly Trevor?'

'All I know is that she left totally of her own free will.'

'I suppose that's something.'

'She'll talk when she's ready.'

'She never has before.'

'She's changing. Growing up.' Louise sat herself in the armchair. 'I think this whole Theo thing has really shaken her up.'

'Really? She hadn't been to see him. I'd written her off.'

'Time to stop doing that. She's all right is Leah.' Louise patted the bed to invite Rachel to sit on it. 'Now. What about you?'

Rachel sat wearily down. 'Need some healing, I think.' She lay herself out on the bed. Louise smiled and took off her jacket, removed the scarf draped perfectly carelessly around her neck and stepped out of her shoes.

Rachel closed her eyes and regulated her breathing, very quickly feeling the warmth of Louise's hands as they hovered over her chest.

'How are the dreams?'

'You know, I don't think I've had one for a couple of days.'

'Oh.'

'Is that weird?'

'What do you think?'

'Probably is. I hadn't noticed till you asked.'

A rush of heat flew over Rachel's heart.

'Hmm. Something going on there,' said Louise. She held both her hands as still as she could, but then took a sharp intake of breath. 'Ouch! Getting too hot for me. Now concentrate your mind on the heat.'

'It's . . . er . . . quite painful.'

'I can see two hands. They're holding a box, a sort of jewellery box. Small. Not small enough for a ring. Bigger than that.'

'Red. All I can see is red.'

'Oh. They're a man's hands. That's funny. They're beautiful hands. Long thin fingers. Well looked after. Manicured even.'

'The heat is getting fiercer.'

'Yes, I can feel it.'

'It's becoming a sort of red light now. No it's not. But it's moving. Oh, weird. It's flying I think.'

'He's opening the box. Oh, how beautiful. It's the most exquisite pair of cufflinks. Silver and look, oh how delightful! They're enamelled with a robin redbreast on each one. One of them has his mouth open, he's singing I think. And the other is hiding his head under his wing.'

'I had them made specially.'

Louise opened her eyes and looked at Rachel lying on the bed. She obviously had no idea what she'd just said.

'You know the old rhyme?

> *The North wind doth blow*
> *And we shall have snow*
> *And what will poor robin do then, poor thing*
> *He'll hide in a barn*

Keep himself warm
And hide his head under his wing, poor thing.

I used to love that.'

Louise was listening carefully, trying to pinpoint the changes in pitch and tone that differentiated this voice from Rachel's own.

Rachel opened her eyes. 'Oh. You've stopped,' she said to Louise. 'It all went cold.'

'Must have been the North Wind.'

'What?'

Louise told her what had happened.

Rachel sat up. 'What do we do?'

'How do you feel about Past Life Regression?'

'You mean doing it? You know how I feel about it. I don't trust it.'

'So what do you think is happening?'

'Stress?'

Louise looked pained by her answer. 'Don't turn your back on everything.'

Tears came to Rachel and fell easily before she even knew they were there. 'You don't know what this feels like.'

'Which "this" are we talking about? Theo's condition or what is happening to you?'

Rachel looked Louise directly in the eye and said coldly, almost cruelly. 'They are *not* two separate things.'

'Good,' said Louise. 'Now we're getting somewhere.' She sat on the edge of the bed and put her arm around Rachel, who leant her head on her aunt's shoulder. 'Talk to me.'

'Before Theo was born, all the visions I had were about death, fear and terror. But since then, I don't know, they've been kind of warm . . . Considering what's happening to Theo, shouldn't it be the other way around? It's like . . . like a story being told backwards.'

'I have only limited skills. But I know someone who can help you.'

'A Past Life Therapist. Do you really think that is what is going on here?'

'Of course I do!' Louise laughed.

Rachel relaxed a bit. 'It's so easy for you.'

'It used to be easy for *you,*' Louise answered.

'Yes, before it became real.' She started to fiddle with her wedding ring, turning it round and round her finger till the edges rubbed her finger raw. 'It's not going to help Theo though, is it?' She looked up at Louise. 'Only the operation can do that. You see, he won't survive without it—'

'And you're not convinced he'll survive with it.'

Rachel said nothing.

'No one blames you for feeling like this.'

'Brendan does.'

Louise took a notebook out of her bag, opened it and wrote down a telephone number. She then tore out the page and handed it to Rachel. 'Ring it,' she said. 'I think it will help you with why you're feeling what you're feeling.'

Rachel took the piece of paper and folded it, folding it again and again.

'But it won't help *him,*' she said.

"Fast Lane? Desperate? Do you really think that is what is going on here?"

"Of course I don't," Louise laughed.

Rachel relaxed a bit. "It's so easy, however."

"Used to be easy for me," Louise answered.

"Yes, before we were married." She started to fiddle with her wedding ring, turning it round and round her finger until it [illegible] her finger [illegible]. "It's not going to [illegible]. I just thought [illegible]" She looked up at [illegible]. "Nobody [illegible] can do that. [illegible] he won't stray without [illegible]."

"And you're not counting. She'll stay with it."

Rachel [illegible] nodding.

"No one [illegible] can [illegible] feeling like this."

[illegible]

Louise took a [illegible] out of her bag and wrote down a [illegible] phone number. She [illegible] and handed it to [illegible]. "I think it will help you with [illegible] your [illegible]."

Rachel took the [illegible] and [illegible] folding it [illegible].

"But it won't help [illegible]," she said [illegible].

Forty – August 1921

'What is it?' There, he's doing it again. When did he ever care how anyone was feeling? But Rachael so infuriates him; his attraction to her is so great. He's never going to be able just to leave it. He has to know everything; until then, there will be no peace inside him.

But Rachael has not been taught to answer those sort of questions, even though she has herself yearned to ask them. Sitting opposite a silent Saul, night after night – the only conversation being of her making: what was happening at the factory? How was the building work going? Must be time for a dinner party, who should we invite? Are Donald and Dorothea expecting us for dinner on Friday? What do you think of the new window boxes? WHY WON'T YOU TALK TO ME? – Rachael discovers a comforting solitude in disinterest.

And here was strange, beautiful Robin asking if anything was wrong simply because she has been momentarily distracted by a thought.

She smiles. He relaxes.

'I was looking at that woman's hat,' says Rachael, pointing out a mess of feathers and net perching precariously on a very small head.

'Not for *that* long.'

'No,' says Rachael, not sure whether to be unnerved or

impressed. 'Then I was thinking about my husband.'

'I wish you'd call him your "late" husband.'

'But we both know he's dead.' Rachael looks at him and that laugh, the one that he had first seen in Hyde Park, again escapes her. Now he's seen it a few times, Robin has decided he doesn't like it. It's patronising. 'Why Robin,' she says. 'I do believe you're sulking.' She lifts the china cup to her mouth, briefly hiding her face behind it. Robin flinches; he hates it when he can't see her expression.

As she replaces the cup she catches the look on his face. 'I'm sorry,' she says and puts a hand on his. 'You don't like being teased, do you?'

'What were you thinking about your *late* husband?' Robin asks.

There he is, asking questions again.

'What was he like?' Gentler, nicer now.

Rachael pours them both a second cup of tea. 'He was . . . he was my husband.'

She looks at Robin, the blues of his eyes flash, sending out bolts of silver lightning. How insensitive of her to remind him. At these moments all her doubts flare up again. He is just a boy. When she walked down the aisle on the arm of her father taking the first steps towards her happy ever after, Robin was . . . what? She knows he is ten years old, but she can't picture what he is doing. A dirty-kneed urchin climbing trees? Part of a raucous gang kicking a can around the streets? Unless he tells her, she will never know that he is walking the streets of the West End, gazing into shop windows, following ladies in fine dresses, breathing in their intoxicating perfumes and 'accidentally' brushing himself against their silk skirts.

'Please,' he asks. 'I'd like to know.' But still he gets no response. 'Start with what he looked like.'

'A spaniel,' she says. 'He looked like a spaniel.'

Robin doesn't know whether to laugh or not. But when he sees Rachael's eyes light up he knows he can join in the joke. 'Big feet and long floppy ears?'

This is the laugh he wants to hear from her; unforced, natural, joyous. 'No,' she says. 'Thick black curly hair and big round eyes.'

'And did he follow you around everywhere and curl himself up in your lap—' He hasn't noticed that she is no longer laughing. '—wanting you to stroke him, tickle him behind his ears—?' The silence makes him look up. He doesn't expect to see tears in her eyes.

'Is it always like this?' Rachael thinks to herself. She knows none of the men she has spent any time with since Saul died, have known how to talk to her about him. She doesn't realise that is because she doesn't know how to talk about him herself. But, she reminds herself, Robin is different. He is not a man, for one. He is not interested in her in the way they had been. He doesn't want a companion. He wants what she wants. It's the only thing that keeps them going through their difficult conversations, their awkward meals and their half-hearted attempts to be interested in each other's lives.

Passion.

In their passion they can forget. In their passion they feel no pain. They have no memories, they are not themselves. They are simply a mesh of nerve endings, sparking, fizzing, exploding. She can feel intense pleasure if he touches a single hair on her head; he will faint with desire if she breathes on him.

In their passion he tells her she is beautiful. In their passion he tells her that the loves her. She cannot accept that this is what love is. Yet when she lies there on his bed, in his funny room, naked, expectant and his perfect body, a thing of beauty, looms over her, before she loses herself she wonders what other name you give to it, how else you express the intensity of the moment.

'Rachael, I—'

'What is it?'

'Don't laugh at me.'

'I'm not.'

'You know I love you.'

Rachael is shocked; he's never told her this out of bed

before. She doesn't like the look in his eyes. 'I've got an idea,' she says. She wants to distract the moment.

Robin is confused. He thinks he's being rejected. 'Rachael?' he offers, by way of giving her the opportunity to recover the moment.

'Why don't we go away at the weekend?'

The cloud hovering races off like an athlete in response to the starter's pistol. 'Yes,' he says. 'Where?'

'Uffington.'

Robin laughs. '*Where?*'

'Uffington. The White Horse. I'm longing to see it. Dulcie's told me all about it. There's a small inn there where we could stay and we could climb the hill and have a picnic and be where George slew the dragon.'

Now he knows what it would entail, Robin panics. 'Why?'

She can't tell him though. She doesn't want to hurt him, he's so young and often seems so fragile. She doesn't want to tell him that it's a test. She needs to know if what she feels for him exists outside the rituals they have very quickly established. She needs to know if any of this is real.

'Why not?' she replies.

And he doesn't want to tell her that he has never left London before and he realises now that this will test how much he loves her. For he must put all his trust in her, in both of them and their love, because he'll be lost. He won't know where he is, and if he feels that then he won't be able to impress her. And if he can't impress her—?

'It will be fun,' she says and he is immediately reassured because she must have seen the fear in his eyes.

'Come home with me.'

'Robin! We've just come from your home.' She runs her fingers through her hair as if to tidy it, as if to remind him of how it had come untidied in the first place.

Under the table he runs his foot up her shin. She responds

by straightening out her leg so that her foot runs along his thigh.

'All right,' she says.

But now she's gone, left him again. He rolls around in the crumpled sheets breathing in her smell, the only thing she has left behind. And he remembers the couple in the park and knows he was right. Love is dreadful, love is terrifying. He can't find the way to fit it into his world. His life, for what it was, no longer exists, yet only three weeks ago, it was everything to him.

He can't even contemplate going back to work. How could he attempt to please another woman? A woman that wasn't Rachael. He tries to imagine the rewards: the clothes, the jewellery, the fine meals, the good wines. Has he really given up all that in order to spend hours in his own, less than adequate rooms? Rooms that he couldn't wait to get out of in the mornings, that now he doesn't want to leave because her presence is here. As soon as she first lay on his bed, his home became the only place he wanted to be.

How to fill the hours till he sees her again?

It is six o'clock. She said she couldn't meet him tomorrow. He knows why. It's still there, hanging unsaid between them.

Yiskah.

Damn her!

He hears the dog barking. Florrie's home. She'll be up here in a minute, sniffing about for her rent. He has the money but he enjoys taunting her; enjoys making her believe that he doesn't have it, enjoys letting her think that he would sleep with her. The sad, stupid woman. That will amuse him, watching how far she is prepared to go and then he can humiliate her.

But as he recognises her shuffle up the stairs the idea bores him. He can't be bothered.

Knock knock. 'Mr Sweeting?'

He can't even entertain the thought of being civil to her so he goes to the bedside table, opens the drawer, takes out an envelope and slides it under the door.

Silence.

Then he hears her bending down to pick it up, a gentle wheezing accompanying the effort.

'Mr Sweeting?' Questioning this time. He doesn't answer. She goes.

He looks at his watch. Five past six.

Now what?

He dresses slowly. His body weighed down with the absence of Rachael. He searches for the shoes he was wearing. After he finds them, under the eiderdown that fell onto the floor, in passion, the image of Rachael open, receiving and loving comes to him and he realises he had forgotten about her during the search. He is angry with himself; he cannot afford to get so distracted.

He can't wait two days to see her, not if he's going to keep forgetting to think about her.

The panic, the fear, her absence, his love. It's bubbling up inside him, threatening to spew out in a torrent of rage.

He grabs his jacket, flies down the stairs, forgetting to lock his door and runs up to the Angel to get the train that will take him to her.

Forty-One

'Surprise!'

'Shoshi?'

'Look, I've repaired and washed her.' Leah handed Rachel the floppy rabbit, who was glowing a golden auburn that Rachel hadn't seen on her for years. 'It's for Theo.'

'Oh, Leah!' Rachel hugged her sister then dangled the legs in front of Theo as he lay carefully positioned in his bouncy chair, a large syringe dripping nourishment through the ever-attached tube into his tiny stomach.

Theo's barely focusing eyes followed the swing of the rabbit's legs, mesmerised by the gentle to-ing and fro-ing.

'Oh, this is such fun,' said Leah, snatching Shoshi from Rachel and taking over. 'Look, we could hypnotise him.' She stared at Theo through the pendulum legs of the rabbit. '"You are getting sleepy". Or, or "You will be well, you are getting stronger. Your heart doesn't have a hole in it". That would be so cool if we could make him better like that.'

'Thank God for Leah,' thought Rachel. No one, not even Brendan, had the ability to face Theo's condition head on.

'Oh, forgot to tell you,' said Leah, giving the entranced baby a much-needed break. 'Twin's coming over later.'

'Jonno? When did he get back?'

Leah sat upright at the table and put Shoshi down, not even

where Theo could see her. 'It was going to be a surprise. You don't mind do you?'

'Of course not. I'll be pleased to see him.' Rachel folded another baby-grow from the washing basket. 'Here, make yourself useful. Fold these.' She threw a bundle of muslins at Leah.

Leah engrossed herself folding the squares, smaller and smaller.

Rachel placed a mug of tea in front of her, checked Theo's syringe, then sat down.

'OK. About Trevor—'

Leah looked up. 'Nothing to tell. He used me. When I was no longer of use, he asked me to leave. End of story.'

'What do you mean "no longer of use"?'

'His creativity dried up. Nothing was coming through anymore. So, I guess I had to go.' She looked around her. 'God, you must be pleased to be home.'

'Don't change the subject.'

'Why do you want to know?' Leah snapped.

Rachel turned in her chair, now facing away from her sister and towards her son. 'One day, maybe, I won't have to answer that question anymore, because you will know, you will understand and accept that *I* care.'

'Yes, I know.' Leah put her hand out to touch Rachel's. 'But, I know how you see me. You've got to also see how hard it is for me to . . . to—' she sighed. 'Oh, fuck it, you know. To admit that I made a mistake.' She was almost shouting. Even Theo looked to see where the sound had come from.

Rachel took Leah's hand and squeezed it.

'Can we not talk about Trevor?' Leah asked.

'Can we settle for, "not yet"?'

'Jesus, you're impossible. While you're at it, why don't you make it hard for everybody?'

This was a new Leah, a different Leah. Previously she had challenged with her silence and her absence. Rachel didn't want to think that whatever ghastly things had been going on at Trevor

Rushcliffe's, it may have done Leah some good? She stopped herself. What was she thinking? How could it be good that her sister was turning into Brendan?

Theo's response was to let out a small cry. A single sound. Not unhappy or uncomfortable or even joyous; a simple reminder that he was there. It worked. Both women got up and went to him as the doorbell rang.

'That'll be Twin. I'll go,' said Leah, skipping out of the kitchen.

Rachel removed the empty syringe and replugged the tube. This was not how she'd imagined feeding her baby. She lifted him out of the chair and placed him so that he was looking over her shoulder, then remembered just in time to put one of the muslin squares there too. She didn't want to have to change her top again. Which reminded her, she needed to wash some of her own clothes. Better do it now while she thought of it or she'd get distracted and forget, then she'd get up in the morning and have nothing clean to put on . . . Tears of exhaustion hovered but she breathed them back.

So the first thing she said to her deeply tanned stepson whom she hadn't seen for six months was, 'Here, hold him. I'll be right back.'

In the bathroom, she sat on the dirty washing box and breathed deeply. 'Would it be like this if Theo wasn't ill?' She was doing all the things she knew had to be done, feeding, changing, bathing, dressing him. And the washing – the constant washing; the sterilising, making up the feeds. Then there was the playing, the cuddling, the dancing, the holding – the relentless holding. It was hard to find any enjoyment or (dare she even think it?) fulfilment.

She couldn't even remember why she had wanted this baby. Oh, that's right – because she got pregnant. Maybe the desire for motherhood had always been there lurking somewhere, but she certainly excluded herself from her peers in their race against the biological clock. So many things had seemed more important to her. Her work, her friends, her family, her life. This is what she'd always feared – exactly what was happening – that she would lose all that; that there would be nothing left of the person who'd wanted the baby in the first place. She knew she didn't want to give herself up.

And Brendan. Choosing Brendan who wasn't looking for that. Many a three-month relationship had floundered with men of her own age, still locked into an advertiser's dream, a Sunday supplement fantasy, when she told them a family didn't figure in her future.

But she'd always known. Her occasionally infuriating psychic abilities that gave periods of her life the feeling of an elongated *déjà vu* (sometimes an awful inevitability) told her so. She was in one now; this one being different only because she couldn't remember how it was going to end.

'Rachel? Are you all right?'

She opened the bathroom door. 'Jonno! I'm sorry about before. How lovely to see you.' She over-enthusiastically flung herself against him. 'You don't have to ring the bell. Why didn't you use your key?'

'It's been a while.'

'We noticed. You look fantastic, by the way.'

Jonno smiled. 'Thanks. Look, are you OK?'

'Is that a professional question?'

'Oh, fuck off. You're my stepmother.'

'Then, as your stepmother, I'm fine. Come,' she said, taking his hand, 'let's go downstairs. Oh, the washing. You go down. I'll be right behind you.'

'I'll give you a hand.'

Rachel laughed. 'You can leave me on my own, you know.'

'I didn't mean it like that.'

Rachel softened. 'Go downstairs, hey? I promise I'll be right down. God, I haven't seen you for months. I want to hear about everything.'

A cry, a baby cry, an unmistakable 'I need you and I need

you NOW' cry wafted up the stairs like a cartoon baking smell.

'Be right there,' Rachel called out, brushing past Jonno.

Jonno brushed his fingers through the sun-streaked blond fringe flopping over his forehead and followed her.

Leah was bouncing Theo on her lap.

'No wonder he's crying,' said Jonno.

'You should have heard him before,' she retorted. 'I think it might be his—' She pointed to his bottom and screwed up her face.

'You could have done it,' Rachel said.

'Oh no. I don't do nappies, especially if they smell like this. God knows what I'd find in there.' She handed Theo to Rachel, who reeled from the stench.

'I see what you mean. Come on littley, let's get you sorted.' She laid him down on the table.

'Oh gross. You're not going to do it here, are you?'

'Why not?'

'We eat off this table. At least we used to.'

Jonno laughed. 'Don't be silly, Leah, he's on his changing mat.'

Rachel listened to their banter as she removed the offending nappy, cleaned him up and put on a clean one.

'Has Dad been on at you about the circumcision?' Leah asked.

'What?' Rachel stopped what she was doing, leaving one of Theo's legs unsecured inside his sleep suit.

'Oh. Ooops. Sorry. Shouldn't have said anything.'

'This is a new one on me.' She looked over to Jonno, distracting himself by browsing at her cookery books. 'Let's go inside. I'm dying to hear what's been happening.'

But as they walked through to the sitting room, the impact of Leah's comment hit home.

'Circumcision! What? Why would I?'

'Because Theo's officially Jewish?' suggested Jonno's voice of reason.

'No,' said Rachel. 'That's not what's going on here. This is one of those weird "what if he doesn't make it" things.'

Jonno's eyebrows shot up in surprise. 'Go on.' He held his arms out to take Theo from Rachel and expertly, confidently held him, rocking him gently. The blue-black eyes very quickly closed.

'I know Dad and how he thinks. If Theo dies and he's not circumcised it's like an unbaptised Catholic baby dying. How would they know? So he'd be in the equivalent of limbo.'

'Why do you think Aza thinks that?'

Rachel hated it when Jonno assumed his professional tone.

'Because he told us, didn't he Leah?'

Leah shrugged her shoulders. 'I don't know.'

'Didn't you listen to any of his stories? He knew why so many of them marched willingly like lemmings into the gas chambers.'

'Because they didn't have a choice,' snapped Leah.

'No. Because if they denied their religion—'

'Rachel, we don't have to talk about this.'

Rachel looked at Jonno. He was right. She took a deep breath. 'I'm sorry. I'm over-reacting. I'm overtired. It is good to see you, Jonno.'

'And it's good to see you too.' Jonno smiled his special Rachel smile. Theo stirred slightly as if he were dreaming.

'Funny, isn't it?' she said.

'What?'

'You being so blond. Pale skinned and blond. And Brendan being so dark and Theo being dark haired and light skinned.'

'Pick 'n mix at the gene pool.'

'Do you think it might be more than that?'

'Like what?'

'Well, like if we carry any physical characteristics from our previous lives.'

'I don't know.'

'Trevor thinks—' Leah began. They both looked at her. 'Oh, never mind.'

'No, tell us,' said Rachel.

'Oh nothing really. He just thinks we do.'

'Well he would do. I mean, his is a visual approach to spirituality.'

'Mmm. Yes.' Leah crossed her arms and sank a bit in the armchair.

'Who's Trevor?' asked Jonno, over-exaggerating his interest.

'I'll tell you later. We are going out for a drink, aren't we?'

'Yes, of course.'

'Great. Look, I'll leave you two alone. I'm just going to lie down for a bit. I'll see you later.' And before Rachel could comment on levels of tiredness, Leah was up the stairs.

Rachel and Jonno sat on the sofa. He held her baby who slept soundly and dreamfully and her awareness of all this having happened before was stronger than she could ever remember. She listened to Jonno and watched him, and as she fought off visions of emaciated bodies in calm silent queues, she knew for certain that he wasn't now, nor ever had been, happy.

Forty-Two – August 1921

Robin watches Rachael sleeping, her head bobbing back and forth, dancing to the tune of the train. Outside greenery slips past. He has no interest in the never-changing view, he is far too busy enjoying the sight opposite him and thrilling to the fact that she doesn't know he is watching her.

He got the same thrill standing outside her house, that night. She'd never given him her exact address, but he knew it was Wildwood Road, that it was opposite the Heath and that it stood on a bend in the road. She had described this much to him. It hadn't taken long to find.

It is a dark, badly lit road. Random squares of orange light glow through exposed windows illuminating his way. He arrives outside her house just in time to catch Rachael drawing the curtains on the upstairs front room. A crack of light is visible where the curtains haven't quite been pulled together and Robin latches onto this, his peephole into the other life she lives, the one that doesn't include him. But here, only yards away from her, he can feel included. He stays until the crack is no longer visible, when the light goes out, and then just a bit longer. Before he knows it the birds are celebrating the start of the day. She will sleep on but he must tear himself away, finally, after all these hours, calmed and reassured by the nearness of her.

The train lurches. Rachael wakes. She smiles at Robin and says, 'How long have I been asleep?'

'I don't know,' he answers.

'Did we stop anywhere?'

'Reading.'

'Won't be long then.' She opens her handbag and retrieves a compact. 'Oh God,' she says, looking at herself in its mirror.

'You look lovely,' he says.

She ignores him and removes the puff and begins to powder her face.

'I said you look lovely. You don't have to do a thing.' He leans forward across the divide and puts his hand on her to stop her. 'Please don't,' he says.

Rachael is confused, but she complies. She shrugs her shoulders, 'Force of habit, I suppose.'

He gets up and sits next to her, puts his lips on hers. She giggles and pulls away. 'Now I'll have to put some more lipstick on.' He responds with a stronger kiss, trying to force her lips open with his own. She relents uneasily. They may have the carriage to themselves but she still feels exposed, on display.

'I've been so looking forward to this,' she says when he finally releases her. But something in her doesn't mean it. Occasionally she feels troubled by his kisses. She replaces the compact in her handbag and sees the small box, nestled against the lining and her confidence is restored as she fills with pleasure in anticipation of giving it to him.

'Will we see it from the train?'

'What?'

'The White Horse.'

'Yes, I believe so.'

Robin dares to take his eyes from Rachael and glance out of the window. He doesn't like what he sees of the countryside, can't grasp its appeal. There so much . . . space. So few people. Robin feels safer in crowds, amongst buildings, where there are shops – shops full of things that he wants. There is nothing here he could want, except Rachael, and, he believes, he has got her.

Rachael catches the look of distrust on his face and laughs. He turns back to her. 'It's only fields, trees and animals,' she says. 'It's not going to harm you.'

'Don't laugh at me.'

She stops. She has been warned before. She should have remembered.

They alight at Uffington station. Rachael automatically calls for a porter. Robin allows her to, even though he could quite easily manage both their bags. There is an awkward moment when the porter waits for his tip. Rachael, being used to travelling on her own, would not hesitate in searching for coppers but she sees a curious look in the porter's eyes that she reads as disapproval, suddenly making her aware of what she and Robin, as a couple, must look like. So she does nothing, waiting for Robin to take the lead. Robin is, however, used to never paying for anything and it is a couple of silent seconds before he realises what is expected of him.

Rachael says nothing about it. Robin thinks proudly of the well-bred women who would hand him money at the beginning of the evening for such a purpose, thus saving both their faces, and has to remind himself that this is different. This isn't work.

Although it is Rachael that made the booking, she expects Robin to take charge when they arrive at the inn. A quiet, gentle, 'You do it,' is all that Robin requires. But he is so unused to it.

They are led up to their room, which is perfectly comfortable, if a little short of luxurious. Robin thinks about the hotel bedrooms he has seen. They have satisfied his craving for the opulent, but they haven't had Rachael in them. They unpack their few things and lie on the bed together.

Rachael closes her eyes and breathes in the country sunshine pouring in through the open window. Robin leans up on his elbow then stretches his free arm down to lift her skirt and walk his fingers to her stocking tops. He then fans his hand over the flesh on the inside of her thigh; double excitement – the stroke of skin against his palm and the tickle of silk on his fingers.

She hasn't moved, hasn't responded.

He pulls his hand away and sits up.

Rachael opens her eyes. 'What is it?'

He glares at her, hurt, rejected. They should never have come. It's already changed things.

'Robin?'

He says nothing.

'Shall we go for a walk?'

'No. I'd like to make love to you.'

But then she smiles. 'But it's not like it is in London. We've got all the time in the world. I don't have to rush anywhere. We can take our time.'

'Yes, you said that,' he snaps at her. And they both know the moment is lost.

'A walk then,' she says.

'Tea first.'

'A walk to find a tea shop.'

He nods.

'I'll be right back,' she says and goes to find the bathroom.

As the door closes behind her, he kicks the bed.

They walk to the village and have tea. They see the Horse way up above them arching towards the horizon, flat, white but as commanding as a rainbow.

'Tomorrow,' she says, 'A picnic.'

'Up there?'

'Of course.'

The day winds down. Returning to the room, they make love before dressing for dinner. It's not as it has been, it's slower, gentler. They look at each other a little differently now, and it scares them both, because it's never been like that before. At least not for Robin without effort or performance. He can do slow and gentle, fast and furious, whatever madam requires, after all madam is paying. For Rachael, she wonders, really wonders what this is that they have between them.

Dinner is delightful, easy, laughing. They go to their room, full of red wine and good brandy. And their passion is back. There is no mistaking it. This is when they are at their best.

Rachael awakes suddenly. A glorious light is pushing against the curtains, demanding to be let in. Her nightmare has left her momentarily disoriented by her surroundings. She looks around her and sees a pale body lying face down in the bed next to her. She can't see his head because it is under the pillow. He looks like the headless corpse she has just seen in her dream. She screams. The body jumps then turns. Two arms lift the pillow and a mass of blond hair covering a perfect face reveals itself.

Rachael is only slightly comforted.

'I'm . . . sorry.'

The hair is pushed off the face. The eyes have changed colour, darkened like an angry moonstone.

'Sorry I woke you. I was having a bad dream.'

He is growing larger. She pulls the sheet up to cover herself – an impotent shield.

'You don't do that,' he says edging towards her.

She pulls the sheet tighter.

'Why would you scream?'

'Go back to sleep,' she says. This wasn't how she'd imagined waking up next to him.

'You're not frightened of me, are you?' Robin is still possessed by his dream-time demons.

He rips the sheet from her hands and pushes her back onto the bed. He lets himself down on top of her, trapping her and lunges, tearing her open. It doesn't take long. Not long enough for Rachael to protest or to work out a way of fighting him off. But long enough for his blond hair to turn to black curls and for her to remember.

When his terrifying convulsions have subsided he collapses on her, passed out, back in his deep sleep.

Rachael lies there. A single, salty drop leaves her right eye from the outside corner and makes a wet trail behind her ear and down the back of her neck.

She makes a plan.

They will have their picnic.

She will give him the cufflinks that she has had specially made.

Then she will tell him that she can't love him.

And it will be over.

PART FOUR

The first thin crescent is wheeled round once more

Forty-Three

Rachel opened the front door with her right hand, her left one pressing firmly against Theo's bottom as he balanced over her shoulder.

'Mum!'

'Hello, dear.' Ella put her face forward to be kissed.

'What a nice surprise. You on your own?'

'Your father's at one of his RHS lectures. I thought I'd be better employed coming to see you.' She marched past Rachel into the hall and took her coat off. 'I did leave you a message telling you we were up for the day.'

'I've not listened to any messages. Can't seem to find the time.'

'How's my lovely?' said Ella, holding out her arms for Theo.

'He's doing all right. Do you want to go to Grandma?' she asked, holding him in her outstreched arms. Theo smiled. 'That looks like a "yes", to me.' She swapped him for Ella's coat.

'Oh, dear,' said Ella, following Rachel into the living room.

'I know, it's an awful mess. Brendan will go mad when he gets back.'

'When's that?'

'Today.'

'Stayed away a little longer than you expected, didn't he?'

Rachel flinched at the implied criticism. 'It's been OK. I've got Leah to help me.'

'Yes. I can see what a help she's been,' said Ella, removing the empty packaging from a baby alarm before settling herself in the armchair. 'Bet you'll be glad to have him home though.'

Rachel took a breath and tried not to sound agitated. 'Of course I'll be glad to have him home. And so will Theo, won't you?'

Theo responded by yawning.

'Is he ready for a nap?'

'No, not yet.'

'Have you been out today?'

'No,' said Rachel. 'We were at the hospital yesterday. It always takes it out of both of us.'

'But you should get out. Fresh air will do you both good.'

'We've been given a date for the operation.'

Ella sighed with relief. 'Oh, I'm so glad. When?'

'First week in March.'

'Does Brendan know?'

'Yes of course, I phoned him last night.'

'Why didn't you call us?'

Rachel breathed in sharply. 'No reason. I'd have phoned you today or something.'

Ella raised an eyebrow but said nothing. 'Ooh, I've got something for you. In my bag.' She waved her finger towards the floor. 'You find it.'

Rachel opened her mother's excessively large handbag and saw an old book. 'Do you mean this?' she asked, lifting it out.

'Yes. I thought you might like it. It's got some wonderful illustrations.'

'*Nursery Rhymes for Boys And Girls.* It's lovely.' Rachel let the book fall open. A chill blew across her heart. 'The North Wind again.'

'What's that dear?'

'The North Wind.'

'Oh yes, it doth blow and we shall have snow. I think it must be blowing today.'

'Yeah. That one.' She looked at the drawing. At one time she would've called it 'manipulatively sentimental'. As if there were any other kind, Brendan would argue. But the little bird, curled up against himself, hiding his head under his wing as a blizzard rages outside the barn reminded her of Brendan. He had been gone for nearly two weeks.

'"Little Polly Flinders" used to be your favorite,' said Ella, at the same time as Rachel turned the page to reveal a picture of a little girl being whipped by her mother.

'God! Can't think why.'

'You were always telling me that you had "pretty little toes – just like Polly Flinders." In fact you wanted us to call you Polly for a while. Don't you remember?'

Rachel did a half-laugh. 'Yes I do. I still like it. If Theo hadn't been Theo, he would have been Polly.'

Ella looked horrified.

'I mean if he'd been a girl. Obviously.'

'Where's your helpful sister then?'

'I don't know. Out somewhere.'

'She must have known I was coming.'

Rachel decided not to rise to that bait.

'I've not spoken to her, you know.'

'Well, whose fault is that?'

'Your father can be rather possessive of her.'

'Perhaps "protective" might be a more appropriate word.'

Ella said nothing.

'She really is wonderful around Theo.'

'I'm glad to hear it. She needs something to take her mind off herself.' Theo gurgled. Ella smiled. 'So don't I get a cup of tea?'

'Yes of course. I'm sorry. I was enjoying sitting down with nothing to do. That'll teach me.' Rachel went to the kitchen.

Ella was still there an hour later when Brendan rang from the airport to say he'd landed safely and was on his way home.

'Are you all right with Theo, Mum, while I just clear up a bit?'

'Yes, of course. We're fine, aren't we? but I must be back in Kensington by four o'clock.'

'It's not going to take you an hour and a half to get there.'

'No, but—'

Rachel let out a sigh of exasperation. She should have learnt by now. Ella would have been quite happy playing with Theo while Rachel tidied up if Rachel hadn't specifically told her that that's what she wanted her to do. And she repeated her silent prayer: 'Don't let me be like that with Theo.'

Very little got done.

Ella left allowing at least an extra half-hour for possible delays on the Underground and Rachel attempted to have a minimum of one clear space that was uncluttered by baby things, by the time Brendan arrived.

Of course he didn't even notice the state of the house. He was so pleased to see the two of them he hugged them for minutes, then went straight upstairs for a bath. Rachel had a sneaking suspicion that she hadn't let out the water from Theo's bath last night, again. But Brendan didn't say a word.

She fed Theo, put him down for a sleep and lay down on their bed. Brendan came into the bedroom, a giant bath sheet wrapped tightly around his middle, exposing his hair-blanketed chest and thick shoulders. His long hair was slicked back, wet, against his head and his beard dripped water. He sat next to Rachel.

'Well,' he said. 'thank God for home. It feels like nothing's changed.'

Rachel thought of the robin, his head tucked neatly under his wing. 'You glad you went?'

'I'd rather have been here with you and Theo.'

The wing feather rustled and an eye was just visible.

'But it was really good to be out there again.' The head hid again. 'I met some wonderful people.'

'Tell me.'

'I told you about the guy who knew my Da, didn't I? He said

he still had some sketches he'd done of him. But of course when I went round to see him, we started on the Irish and never quite got round to looking at them.'

Rachael smiled.

'But what I didn't tell you is—'

'What?'

'You won't believe this. On second thoughts, of course you will. But his daughter has just bought a new house. He's ridiculously proud of her, she married some showbiz lawyer, or something ghastly, so he thinks she's done really well for herself. And you know what they're like out there. He knew my father so therefore I must get to know his daughter and we both live in London, blah blah. So guess where she lives?'

'In this street?'

'No.'

'Where?'

'Hampstead Garden Suburb.'

Rachel got that sting at the back of her eyes.

'Wildwood Road.'

Rachel always felt reassured when she could still be amazed. Sometimes she felt that being psychic threatened to remove the element of surprise. 'You didn't tell him, did you?'

'I just said that it was a weird coincidence because we'd been to see it, that's all. But they've just had a baby too. Well, he's about five months old, their boy. It might be good for you to meet her.'

Rachel let the idea float around her head to see what would attach itself to it. 'Perhaps,' she said.

'Good, I'm glad you said that because they've invited us over for lunch on Saturday.'

Rachel sat up. 'I don't know if that's a good idea. We've got to be careful with Theo. We can't risk him getting any infections. You know what babies are like, they've always got a cold or something.'

'Did anyone ever tell you he shouldn't mix with other children?'

'Er, no.'

'Check it with the hospital if you're at all concerned.'

And Rachel was surprised for the second time in two minutes. This was most unlike Brendan to accept her anxieties without argument or reprimand. But her ungenerous side settled for Brendan not wanting to admit that he had similar worries of his own.

He shivered. 'Better get some clothes on.' He let his towel drop, opened drawers, pulled out clothes. Brendan was back. Rachel had been so preoccupied with Theo that she hadn't had time to notice the absence of Brendan's things around the place.

'Then I'd better go and spend some time with that son of mine.'

'Brendan?'

'Yes?'

'Put your towel back.'

'Said the woman who hadn't emptied the bath water.'

'It's not easy on your own.'

'I know.'

Rachel didn't think he did, but said nothing.

'I know it was bad timing. But it couldn't be helped.'

'It would've been nice if we could have brought him home together.'

'Yes, but it's not as if—'

'What?'

'No, never mind. I'm here now and I'll be here for when we bring him home well and strong, after the operation. That will be the real start of family life.' Brendan placed a kiss on Rachel's head and left the room.

His words ripped through her like the North Wind. Yet he was only confirming what she was already feeling, that somehow this bit didn't count. She thought about Louise persuading her that the reasons for her detachment from her son, never mind all the visions and dreams, lay in a past life, something unresolved – an old drain that needed unblocking that she didn't even know she used. And here was Brendan expressing the same feelings without any apparent guilt.

How else could he have left a sick child and disappeared for a fortnight?

But then she realised; Brendan could never, would never have done that if he'd held any doubts that Theo was going to make it.

And that was the main difference between them.

caused and here was [illegible] expressing the same feelings without any apparent guilt.

How else could he have left [illegible] child and disappeared for a fortnight?

But then he returned [illegible] would [illegible] have done that [illegible] to make it.

And that was the main difference between them.

Forty-Four – September 1921

Dulcie held Rachael tightly. She stood still, letting Rachael take the lead. She would disengage herself from this fierce comfort when she was ready.

Rachael was still. Silent tears racing down her cheeks. Today they are noiseless, yesterday they were accompanied by exhausting sobs, the day before, she screamed out loud with the pain.

Finally she moved. Only an inch but it was enough.

'I presume this has something to do with why I've not seen you for ages?'

Rachael pulled back from Dulcie's hold. 'It was awful,' she said. 'I feel so, so, stupid, dirty, pathetic.' She looked around her and something came back. It hadn't been a good idea to come here, to her old home, sit with Dulcie in her bedroom, on the bed – the same bed . . . No wonder she had cried when Dulcie asked her how she was. 'Can we . . . go somewhere?'

Dulcie stood up. 'Of course. Come on. We'll walk up to the Village.'

But suddenly Rachael didn't want that either. She put her head down and shook it.

'Over the Heath?'

God, no! That would be worse. She needed to be somewhere that bore no traces of Saul and therefore of Robin. 'I know. The Summer House.'

'That's not much of a walk, down to the end of the garden.'

'I know, but—'

Dulcie smiled. 'That's fine. I'll organise some tea.'

Rachael followed Dulcie out of the room, along the oak-panelled landing and down the wide stairs. Dulcie disappeared through the swing door that led to the kitchen and Rachael went out into the garden through the dining room's French doors.

The garden was not looking good. It was maintained but not cared for. Rachael had constantly been complimented on the verdancy of her garden. It was certainly not how you would describe it now. She turned behind the laurel hedge she had planted to make a secret place for herself, hidden from view, and turned the handle on the door of the Summer House; a present from Sydney, something to help her through her mourning.

Dulcie obviously never used the place. The floor had not been swept for months. The remains of last year's fallen leaves dusted over the tiles. Rachael felt a chill. There were cobwebs on the furniture. But the eyes of the stone Pan still twinkled, cheekily, invitingly as he blew on his pipes facing one direction, his fawn's legs dancing away in the other.

'I'm sorry Rachael. It's a mess. Let's sit in the garden.' Rachael jumped. She hadn't heard Dulcie arrive.

'No.' The strength of Rachael's refusal caused Dulcie's eyes to widen slightly. 'I want to be here.'

'All right then. I'll get Becky to give everything a dust down.'

'No, wait. Sit with me.'

Rachael sat on the window seat, disturbing at least a year's worth of dust as she did so. She told Dulcie that this was where she used to sit, for hours at a time. Sometimes reading, sometimes sewing and sometimes painting. 'Daddy was always on at me about my painting. He made me carry a sketchbook around.' She looked away from Dulcie out of one of the windows, recognising a particular view she had tried in vain to capture in pastel. 'But the thing is, I can't draw.'

A puzzled smile unveiled itself across Dulcie's mouth. 'Does it matter?' she asked.

'Only if you're my father's daughter.'

'Or wish to become an artist, then it might be a problem.'

'He used to say, "You'll never get a husband if you can't draw."'

'Oh.'

'What?'

'When? I mean, when did he used to say that? I thought you were always going to marry Saul and everyone knew.'

Rachael leant back against the glass, brushing a cobweb away. 'I don't know,' she said. 'But you're right. Maybe it's just a thing fathers say.'

'A thing architects say. I know what *they're* like.'

Rachel smiled with her mouth but nothing else.

'Do you want to tell me what's happened?'

'One day. I feel so much better now.'

'Anytime you want to come and sit here, please do.'

Rachael said nothing.

'We're missing you down the mission. Will you be coming back? We're desperately short of volunteers at the moment.'

'I don't think so. Not for a bit anyway. I've been neglecting things, people, you, Yiskah—'

'We noticed.'

The thought of Yiskah started the tears again. The relief from the guilt, now Robin was out of her life, was so huge she had been unaware of quite how much she had been carrying. She needed to make it up to her.

'Please tell me what you know about Shoshi's father,' she asked Dulcie.

'What has she told you?'

'Only that she wasn't married.'

'I don't know much more—' Dulcie's voice trailed off.

'Yes you do.' Rachael shocked herself with her severity. Dulcie looked up in surprise.

'I know that he wasn't Jewish and,' Dulcie took a deep breath, 'and that he forced her.'

'Rape.' Rachael said it quietly, calmly, coldly. She put her hand up to her mouth. She thought she was going to be sick. 'Oh God. Poor Yiskah.'

She remembered her look when she had recognised Robin. She could see her, as if she were here, right here with them in the Summer House. That terror. But she could also see what she hadn't been aware of before, disgust and shame, because that was what she was feeling herself.

And she knew for certain.

Becky arrived with a tray which she placed on the bench, laid a tablecloth, then lowered the tray onto the table.

'Thank you, Becky.'

But Becky didn't go. Dulcie was anxious to bring her friend back from wherever her thoughts had taken her. 'Was there something else?' she asked her maid.

'Yes, Ma'am. A gentleman—'

Rachael turned.

'He left this.'

Dulcie reached out for the card.

'No. It's for Mrs Silverman.'

Rachael didn't move. Becky didn't know what to do with it.

'I'll take it. Thank you Becky.'

Rachael watched until Becky's shadow was no longer visible behind the laurel hedge. 'Read it,' she said.

'"Robin Sweeting". That's all.'

'No,' said Rachael. 'There's something written on the back.'

Dulcie turned it over. 'Oh yes "*Selfridges. Main entrance. Two o'clock. Tuesday*" What tiny handwriting!" Rachael, what is this?'

'Give it to me.' Rachael snatched the card from Dulcie. She was about to tear it into tiny pieces, when she noticed a dirt stain on one corner.

A stain she was familiar with because she had spent hours

staring at it, trying to make up her mind whether to go and meet him that day.

A stain that had been acquired as she tapped the card against the bench that Sunday in Hyde Park, before slipping it into her handbag.

Forty-Five – September 1921

Robin opens his eyes. He has a full second of consciousness before he remembers. He closes his eyes again; he wants to be back on that hill, the sun shining, that plane circling them, the noise from its engine getting louder and louder so that he has to shout to tell her how much he loves her, how he never wants this moment to end.

Of course, he doesn't believe her. You don't give someone so special a gift if you don't love them. He had not been encouraged by the sight of the small box; he had seen so many of them before. But then it sprang open and he knew he would never receive another gift like this one.

They sit in their open box on his bedside table. One of the things that makes being awake bearable. He leans over for it and runs a long, well-manicured finger over the enamel as if to coax the little robin out from under his wing. His eyes move to the other one. There he is, singing his tiny heart out. Robin imagines the sound, at once both joyous and mournful. A beautiful moment made awful.

Like the plane flying over them invading their peace.

Like Rachael telling him she could never love him.

Like his mother handing him a brown paper parcel tied up with silk ribbon, him knowing what was inside, and then her leaving him, for ever.

Then he tries to think of awful things made beautiful. And he thinks of himself.

'Today is the day I will get her back,' he says, getting out of bed with a huge effort. He pours water from the jug into the bowl and splashes his face, shivering as he does so. He is never ready for how cold it feels.

Once dressed, he removes a box from the wardrobe. He opens it. The brown paper parcel lies on top, where it lives. He peeks inside, gets his rush of pleasure but puts it aside. He lifts out a photo album.

It is covered in lace. He opens it.

On the first page a gold-edged, stiff, white card announces:

Mr Sydney Cohn
would be honoured if you would attend
the Wedding of his beloved daughter
Rachael Leonora
to
Saul Ethan Silverman
son of
Donald and Dorothea Silverman
on
Sunday 11th June 1911

Robin turns the page. And there they are. Her arm in his. Rachael smiles. Saul doesn't. Robin hates him. If that were him, he would have been the happiest man alive. Nothing could have stopped him smiling for the rest of his life.

He studies her face and thinks about how meeting her has helped him. Had helped him. Because now the pain is back worse than ever and only the knowledge that they *will* be together makes it bearable.

He glances through the half-dozen photographs in the book. Rachael looking more beautiful in each one and that ugly, bug-eyed husband of hers looking worse. In one of them Rachael's long pearls have caught on the jacket button of Saul's suit. Robin hates this one for he imagines how that could have happened: she must have been standing facing him, leaning close, then, as they parted the necklace got hooked and there it is, the evidence of an intimate moment that stabs at Robin's love. The terrible reminder that she has been loved before.

He takes out his favourite, the one where Rachael looks the most beautiful and carefully cuts it in half, discarding the dead husband. The picture looks so much better that he decides to do the same to all of them.

He puts the album down and sits down to write today's letter.

September 2nd
My darling,

I awoke with a thought today: we haven't discussed where we are going to live! Maybe you've just assumed that I will move into your house. I want you to know that this is perfectly acceptable. We would hardly be comfortable here in my two rooms or with Mrs Grix and her ghastly dog, not to mention her endless pots of tea.

No, you are used to your own home, which you have made extremely comfortable and I would not dream of asking you to leave it. The only thing I ask for is a wardrobe for my clothes.

I hope you will forgive such a short letter today but I have an awful lot to do. (As if you weren't aware of your approaching birthday – I have so much to organise).

Please be assured that I am thinking of you always, reliving our pleasure with each other every moment in my head and will not rest until you are where you were born to be, forever by my side.

With more love than can ever be expressed,
Robin

He folds up the grained paper and puts it in a lined envelope, carefully licking around the edge with the same delicacy as if it were Rachael herself. He addresses it then opens the drawer of his bedside table to find a stamp. He gives a snort of annoyance at the pile of similar envelopes, returned unopened. He is sure she will read this one.

Her birthday! That has reminded him. He checks his watch. His first appointment of the day is not for another couple of hours. But he heads out, anyway.

Forty-Six

'I don't really want to be doing this.'

'Could you perhaps have made that a bit more explicit?' said Brendan, putting a bottle of water and a bottle of milk in Theo's changing bag. 'I mean, we should have been there half an hour ago and you're not even dressed.'

'You go, I'll stay here.'

Brendan threw a jumper at her. 'No. Put this on and let's go. Theo's nicely full and comfortable. We won't stay long. About an hour. As soon as he starts to get restless, we'll leave.'

Rachel's head appeared through the polo neck. 'What about when I start to get restless?'

'Don't you want to go back to the house?'

'I don't think it will help anything, to be quite honest.' Rachel searched around the floor for her boots.

'Is it not still bothering you?'

'Actually, more than ever. Ah, found one.'

'So?'

Rachel collapsed into a chair then forward onto the table. 'I'm just so tired. I'm tired of it all. The trips to the hospital, the worrying, the caring; the worrying about not caring enough, the caring about not worrying enough. When's it going to end?'

'You're letting it all get on top of you. Leaving your clothes lying around the kitchen is a perfect example,' said Brendan handing her the other boot. 'If you just took that small effort and started to deal with the manageable stuff, then the big things wouldn't be nearly so daunting.'

'When did you get to be so wise?' She pulled her boots on. 'OK. Ready.'

'So we're going then?'

'Yes. Because you're right. You're always fucking right,' she said, picking up Theo who was safely strapped into his car seat, and walking out of the room.

Driving along Wildwood Road, Rachel watched a group of boys playing football on the Heath. 'I'm going to hate what they've done to the house,' she said without turning her head.

'Oh, you know that, do you?'

'Of course I do. I'm psychic. Remember?'

Brendan laughed. 'Bleedin' psychotic, if you ask me.'

They drove round the small roundabout and parked opposite the house.

'And be nice,' said Brendan, unclicking his seat belt and getting out of the car.

Rachel got out and let Brendan deal with Theo. She stood and looked at the house. It already looked different. She took a deep breath and tried to talk herself out of her crabbiness. For a moment she felt able to cope but the tiredness returned with her next breath. It was no use, she told herself, going in expecting to find answers. At best she could leave with more questions, but even this seemed too much to have to deal with.

From the moment a dark, curly-haired man in his early thirties opened the door, introducing himself as 'Dave', sticking his hand out to be shaken, Rachel felt the disappointment that comes with being proved right.

Rachel didn't like men, particularly young men, who relaxed in pressed chinos, Ralph Lauren shirts and loafers. 'Bet he's got a suede bomber jacket,' she thought.

Dave crouched down to be on Theo's level, to introduce himself. Rachel bent over and took of Theo's hat, catching Dave's slight recoil as she did so. With his hat removed his tubes were fully visible. Dave mumbled a loaded 'How is he?'

'He's great,' said Brendan, smiling a broad smile that reassured Rachel.

Dave led them from the hallway (dried flower arrangement on a radiator shelf, Rachel noted with dismay) into the living room.

Rachel sighed. Naturally their furniture was completely wrong for the house.

'Where's . . . I'm sorry, I can't remember your boy's name?'

'Connor,' said Connor's father proudly.

'Oh, yes of course. Good Irish name.'

'By way of North London,' thought Rachel.

'He's just waking up.' A small cry came down the stairs. 'That'll be him.' And, perfectly groomed to match her husband, in came Mary, carrying Connor, a no-haired, no-chinned brute of a baby.

'So nice to meet you at last,' gushed Mary.

Rachel warmed to her only because her Belfast accent was thicker even than Brendan's.

'Da's told me so much about you.'

Rachel let Brendan and Mary get acquainted, which they both seemed quite happy to do. It was good to see Brendan relaxed, but he always was at his best enjoying conversation. She pretended to be interested in their reminiscences about where they grew up, all the while trying to reconnect herself with what had drawn her so strongly to this house. It was hopeless; she could feel nothing. Dave and Mary, with their three-piece suites and voluminous curtains, had soft-furnished the soul out of it.

The sun briefly shone through a break in the clouds. She thought she heard a voice. Something at last. Rachel looked up and out of the window.

'Do you mind if I look at the garden?'

'Yes. Why not?'

Brendan smiled at her and mouthed something she couldn't get, but she assumed it was approval, and she followed Dave into the kitchen.

Past caring whether she was being rude or not – she simply had no energy to spare being civil to someone she didn't care about – she let Dave open the back door and marched past him, indicating that she wanted to be by herself.

In the garden Rachel heard that rush of water again.

'Thank God something is coming,' she thought.

She had that same feeling of something terrible having happened.

This house. She had been brought to it by so many routes. If she'd let an opportunity pass her by, then another one came by sooner or later. Louise, Jonno and now Brendan had all led her here.

She was feeling the burden of the past; beginning to recognise that it must be faced head on. And with that came the final burying of any romantic notions attached to the idea of a past life. There was no comfort in it for her anymore, only questions.

Mary and Dave, with their self-evident 'why-buy-something-old-when-you-can-buy-something-new' philosophy were showing her was how easy it was to smother the past. Even if she never got the answers, she could never give up her passion for keeping the past alive.

Rachel made her decision. She would make that appointment.

As she turned to go back into the house she heard the plop and splash of a heavy object falling into water and a woman screamed out the name of Rachel's most favourite special toy.

Forty-Seven – September 1921

'Rachael! You look beautiful. Happy Birthday, my darling.' Sydney gently placed his hands on his daughter's shoulders and kissed her lightly on each cheek. 'Come into the drawing room. Isaac and Dulcie should be here any minute. Why didn't you share a taxi?'

Rachael shrugged. She hadn't thought. She was feeling guilty about leaving Yiskah and Shoshi alone tonight. Shoshi had been so excited at the prospect of Rachael's birthday; she drawn her a card, picked some flowers from the garden and tied them with a special ribbon and had not left her side all day. Yiskah had seemed worried, distracted, but Rachael was so used to her being like this, she hardly took notice of it anymore.

'Champagne? Or shall we wait for our guests?'

'Better wait, I think.' Rachael sat in the armchair by the fire generally reserved for her father.

'Are you all right?' Sydney leaned over her and gave the top of her head a kiss.

'Yes, of course.' Rachael suddenly brightened up. It was hardly fair on Sydney for her not even to attempt to enjoy her birthday.

'I know traditionally presents come after dinner with coffee, but I wanted to give you this, privately.' Sydney handed Rachael an envelope.

She looked up at him.

'That's better,' he said. 'I haven't seen that twinkle in your eyes for a long time.'

'Thank you.' Rachael took the envelope and felt it, then shook it, then held it up to the light.

Sydney laughed. 'Why don't you just open it?'

'I will,' she said.

'Well let me know when you have,' said Sydney, crossing to the drink's cabinet and pouring two whiskies.

Rachael edged her finger under the envelope's flap and pulled out a letter. She read it carefully, folded it and put it back in the envelope.

Sydney had been watching her.

'Well?'

'Who'll come with me?'

'Whoever you like.'

'Would you?'

Sydney closed his eyes and breathed in, utterly unable to prevent the smile that was bursting out of his lips. 'I'd have thought I was the last person you'd want to do New York with.'

'Wrong,' she said, jumping up and flinging her arms around his neck. 'You're the only person. When shall we go?'

'It's an open ticket. Whenever you – whenever *we* like.'

'Thank you, Daddy, it's a wonderful present.'

'I thought you needed cheering up.'

Rachael looked terrified as the doorbell rang.

'It's only Dulcie and Isaac.'

But Rachael didn't relax until they were in the room.

Dinner was difficult. She tried her best to be cheerful but it was so hard, what with Dulcie sending sympathetic glances at her all night and Isaac, who obviously knew something, being extra loud and jovial. Sydney knew something was wrong and was more concerned than curious.

Every time the door opened Rachael jumped and took a couple of minutes to recover, while empty plates were removed or wine glasses refilled. It did not go unnoticed that Rachael's glass was filled more frequently than anyone else's.

But as it got later and the wine had calmed her down sufficiently, she began to relax a bit, although there was a part of her that was alert to the fact that it was her birthday and Robin had, as yet, not acknowledged it.

All day she had been dreading the doorbell ringing, feeling sure that he would be sending flowers, gifts, a card, or appearing himself. His absence was unnerving her more than his presence.

Davis wheeled in a small trolley laden with parcels, which he piled up in front of Rachael. He then served coffee.

Sydney, enjoying the ritual probably more than Rachael, placed them in the order in which they should be opened. Rachael tried so hard to be thrilled, for his sake, but it was just another bottle of perfume, volume of poetry, pair of earrings. She smiled gratefully, if unenthusiastically.

There was a stunning beaded bag from Dulcie and a small framed print from Isaac. One present remained.

'Sorry, Daddy. When should I have opened this one?'

Sydney looked up from lighting his pipe. 'That's not one of mine.'

'Dulcie?'

'No.'

'Isn't there a card with it?' asked Sydney.

'No.' Rachael picked it up. It was the size of a large book.

Davis entered with brandy and port.

'Is this from you, Davis?' asked Rachael. He had been known to give her a small gift, from time to time.

'I'm afraid not, Mrs Silverman. Do forgive me.'

But Rachael knew who it was from. She left it on the table and took a glass of port.

'Aren't you going to open it?' asked Sydney.

Rachael looked at Dulcie.

'It's safe to open it here,' Dulcie said.

Sydney was about to ask Dulcie what the devil she meant, but he stopped himself at the sight of Rachael's hands trembling as she struggled to rip the paper.

'That looks just like your wedding album,' said Sydney as Rachel removed a lace-bound book.

'It is my wedding album,' said Rachael, slowly.

Dulcie got up from the table and went to Rachael's side. 'Show me,' she said.

She picked it up and opened it, looking carefully at each page, not saying a word but breathing louder and louder. 'I'll take it,' she said.

'I want to see,' said Rachael.

'No,' said Dulcie.

'Will someone please tell me what is going on?'

Rachael looked at Dulcie and nodded her head in the smallest of movements. Sydney took the album and opened it.

'Rachael? Who is this man?'

Rachael leaned over the table to her father and snatched the book from him.

There was Rachael, on her wedding day, as she remembered herself. Ivory silk, tight bodice, small bustle. Simple hat and net veil tucked neatly under her chin. Bouquet of mixed lilies and ivy trailing to the floor.

As she always did, Rachael studied the expression on her ten-years-younger self, looking for signs, anything at all that pointed to the unhappiness to come.

But the man next to her was not Saul. His hair was not dark, but blond. His eyes not brown, but blue. He wore a morning suit, carried his top hat and displayed a Star Lily in his button hole.

Rachael screamed.

Now it was Isaac's turn to look at the pictures. 'Now that's what I call chutzpah!'

'I think it's a little more than that sweetheart,' said Dulcie gently.

'Who is this man?' repeated Sydney.

Rachael couldn't look at her father. 'At a guess,' she said. 'Someone who wants to marry me.' Then the tears that she had been holding back exploded out of her eyes.

Sydney pressed the bell for Davis. Thirty seconds later he entered.

'Yes, Sir?'

'Did anyone deliver a parcel today?'

'No, Sir.'

'How did this present get into the house?'

'I afraid I can't tell you, Sir.'

'Do you mean that you don't know?'

'Yes, Sir. That is what I mean.'

'Then why the devil didn't you say so?'

Davis didn't reply.

'Thank you, Davis. But I'd be obliged if you asked amongst the staff, to see if any of them know anything about it.'

'Yes, Sir.'

Davis left.

'Don't worry my darling. If there's even a sniff of any criminal activity we'll have the scoundrel behind bars before you know it.'

'There already has been.'

'What do you mean?'

'Well he must have somehow got into my house to steal the album in the first place. I've never invited him to my home.'

'Maybe Yiskah let him in. All he'd have to do was say he was a friend of yours.'

'NO! I mean, no. Yiskah would never let him into the house.'

Rachael saw the look that Sydney gave Dulcie. She sank back into her chair and sighed.

She was going to have to tell him everything.

Forty-Eight – October 1921

Robin snatches the pile of envelopes from Florrie. She's been eyeing him suspiciously lately. It can't have escaped her notice that almost every day now, Robin receives in the post a handful of letters, all addressed by the same person, that have been returned to him, unopened.

'Your rent, Mr Sweeting?'

'You'll have it by Friday,' he says and shuts the door of his room before she can respond that he told her that last week and the week before and the week before that.

She is only partly placated by Robin's decision to give up the second room. It has been let to a small, quiet man who dresses in a grubby suit and leaves the house at ten to eight precisely every morning, carrying a highly polished black briefcase, and returns every night at twenty five to six. He closes the door and no one hears a sound until he leaves the next day.

The quiet unnerves Robin. He can't imagine what this man gets up to, alone, noiselessly for an evening and a night. Sometimes it upsets him so much he makes as much noise as he can, hoping he will disturb his neighbour into some human contact. But he only seems to succeed in making that damn dog bark.

Robin now has so many of Rachael's letters he has had to find somewhere special for them. He even spared a small piece of his mother's taffeta to cover an old shoebox. As he runs his hand over its lid, he has an idea. A wonderful idea that lifts his spirits to a happier place than he has been in a long time. An idea so perfect that he forgets the despair and hopelessness he usually feels when putting away his unread, unshared intimacies.

He will do it for Christmas. They will spend Christmas together, of course; waking up as they had slept, entwined. A champagne breakfast as they exchange gifts. He can already see her face, the joy and the delight as she removes from its tissue wrapping—

Six weeks. He has six weeks to wait. That's good. That gives him time to do it properly. It has to be the best, the most perfect.

A knock on the door.

Robin jumps up. 'Yes?' he calls through the wood.

'I have a letter for you.' It is Florrie.

'I have my post, thank you.'

'No. This one got mixed up with mine.'

'Just slide it under the door.'

'But Mr Sweeting—'

'Slide it under the door!'

A long, cream envelope slithers onto the edge of the rug. He waits until Florrie's footsteps have receded.

He walks the few steps and stares at it before bending down to pick it up. But he knows. He can smell her scent on it from here. He knew, just knew that she couldn't ignore him for ever; that eventually she would regret her decision, come to her senses, see that there is no escape from the kind of love they have for each other.

He kneels down and takes the letter, breathing in Rachael. He opens it carefully. Only one sheet. Only three lines.

I implore you to stop your pestering. I have taken what steps I can to protect myself. My father and my friends are all alert to you. None of us will have any hesitation in contacting the police should your actions continue.

No name, but signed with a gentle, human touch. Two words: *Forget me.* Two words that fill the reader with hope. This is why he loves her. She has kindness, she has sincerity. She cares.

He must go to her immediately.

He takes up his position on the wall by the post box. He has a perfect view of the house and the front door but he cannot be seen out of any of the windows. He knows because he has checked this. If the front door opens he simply hides behind the wall until whoever it is has gone. He also has a clear view of the Heath so if anyone should approach he has plenty of time to disappear. He believes he has no chance of being discovered.

He sees Shoshi first. She comes skipping from behind some trees. Robin climbs over the wall and leans against the garage that runs at a right angle to the wall. He can't be seen as there is a tree between himself and the view from the Heath. Yiskah and Rachael walk arm in arm a few yards behind Shoshi, who waits patiently at the edge of the road.

Rachael and Yiskah seem deep in conversation, barely looking out for Shoshi as they cross the road. Shoshi continues to skip, opening the gate, up the path. Suddenly she turns to where Robin is hiding and peers intently.

Robin is sure he can't be seen, but sidles along the garage just to make sure he is completely out of sight.

Rachael opens the front door, they all go inside. Robin waits a couple of minutes then goes back to his place.

But minutes later the front door opens again and Shoshi comes out. Robin ducks behind the wall.

'I've seen you before.'

He looks up to see Shoshi's face peering at him.

'What are you doing?'

'I dropped something,' he says.

'What?'

'A button. Never mind, can't find it.' But he doesn't get up. 'Why don't you go back in the house?'

'Mummy told me to play outside.'

Robin is caught off his guard. He's not sure what to do. He thinks he wants her to go away, but there is something compelling in her nearness. Of course he's observed her a hundred times as she's played with her mother. But he's never been this close to her before.

'Surely Mummy meant the back garden.'

'You're always here.'

Robin laughs nervously. 'I like your Mummy,' he says.

'Why don't you come in? Why do you always sit outside?'

Robin wants to feel comforted by Shoshi's presence. He wants to feel that if he can't be close to Rachael, then being close to her daughter should be the next best thing. He is disturbed by how little he feels.

He reaches out and pulls one of her curls. 'You've got your father's hair.'

Shoshi looks down.

'I'm sorry,' he says. 'I didn't mean to upset you.'

'I haven't got a father,' she says.

'I know. I'm sorry.'

Shoshi is trying to form a thought. Robin watches her carefully.

'Everyone has a father, don't they?' she asks eventually.

'No. I don't. My father is dead, like yours.'

Shoshi is very confused. 'But, Mummy said—'

'Mummy said what?'

'That I mustn't talk about him.'

Robin says nothing. He guesses correctly that if he stays silent she will ask him another question.

'Do you know my father?'

'No. But I've seen a picture of him.'

Shoshi's eyes widen with disbelief. She hears her name being called from inside the house. She is torn; she wants to go but she wants to hear more about her father. Her name again, louder.

Robin tells her she must go. 'This is like a secret,' he says, putting a finger to his lips.

Shoshi nods her head and smiles.

'Don't tell your mother you spoke to me.'

Shoshi thinks about it. 'But can I tell Rachael?' she asks.

A voice, louder, calling out for . . . who? Who is this child? The change in Robin's expression makes Shoshi run away, screaming.

The front door opens.

Rachael bends down to the hysterical child. Puts her arms around her. Lifts her up. The child's legs grip around Rachael's waist, her arms tight around her protector's neck.

'What happened? Shoshi? It's all right.'

But they don't move. They stay on the doorstep.

Robin stands backed against the garage, shaking with rage and humiliation. But he is not in control of his body, which suddenly leaps over the small wall, and storms through the open gate to face the lying bitch.

The hand that flies against her face is open. A slap, not a punch. But the force of it causes Rachael to stumble. Shoshi's grip tightens. Rachael cannot work out how to stop herself from falling over or how to hold onto the child whose screams are now deafening.

Robin sees another figure emerge from the house. She removes the clinging monkey and carries her inside. Shoshi goes willingly. Of course she would. Robin understands now. Of course she would go to her mother.

Rachael tries to straighten herself. She turns on the spot, hands feeling around in front of her. She looks at Robin, trying hard to focus on him.

'The song's not finished yet,' he says and watches while Rachael faints, falling slowly to the ground, reaching out for something, somebody to help her.

She lies half in and half out of her home.

He leaves her there. Crosses the road and doesn't turn back.

[illegible] neck, her head and shoulders.

[illegible]

[illegible] you [illegible]

[illegible] 'Who [illegible]

[illegible]

screaming.

'Whatever that means.'

[illegible]

[illegible] around. [illegible]

[illegible] her protective [illegible]

'What happened?' [illegible]

[illegible]

[illegible]

[illegible]

[illegible]

[illegible]

[illegible]

[illegible]

[illegible]

Forty-Nine

Rachel left Louise at the nicest-looking pub they could find. 'Are you sure this is all right?' she asked her.

'Of course it is. It's much better you go on your own. I know Valerie too well. This isn't a social visit.'

'You know how to work the pager, don't you?' Rachel asked, handing her the small black square.

'Yes, but please don't worry about Theo or about me. You need to keep your head as clear as possible.'

'I'll try. Let me get you a drink before I go.'

'I'll have a coffee, thanks.'

Rachel went to the bar and ordered Louise's coffee. She checked her watch. She was still early so she ordered one for herself as well.

'*How* nervous are you?' asked Louise, laughing as Rachel placed in front of her a saucer with more coffee in it than the cup. 'Don't worry.'

'Do you know what she told me?' Rachel sat down and looked around her.

'You're behaving like you're about to do something illegal.'

Rachel was not amused. 'She told me that we're not meant to know about our past lives.'

Louise nodded slowly.

'She said it shouldn't be necessary to regress as we are given the chances in each life to put right the things that went wrong before.'

Louise nodded again.

'But don't you think that's an odd thing to say if that's how you make your living.'

Louise half smiled and raised an eyebrow.

Rachel sat back in her chair and flicked her spoon around her cup. 'Oh, right. That thing again.'

'What's that?'

'People involved in spiritualism are beyond making a living. They're only there to help.'

'Invites instant trust though, doesn't it?'

'Mmm. Yes, I suppose so,' said Rachel distractedly. 'Maybe I should just check on Brendan and Theo.'

Louise put her hand on Rachel's to prevent her from getting up. 'No. They're fine.'

'Of course they are. Well. I should go.' She didn't move. 'I am doing the right thing, aren't I?'

'I don't know the answer to that.'

'Good old Louise.'

'You're looking for an answer. You never know.'

'Right. I'm off then.' She got up and gently squeezed Louise's shoulder as she went by.

'Good luck,' said Louise. But Rachel had already gone.

Number 26 was the only house not to have turned the front garden into a driveway. While all the other houses' front windows looked out onto the bonnets of cars, number 26 had window-boxes and a gravelled area with a dozen or so terracotta pots. Some snowdrops were already in flower and elsewhere green shoots were pointing upward, trying to get the benefit of the wintry sunshine.

Rachel always got a small thrill from the first shoots of spring, but this year, for the first time they seemed burdened, seemed still to be carrying the memory of winter.

She searched for a doorbell and couldn't find one so banged

the brass letterbox instead. Heavy footsteps came towards the front door and Rachel was surprised to see the door opened by a small, slim woman.

'Valerie?' she asked.

'Yes. You must be Rachel. Come in.'

Rachel followed Valerie into the dark hallway, then held open the door of the front room and Rachel stepped into the light.

'What a beautiful room,' she said, basking in the sunlight bouncing off the ice-blue walls.

'Thank you. Where would you like to sit?'

Rachel looked around. There was a blue velvet *chaise-longue* in the bay of the window, an old pine rocking chair next to the fireplace and a small, two-seater sofa whose fabric was fading and ripped. She went to the rocking chair.

Rachel sat down and, turning to the window, immediately fixed her eyes on a cherry tree across the road, searching for buds.

Valerie relaxed back into the sofa. 'Do you mind if I take my shoes off?' she asked Rachel.

'Of course not,' she answered, then felt a sudden urge to do the same.

'Take a few moments to arrive and then we'll start.'

Rachel leant back and closed her eyes. She felt sudden warmth on her lids and opened them to see rainbows skipping off a crystal, hanging from a wind chime in the window. There were crystals everywhere. The largest chunk of amethyst Rachel had ever seen dominated the mantelpiece.

Valerie started to talk Rachel through a relaxation process.

Rachel surprised herself by how easily she responded.

'Say anything. Anything at all that comes to you.'

Rachel began to talk about Theo. Theo's heart. An incomplete tiny pulsing organ, working hard. Beating away. The hole expanding. Reducing.

Beat beat. Thump thump. Adore withdraw. Close it with love.

Rachel could feel her unconscious opening up like a crack in the earth. Wider and wider. She stood on the edge, peering over into the darkness. Then she sat on the side, testing the water with her big toe. Then a whole foot. Both feet playing with it now, splashing the contents over the side. She supported herself with her hands and gently eased herself in.

She landed at the head of the Horse.

She runs about the sunshine.

Sudden cold and dark. She looks up to see where the shadow has come from.

It's a small plane. She can just about see the pilot; a handsome moustached Air Force type. The sound of the propellers mesmerises her, getting louder and softer as the plane circles the hill.

'Tell him now. Tell him now. Tell him now.'

She is sitting on a camel-coloured rug, playing with its fringes. She sits legs to one side and runs her hands over her stockings. A blast of warm wind. She puts her hand up just in time to prevent her hat from blowing away. Sitting next to her under a black cloud is an angel. He smiles a smile she knows so well but her eyes are drawn to his chest because she can see straight through his shirt to his heart. As she watches, it snaps. Breaks in two.

And when she looks up into his face it is blue and bloated.

The brown bead eyes on a copper-coloured fur rabbit turn blue and wide. Her ears shrink, her face flattens and the fur on her head grows into thick curls.

'I know who her father is.'

But the child's face sinks backwards, losing definition, a watery veil distorting Rachel's vision. Bubbles disgorge from her mouth as she tries to speak. Further and further, deeper and deeper, the brutal bubbling reducing to a gentle fizz.

Rachel is talking fast – the part of her that remains conscious, aware of who she is, where she is and why, stops to ask Valerie if she is making sense.

Valerie bats back the question. 'Do you think you are?'

Now it is Christmas. A fairytale Christmas. A tree that's a green you never see anymore decked with boughs of golden beads. A star does more than twinkle. A perfect fire glows warmth, comfort and safety. The sense she gets of the room is wood. Masculinity. This is a man's house. A man who has lived on his own for many years. Looking round the room her eyes catch sight of a faint pencil drawing surrounded by a wine-coloured mount and a thin gold frame.

Suddenly the room is filled with people and laughter. But not happiness. Rachel watches the crowd, removed, anxious, waiting for something to happen. For she knows that it will and she knows that it will horrify her.

A flash then everyone is quiet. They are all looking at her as she stares at the figure in the gloriously rich, deep red dress, the colour of fine wine, shot with a silver that reflects tiny sparkles of light. She screams then it all goes black.

When she opens here eyes she is on a bed. A brass bed covered in a quilted pink and gold eiderdown. A floppy rabbit lies next to her. A man with grey hair sits with her.

'Has he gone?' she asks.

'Yes,' he answers.

But lying over a chair she can see some fabric that makes her think of—

'What's that?' She points to the other side of the room.

But it's very plain what it is; it's the burgundy taffeta dress.

'GET IT OUT OF HERE!'

There is a note on it:

'The only thing I have that belonged to my mother. Now it is yours. That's how much I love you.'

Rachel leans over the side of the bed and empties herself. Out pour fear, rage, humiliation, disgust. But when she looks again at the chair a tiny, blue-faced baby reaches out his limbs to her. She can see right through his chest. His heart is broken in two.

'I'm sorry,' she says. 'But I know I could never love you. Not how you love me. I'm so sorry.'

Rachel fell into a deep, dreamless sleep.

When she woke the light was fading. Night-lights shone in oil burners, filling the room with a sweet spicy smell. She felt rested and well, a small spark of excitement flickering around the inside of her chest.

She sat up but lost her balance and the noise of her falling back into the rocking chair precipitated a gentle knock on the door.

'Yes, come in.'

Valerie came in, followed by Louise.

Rachel ruffled her hair in an attempt to straighten it. 'How long have I been asleep?'

'About half an hour.'

'I phoned from the pub,' Louise said. 'Valerie said you were asleep, so I came round. I'll leave you two alone now.'

'No,' said Rachel. 'I want you to stay.'

Valerie nodded her approval. Rachel got up and went to sit on the sofa. Louise sat next to her.

'How are you feeling?' Valerie asked, switching on the table lamp before sitting herself in the rocking chair. 'Can I get you anything?'

'This is fine, thanks.' Rachel helped herself to a glass of water from a filter jug on the coffee table. She drank it in one then poured another. 'I'm feeling amazingly clear headed. Like . . . like—'

Valerie waited for Rachel to find the words.

'Like a curtain's been raised.'

Valerie sort of smiled.

'I think it's very clear. It couldn't be clearer.'

'Go on,' said Valerie.

'This is why it's been so hard for me—' Rachel's voice choked. A sob bubbled up, waiting to release itself. 'I broke his heart before. That's why he's come back to me. His heart is broken because I couldn't love him. And now he's come back to me so that I can mend it.' She allowed tears to fall. Louise handed her a crumpled tissue.

'You're privileged,' said Valerie.

Rachel looked up at her.

'It's not many people that can have so clear an understanding of why they are here.'

Her words rained down on Rachel like stones. A purpose. She had a purpose. A destiny to fulfil; a responsibility, a burden.

Rachel looked at Valerie as if she were seeing her for the first time. A shrinking old lady lost inside baggy trousers and a loose tunic, thinning hair cut into an unkind bob, tired, weary, worn down by the amount of lives she had glimpsed. The air felt heavy with centuries of despair.

A panic fluttered inside Rachel. She wanted to reject what she had willingly come here to learn. She wanted a life of free will, her own choices, her own mistakes. But where did that leave Theo?

Needing time to think, she focused on a black-stoned ring in a silver setting, on the middle finger of Valerie's left hand.

'Obsidian,' said Valerie, taking it off and handing it to Rachel. 'Hold it up to the light.'

What had appeared solid black turned translucent. A golden streak ran through it that made Rachel think of the rings of Saturn.

Valerie reached for a small bowl of crystals. 'Here, choose one. Obsidian is particularly effective in past life work.'

Rachel concentrated on the mass of stones.

'We only live one life at a time. You must try to bring the jewels with you and leave the trauma behind.'

'But when it spills over—'

'Then you must try harder. Call me anytime. You have support and warmth and light here.'

'But what about Theo?' Rachel dropped the crystals she was playing with into the bowl. They clattered and clinked like milk bottles.

'You can't take on Theo's work for him.'

'But I'm his mother!'

'Rachel.' Valerie's voice was forceful yet calm. 'You came here to investigate your past life. One thing at a time.'

Rachel retrieved her shoes and wrote a cheque. She always found that a disturbingly unsatisfactory act cruelly grounded in reality.

She was silent as Valerie and Louise made their fond farewells.

'How do you feel?' asked Louise as they walked arm in arm to the car.

'Confused, threatened, scared.'

'Do you think you've found the answer?'

Rachel stopped and flung herself at her aunt, throwing her arms around her neck and crying into her shoulder. 'How can I believe that once upon a time I broke the heart of a boy that I couldn't love. Do you know why I couldn't love him?'

Louise stroked Rachel's hair.

'I couldn't love him because he scared me. He was trying to frighten me into loving him.' She ran her fingers under her eyes to catch the tears. 'And don't you think that I haven't already believed that Theo is doing just that?'

'Theo isn't him. It's only his soul.'

Rachel pulled away. They stood by the car. Rachel opened the door. 'Thank God for you,' she said.

Louise responded by clutching her guts and collapsed white faced into the front seat.

Fifty – October 1921

Rachael opened her eyes to see the pale face of Yiskah.

'I telephoned your father. I hope that was all right.'

Rachael tried to lift her head. She put her hand up and felt softness, feathers.

'I put a cushion behind you. But I couldn't move you.' Yiskah had also covered her with a blanket.

'Where is he?' Rachael asked.

'Gone.' Yiskah looked away. 'I wish you'd told me,' she said. 'Then I could have warned you. I could have told you that this would happen—'

Rachael slowly lifted herself into a sitting position, dragging her legs in from the outside.

Yiskah stepped over and finally closed the front door. 'Here,' she said, helping Rachael up. 'Come and lie down.' She led her into the drawing room and settled her down on a settee. 'I'll get some more coal for the fire.'

Rachael lay back against the high arm, moving a cushion, here, there, trying to get comfortable. The side of her face stung and she felt heavy-headed, nauseous. She closed her eyes but the room spun round so she kept them open. Suddenly she felt a gentle stroking of her hair.

'Who was that man?'

'Shoshi, darling. Did he frighten you?'

The little face nodded fiercely.

'Come, sit with me.'

Shoshi climbed onto Rachael's lap and, curling into a ball, snuggled herself against her.

'Why did he say he knew my father?'

Rachael closed her arms tighter around the tiny body. 'I don't know.'

Yiskah came in with a bucket of coal and, with the tongs, carefully built up the fire.

'Mummy?'

'Mmmm?' Yiskah continued her task without turning around.

'Did you know that man?'

A piece of coal dropped from the tongs, clattering against the fender as it fell.

Yiskah turned to look at Rachael.

'He's not a very nice man,' Rachael said.

'He frightened me,' said Shoshi. 'But I'm all right now.' She curled herself even smaller.

'I'll make some tea.'

'I think a brandy, actually.'

Yiskah got up and went to get Rachael her brandy.

'Have the fish gone to sleep yet?'

Rachael hugged the little thing curled up like a doormouse. 'I don't think so. It's not quite cold enough yet.'

'Can I go and see?'

'Yes, of course.'

Shoshi jumped up as if there had never been anything wrong with her and ran out of the room.

Yiskah handed Rachael her brandy. 'What do we do now?'

'I'd like you to tell me. Tell me about him. What he did. Who he is.'

Yiskah sat on the floor at Rachael's feet. 'No one must know.'

'Of course not.'

'He . . . he's—'

'He's her father, isn't he?'

Yiskah's silence told the truth.

'How—?'

One tiny word and it all came out. Everything. Yiskah had never said these words before. At first they were disjointed, half-sentences, a spluttering tap that hasn't been used for years, but then memories flowed freely.

A boy who lived in the same street. Different from everyone else. Teased and taunted by her brothers, their friends. But it was her, Yiskah, who was singled out for his revenge. Because she was quiet, because she was shy, because she was a girl and should have been indoors. What they did to him, he did to her. They were only children. But it got worse and worse until one day . . . She thought it was something to do with the war. He was angry that he was too young to fight. 'How will I ever get out of here now?' he'd said, as if it were her fault. And that was when . . . well, that had been the first time.

Rachael listened. Yiskah was not facing her. She had leant back against the settee and was facing towards the fire. 'If only she'd told me,' thought Rachael. But that, she knew, was a purely selfish thought. Yiskah's was a dreadful story. And now she had told it, now it was something that they shared, apart from—

Rachael closed her eyes. It had only just occurred to her. She hadn't had a period since coming back from Uffington.

The plop and splash of a heavy object falling into water.

The two women jump up. They cry out. The doors to the garden swing violently as they run through.

'Where is she?' screams Yiskah, her body running in one direction while her eyes search in another.

'That splash,' yells Rachael. 'The pond. Yiskah! The pond.'

Yiskah turns to the pond. Calls out the name of her daughter again. And again. 'Where is she?' she repeats.

The pond is not deep. It is raised about three feet and there's maybe another twelve inches below ground. But it is wide and long.

Rachael climbs in.

'What are you doing?' asks Yiskah.

Rachael feels around with her hands and looks for bubbles. She brushes against waterlily roots and slime and mud, disturbing fish and frogs.

'Rachael?' Yiskah's voice, a high-pitched squeal now. Panic. Confusion. 'Where's Shoshi?'

Rachael's leg stops against a large object. The water is black. She can see nothing.

'Here,' she says.

Yiskah can't move. She watches Rachael duck under and lift to the surface a small, limp body.

'Shoshi? Shoshi! NO!'

Yiskah, still. Staring at the wet thing. Not understanding.

She tilts her head to the heavens and lets out a long, loud, piteous cry.

Fifty-One

Rachel was dazzled by the blond hair and blue eyes coming straight towards her. She took a step back.

'Rachel! How is she?'

'Oh, Jonno! What are you doing here?'

'I was with Brendan.'

'Why hasn't he come?'

'He's with Theo.'

'Oh God! Of course.' She took another step backwards, searching for the seat she had been sitting on. She found it and fell into it. 'You must think—'

'I don't think anything,' said Jonno, sitting next to her and taking her hand.

Two porters wheeled a trolley past them. Rachel caught a quick glimpse of an old, terrified face.

'She's not said a word to me about this.'

'You've had enough to deal with.'

'But—'

Jonno put his arm around her. Rachel relaxed against his leather coat.

'Fucking hospitals,' she said. 'As if I hadn't seen enough—' She suddenly became aware of Jonno's finger stroking the top of her arm. She sat up. 'I haven't phoned Mum. Do you think I should?'

'When you've got something to tell her. You've rung Roger?'

'Shit!'

'I'll do that.'

'I'll go get the number.' Rachel stood up.

'Where's Louise now?'

'Somewhere with somebody poking about trying to find something. God! I can't bear it.'

Jonno looked at the pile of coats and bags next to the seat Rachel had just vacated. 'Is this Louise's bag?'

'Yes.' Rachel sat down again.

'Have a look inside. She might have an address book with his number in it.'

'OK.' Rachel did as she was told. 'Thanks, Jonno.'

'What for?'

'Looking after.'

Jonno smiled. A smile that cut through Rachel as if he had stabbed her.

'Are you all right?' he asked.

She put her hand to her head. 'No, not really. Look, you do it.' She handed him the bag.

'Here take some of this.' Jonno held out a small bottle of Rescue Remedy he'd found in Louise's bag.

'I've already had some.' Rachel wished Jonno would stop smiling.

'Here we are.' He pulled out a slim, flowered address book, its tattered cover totally incapable of holding together its loose pages.

'Oh my God!'

'What?'

'I bought her that when I was about twelve.'

'She's obviously very attached to it – to you,' he added, unnecessarily, Rachel thought, touching her arm.

'Roger's number? It will be under "W". Whelan.'

'Got it.' Jonno took out his mobile phone.

'They won't let you use that in here.'

'There's no equipment in this corridor.'

As soon as he turned it on a nurse appeared from nowhere.

'I'm sorry, you can't use that in here,' she said.

'I'll be right back,' he said to Rachel.

Rachel leant back and tried to calm herself. She was divided between being furious and terrified. As long as she managed to keep hold of the anger that Louise hadn't trusted her enough to share her pain, then she wouldn't be feeling so dreadfully frightened that she might lose her.

A young man in a white coat, stethoscope draped importantly round his neck, emerged through some double doors and sat next to Rachel.

'Well we've found out what it is.'

'And?'

'It's an inguinal hernia.'

'What? Thank goodness. I mean, I don't mean—'

'No, you don't mean . . . Fortunately it's a relatively simple procedure, but it is an emergency. We'll be operating on her as soon as we can.'

Jonno came back. 'Roger's on his way.'

Rachel told him the news. Jonno took it a lot more seriously than Rachel had done, asking all the practical questions about how long she would be in hospital for and how long the recovery was expected to take. Rachel wasn't listening. Now Louise's life was no longer in danger – apart from the everyday risk of surgery, Rachel could breathe.

'I'd better ring Roger back,' Jonno said and dashed outside again.

The doctor was still sitting next to Rachel. He was evidently glad of the rest.

'Can I get anything for you?' he asked Rachel.

'No, I'm fine now, thanks.'

'Scared you, didn't it?' he said.

'I can't tell you how much.' Rachel wished she could think of a way of carrying on the conversation.

The doctor leant forward, opened his mouth to speak but changed his mind.

'She'll be all right, won't she?'

'Yes, we hope so.' He got up and gently placed his hand over hers for not even half a second. Then disappeared from whence he came.

Jonno was back. 'Let's go get a drink.'

'Did you catch Roger?'

'Yes. He's going to Louise's place to get some things for her.'

'He has a key?'

'Unless he's going to get in some other way.'

Rachel picked up the coats and bags. 'I had no idea it had got that far. I have a key. I could have gone.'

'I'm not sure you're in a fit state to do anything.'

'I must call Brendan.'

'Theo's fine.'

'I know, but I want to speak to Brendan.' She was irritated with Jonno for not recognising that of course she would want to speak to her husband.

Jonno handed over the phone, suitably admonished.

'I'll see you in the café.'

Outside, she watched another ambulance arrive, another suddenly stricken patient carried out on a stretcher, another shocked and frightened relative following uneasily behind.

She found a quiet corner and dialled her number. The answer phone came on. Her watch said half past six. Maybe Brendan was feeding or bathing or changing Theo. She knew how many times she'd not answered the phone. She left a garbled message asking him to ring, then saying no don't because the phone wouldn't be turned on.

Rachel found Jonno sitting opposite a young woman. When Rachel approached the table the woman blushed and apologised, folded her copy of *Chat* and moved away.

Rachel raised her eyebrow at him as she sat down.

'Leave it out,' he said without warmth.

'Jonno?' she asked.

'Yes? Here, I got you a tea.' He pushed a cup across the table.

'Thanks. How's things with Iris?'

'I don't know.' He couldn't look at her. 'I don't know what to do. I came back for the birth because I promised I would, but I don't think I can do it. I don't think I want this.'

Rachel pulled her cardigan across her chest, preparing to protect herself from what she knew Brendan's response would be to this news.

Jonno's eyes slowly came up to meet Rachel's. 'I think about you, you know.'

So it was true.

'It wouldn't be fair to her, to Iris . . . Me being in love with someone else.'

A violent shock bolted through her. Fragments of images. Almost. No. Lost. Gone again. She was left feeling only scared. Very very scared. She stared into his clear blue eyes in which she saw an aching loneliness. The kind of ache that leaked out of a broken heart.

Rachel put her hand on Jonno's. It was shaking.

'Will you be all right?' she asked slowly.

Jonno visibly reeled. He had not mistaken her meaning. 'Maybe I will or maybe I won't. Either way, the song's not over yet.' Then in a sudden, violent, decisive gesture he leapt up from the table and walked away.

Rachel watched him go.

He didn't turn back.

Fifty-Two – October 1921

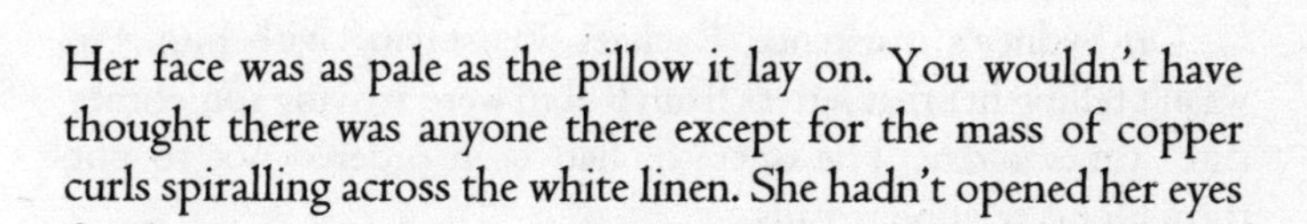

Her face was as pale as the pillow it lay on. You wouldn't have thought there was anyone there except for the mass of copper curls spiralling across the white linen. She hadn't opened her eyes for days.

A small figure sat next to the bed and held onto the tiny hand, squeezing it, stroking it, playing with it. From time to time she would hold it up to her lips and kiss it, then replace it, decorated with a small tear.

Yiskah was brought tea, soup, bread, cakes, but she ate nothing and drank only an occasional glass of water.

No one could tell her how long it would be like this. They said that there was no fluid left inside her daughter. What there had been had done some damage, but until she woke they couldn't know how much. At least, thank God, she was alive. They had got to her in time.

Rachael came every day. But Yiskah could not bring herself to talk to her. If she was to apportion blame then firstly she blamed herself. Then Rachael. If only Rachael hadn't—

She couldn't waste thoughts on that. All her prayers must be with her daughter and bringing her back to life.

After five days the doctor told her they were worried.

But she would never give up hope.

And on the seventh day when Rachael arrived, she found the bed empty and Yiskah gone.

In the early hours she had sneaked out, carrying her oblivious daughter. The night nurse had been away from her desk for only a couple of minutes and no one else had seen, or heard, a thing.

Rachael organised a thorough search. But she knew it would be hopeless. Sydney, with his connections in the Police Force did his bit, as did Dulcie in the East End. Rachael made daily contact with as many hospitals as she could. Not one had admitted a five-year-old child in a coma.

On Sydney's insistence, Rachael was staying with him. He wasn't telling her that letters from Robin were arriving sometimes three times a day. The operator had been ordered not to put through his telephone calls.

Only a small part of Rachael felt safe. She knew that Robin was out there, somewhere. But now she was sure there was a small part of Robin inside her too. Every morning she woke wanting to vomit the intruder out.

Dulcie, of course, guessed. Rachael was more terrified of her apparent pregnancy than the idea of facing Robin again. Every day she prayed for it to be over. Dulcie took control, daring to offer the name of a woman 'who could fix these things'.

Rachael was on the verge of agreeing when one day she fell to the ground, cramped double with pain; thick, black, brown and red blood expelling itself in waves. She lay in a hot bath until the pain subsided and the bleeding slowed down. Then took to her bed.

Sydney asked no questions.

After two days she wanted to get out. She wondered if she should risk a walk in Regent's Park.

Once outside in the damp autumn air, she felt cleansed, light, free. There was nothing of Robin in her anymore.

She crossed Gloucester Place, walked along Melcombe Street

then down Baker Street, a route she had taken a hundred times. She was thankful for the traffic. People meant safety. But once in the quiet of the Park her anxiety returned. She tried to calm herself by glorying in the golds and coppers of the trees, a light wind creating a shield of falling leaves swirling around her. But every blond figure she saw in the distance interrupted her heart-beat, only to have it start up again, twice as fast.

Soreness was returning in her womb. Her steps slowed. A dull ache was forming in her lower back. She wasn't as well as she thought she was. A bench fifty yards away gave her something to aim for. She put one hand on her back and the other over her stomach, becoming increasingly unable to stand up straight.

She was only a few steps away from the bench now. She leant forward, reaching out for it, but her hands grabbed something both rough and soft, hard and pliable. Then something was enfolding her. Her head was pounding. She leant against whatever was behind her, feeling a scratchiness next to her cheek. Breathing in, a sweet spicy smell crept around her memory. It comforted her with its familiarity. It went no further. She needed to be comforted.

She felt herself being eased down to a half-lying, half-sitting position. Long fingers ran over her face, through her hair.

Then a kind and gentle voice, full of love, care and concern, whispered in her ear, warm breath flowing into her and, like his smell, stopping short of recognition. 'I think you need looking after.'

'Drink this.'

The arm enfolds her again, lifting her up slightly. He rests her head back against the stack of pillows and holds the glass to her lips, which she parts for him. The water feels cool but then she becomes aware of a slight bitterness and allows the liquid to dribble out of her mouth, unswallowed.

'It will help the pain.' He pours it into her, then holds her mouth closed, compelling her to drink it, like you would a dog.

Rachael isn't aware of any pain, only a heavy head and an insatiable desire for sleep. She fades to black.

How long has she been here?

She drifts in and out of consciousness only vaguely aware of movement around her. Once she thinks she catches a glimpse of sunlight behind heavy curtains but the next time she looks it is gone. She hears knocks on the door, far away voices, footsteps. Then she is given the foul tasting water and is aware of nothing.

Rachael feels his presence, knows that he sleeps next to her. Occasionally she will feel something like a feather trailing across her skin. She wants to flick it away but she doesn't have the strength.

How long has she lain here?

Rachael tries to open her eyes. She can't lift her head even though her body seems to be floating. Slowly the mist lifts and her vision focuses. There is gold everywhere. Gold, yellow, and cream striped curtains. Ornate guilded furniture.

The years since she last saw a hotel room just like this one evaporate, and briefly she becomes a young bride expectant, thrilled and slightly afraid.

But the figure in a dressing gown, bare legged, walking slowly towards a large door is not Saul. And consciousness returns discarding the expectant thrill but leaving her with the fear.

Another figure enters, a young boy in a sort of uniform. He balances on his shoulder a large silver tray that swoops down to land on a small table. The boy is thanked. He goes.

And coming towards her, a smile she knows so well that stabs at her heart.

'I'm glad you're awake.' He sits on the bed and runs a hand down the side of her face. 'You look beautiful,' he says.

'Where am I?' she asks although she thinks she knows.

'With me,' he answers.

Her mind is slowly awakening. She is aware enough to know that she must show no terror. She tries to think, but she's not ready, yet.

'Is that food?'

He gets up and walks to the table with the tray on it and lifts a silver dome, then carries the plate over to her. 'I thought a lightly grilled sole was probably all you could manage.'

Rachael looks at it, lying there. Thin, white flesh, speckled with the odd brown smear. 'Shortly,' she says. 'When I'm properly awake.' She pulls herself upright. 'Thank you,' she adds. He smiles – she wishes he would stop smiling – and returns the plate to the tray.

Rachel looks down at herself. She is wearing, barely wearing, the lightest, softest silk nightdress that sheens like mother of pearl. Delicate single threads of silk form a lace braid that continues along the edge and becomes the straps that fall over her shoulders.

'Where are my clothes?'

Robin has his back to her. He stiffens before he turns to answer. 'Don't worry about that,' he says.

They stare at each other.

Rachael sees that he knows that she will fight her hardest to escape but will appear the compliant prisoner, the willing victim. His eyes flash red; she sees Hanael, the angel of Blood, and knows that she will win.

'What a lovely room,' she says.

'It's always been one of my favourites.'

'So, you've been here before?' A hint of disappointment.

Robin falls for it and inwardly curses his careless tongue. 'But only you do it justice,' he says.

Rachael keeps the half smile on her face, her forehead straining with the effort of maintaining wide, bright eyes. 'Tell me about them,' she says.

Robin is still hovering around the food. He must think about this. He doesn't see it for the disarming tactic that it is, but something doesn't feel right.

A pain speeds through Rachael's womb. She cannot help the grimace that accompanies it.

Robin rushes to her, holding out the ever present tampered water that sits next to the bed. 'I didn't mean to cause you pain, my darling. Drink some.'

She takes a sip; makes the link between its taste and her languor. Knows now what is in it, what it will do to her and that she must avoid drinking any more. 'Thank you, I'm better now.'

'Please Rachael, forgive me. They were nothing those women. It was just a job.'

Rachael acts out another spasm.

Robin is beside himself. 'It was stupid of me. I should have thought. But I wanted you to be comfortable. I only want the best for you. And this,' his eyes sweep around the luxury furnishings, 'is the very very best.'

'Let me sleep now,' Rachael says feebly.

'I'll be right here,' he says, sitting himself on the edge of the bed and taking her hand.

In her feigned sleep, with her head still pounding, Rachael tries to make a plan. Someone must come to collect the dinner tray, perhaps she could leave a note on it. But it is unlikely that Robin will leave her alone for the time she would need to do this. She knows she hasn't the strength to overcome him physically. But he has a weak spot. And that is her. It is her only chance.

She lets her hand go limp, indicating a fall into deeper unconsciousness. For a few moments his grips tightens, and then, as she has hoped, is removed completely.

She feels the relief as his weight is lifted from the bed. Then a door opens and the sound of water running. Maybe she has a chance after all. But she daren't move yet. She needs to be sure of where she is. The sound of a foghorn releases the memory from where it lay buried in her mind. A boat. The river. The Savoy. A cruel twist of fate.

No time for that. She must find a way out. Then a flash of inspiration.

She rolls over, rustling the sheets. And there he is, beside her.

'Can I get you something? Anything you want, just ask for it.'

'I'd like to telephone my father.' Her voice, her request is all innocence.

He does it again. Tries to stare her out. 'I'm afraid that won't be possible.'

'I see.'

'I've run you a nice hot bath. I think you should have it.'

'I love this hotel.'

He doesn't answer.

'We had our wedding lunch here.'

He flinches slightly. A tiny movement but enough for Rachael to gain confidence. She was right; his weakness is her past. This is how she will overcome him.

'And our wedding night.'

He reels.

'That was the only time I've stayed in a London hotel. Until now.'

His breathing is getting deeper, louder.

'Not this room, of course. But I recognise the decor.'

The cry escapes him before he can control it.'

'The bed was the same.'

He puts his hands over his ears.

'So,' she says. 'It's all right for you to have made love to other women, in *this* bed, but not for me to have—'

'NO!' he screams. 'Of course it's not all right.' He is breathing fast. He can't get any more words out, he can't catch his breath.

Now. Now she's got him.

'Here,' says Rachael, up now, standing before him, holding out the glass of water she picked up from next to the bed. 'Drink this.'

And because his only concern is where his next breath is coming from, he does.

Fifty-Three

'What?'

'What?'

'Why are you looking like that?'

'I don't know what you mean?' But Brendan couldn't control it any longer. He let out a laugh, a delightful baby's gurgle of a laugh; his eyes sparkling as he did so.

'Are you going to tell me what's happened?' Rachel rearranged Theo and turned the bottle.

'It's a girl.'

'What is?'

Brendan looked at her and sighed. 'Well thank goodness I can always rely on you to burst the bubble.' He flopped into the armchair and stared at her, challenging her to work it out.

'You don't mean—?'

Brendan nodded.

'When? Oh my God.'

'Iris went into labour yesterday afternoon.'

'Why didn't they tell us?'

'They didn't want to worry us.'

Rachel put the empty bottle down and lifted Theo into an uncomfortable sitting position, rubbing her hand up and down his back while supporting him under his chin. 'We wouldn't have been worried.'

'We know that.'

'So, tell me everything.'

'Oh, I don't know.'

'I'm so pleased.'

Brendan got up and nuzzled his beard against her cheek.

'Hey, Grandad!' She looked down at Theo. 'Daddy's a grandfather.' Then she laughed too. 'So now you have to tell me all the details, like how long the labour lasted, what sort of pain relief, if any, she had, and how much the baby weighed.'

'You can find all that out when you see her. I said we'd pop in tonight. In shifts, of course.'

'So soon?'

'Of course. Why not?'

Rachel stiffened. 'Hospitals, of course. I'm sick of the sight of them.'

Brendan returned to his armchair. 'I remember you saying it must have been difficult for Iris to visit you and Theo.'

Rachel said nothing.

'So if she can do it—'

Rachel looked down. 'I'll just get Theo to sleep.'

'I hope that's not you walking away.'

Rachel glared at Brendan. 'No. That's me wanting to put my baby to bed.'

Brendan got up. 'I'm going to open a bottle of wine. Do you want some?'

Rachel picked up a handful of Theo paraphernalia and followed Brendan into the kitchen.

He was at the fridge, searching, 'I hope you're not going to use Theo as yet another way to avoid confrontation.'

'For fuck's sake Brendan, what is it with you? You know what time he goes to bed.'

He produced a bottle of wine. 'We don't have any champagne, we'll have to toast the baby with white instead.'

Rachel breathed in sharply and walked out of the room and upstairs.

Theo was restless. She held him close and sang 'Lullaby in Ragtime'. Usually by the time she'd got to the end of 'Goodnight' (which if Brendan were available would be sung concurrently) he would at least be closing his eyes. But his little body was squirming in discomfort and he was trying harder than ever to pull the tubing away from his face.

Rachel sang, 'Somewhere Over the Rainbow' then 'It's A Sin To Tell A Lie', but he would not be still. She put a drop of Rescue Remedy on her finger then let him suck it off. He stopped wriggling but did not seem to be tired. Rachel knew he was picking up all her anxieties. An uncertainty was hovering over all of them and she was convinced that at some level Theo was feeling it too.

She was feeling useless, helpless and angry since her visit to Valerie, all of which were contributing to an increasing detachment from her son.

She walked slowly up and down his room, holding him close against her, every so often checking to see if his eyes were closed. They weren't. She'd run out of songs and out of patience. 'Go to sleep, darn you,' she said. Theo started to whimper. She jigged him up and down. The whimper turned into a cry. The jigging became jumping. 'Go to sleep, go to sleep, go to sleep.' The crying got louder and louder. Tears of frustration burnt her eyes. It was harder than ever to love him.

Brendan burst into the room. 'What the hell is going on?'

Rachel thrust Theo at Brendan and without even waiting to see if he had hold of him, ran out.

She lay in the dark of her bedroom, sobs tearing through her.

Wasn't it hard enough being responsible for your own happiness? Rachel felt she was carrying the burden of being responsible for the happiness of not only her own past life, but Theo's past and present lives. Why? Why should she be given another chance to love someone that she had failed to love before? There was a very good reason why she hadn't loved him before. So, how could she love him now?

*

Brendan found her exhausted by her crying, in a kind of half-sleep. She was aware of him coming into the room, sitting on the bed, putting his hand on her shoulder. He lifted her so that he could embrace her and she fitted herself into him. He let her lie against him. 'You haven't told me,' he said.

She breathed in Brendan, gaining strength; waking up. 'He . . . it . . . everything terrifies me.'

'You're frightened of your son?'

'No, of course not.' She moved her head, snuggling it into his neck. This is the kind of safety she wanted with Theo. This is what she wanted Theo to feel with her. 'It's just very hard to work out how much we still are who we once were.'

'And you've made a lifetime study of it.'

'Nothing I've read, nothing I know has prepared me.'

'Don't reject him. He needs you so much.' He tightened his arms around her. 'Look, OK. Suppose he hadn't been born ill. Suppose he tested your love in other ways, by being removed, distant, unreachable. How would that be different?

Jonno.

'It would be very different,' she answered because she didn't want to talk about him. She sat up and ran her hand over Brendan's beard. 'He was born with a damaged heart because I broke it.'

Brendan shook his head. 'We break our own hearts.'

'I don't know about that.'

'How many failed relationships did you have, before you met me?'

'You know.'

'Go on, tell me.'

'Half a dozen or so that might, with the right timing, have meant something.'

'And how many broke your heart?'

'Well, none. Not really. I was pretty devastated a couple of times because the break came out of the blue. Once or twice I was disappointed that it didn't work out. But none of them were right.' Rachel pushed Brendan down onto the bed and put her head on his chest, against his heart. 'Do you know why you were right for me?'

'Why?' He stroked her hair.

'Because you stopped me being sensible about love. Because if you're sensible about it then chances are you won't fall in it.'

'So you've proved my point. As I knew you would. No one broke your heart because you wouldn't let them. But I could because you'd let me.'

'So what about Theo?'

'It's not about Theo.'

Rachel sighed. 'OK, Theo's past life.'

'He obviously wasn't remotely sensible. He fell wildly, madly passionately in love with you, whoever you were – the one that lived in that house. But you didn't want him. So instead of doing what you did, in this life – just go on with it – he allowed his heart to break—'

'Obviously a deeply dysfunctional person then.'

'Exactly. And then in a grand gesture of supreme melodrama he hangs himself just to prove how badly broken his heart is. Now your job—' Brendan put his hand underneath Rachel's top and walked his fingers up her spine towards her bra.

'Mmm?'

'—is to teach this young man how a whole, healthy, emotionally mature person—'

'Like his mother.' Rachel undid two buttons on Brendan's shirt and put her hand flat against his chest, weaving her fingers through his hair.

'And father,' Rachel's bra sprang open. '—handles the rollercoaster ride of the joy and pain in relationships. Now,' Brendan turned on his side and lay Rachel on her back. 'Does that seem too hard a parenting task?' Then he let his face fall onto hers, greedily searching for her tongue with his lips, his hands all over her.

'NO!' Rachel pushed him over and sat up, putting her head in her hands. 'If only it were that simple.'

'It is.'

She turned to him. 'You're not in it. You can't feel it.'

Brendan sat up. 'So what's your solution?'

'I can't let him go through with it.'

'What?'

'The operation.'

'Are you crazy?'

'It doesn't feel right.'

'Of course it doesn't. It feels fucking horrible. And all wrong. Of course it's wrong that our child, any child, should have to go through this. What do you want it to feel like?'

'I should be able to believe it's going to work. And I don't. I never have done.'

'And I'm supposed to accept that, am I? Look, I've been very patient and very tolerant of all this past life crap. But if it's going to come between my son and his chances of living a normal healthy life—'

'Please trust me. Listen to me. I don't believe that it's going to work.'

'I'm sorry, Rachel.' Brendan stood up and buttoned up his shirt. 'That's not a good enough reason not to do it.' He towered over her, a giant black shadow, angry, menacing, yet full of hurt. 'And you know the worst of it?'

Rachel turned away from the blackness.

'LOOK AT ME!'

She couldn't.

He put a hand under her chin and ratcheted her head around, like a spanner struggling against a stubborn nut. 'I don't think you really want it to.'

Rachel closed her eyes, her mouth quivering with the anticipation of tears. His hand on her jaw was pressing hard, bruising, paining.

'Has it never occurred to you that you might be wrong?'

Rachel closed her eyes tighter.

'Damn you and all your past fucking lives.' He let go of her head, pushing it backwards as he did. She fell back, hitting her head against the wall.

Rachel curled herself up on the bed, her hands covering her head. 'I'd like you to go now,' she said quietly, calmly as she rocked herself back and forth.

'No,' he said. 'I'd like *you* to go.'

Fifty-Four

She heard the front door slam. Then a car door do the same. An engine revving. 0 to 60 how quickly? The sound faded, a volume control turning right down.

She got up slowly. The pain in her head was more localised now, shrunk to the size of a small bump. Reaching into the gap between the wardrobe and the wall, she pulled out an overnight bag. Into it went underwear, trousers, tops, a jumper or two. She went to the bathroom and piled her beauty regime into a sponge bag, then grabbed the robe hanging on the inside of the bathroom door. The zip struggled to close.

Theo's room next. A second bag was stuffed with nappies, sleep suits, tiny clothes. Down to the kitchen; bottles, tubing, miles and miles of tubing, syringes, his food, the steriliser. Oh shit. Brendan had the car. Phone for a cab. Get Theo up. Wrap him warmly. Blankets. Damn! The car seat was in the car. She'll have to carry him and the two bags. Should she take the buggy? Of course she should.

A pile of things in the hallway. A sleeping baby in her arms. The doorbell. The cab driver reluctant to help her with all her things.

'Paddington Station,' she told him.

As she was getting herself in the back seat a voice made her jump, a face suddenly in front of hers.

'Rachel? What are you doing? What's going on?'

'Leah!'

'What's happening?'

'I'm going to stay with Mum and Dad.'

'You didn't say.'

'No. Spur of the moment decision. You couldn't phone them for me, could you, and tell them I'm on my way?'

'When will you be back? I thought you were going to the hospital tomorrow?'

'Leah, for God's sake just phone them will you and cut out all the questions.' Rachel pulled her leg into the back seat.

Leah looked hurt, puzzled. 'Look, why don't I come with you to the station, help you with all the stuff?' She climbed into the back seat next to her.

Bump. Right back on earth. Weak and helpless once more. Depending on the kindness of a hopeless sister. Stealing away in the dark, turning her back on an intolerable situation had been giving her a kind of strength. Heroines of Gothic Novels could lock themselves away in country houses, haunted, in their heads, by ghosts and living in fear of violent men, but not Rachel. No dramatics allowed.

They were silent on the journey. Leah put a finger out for Theo to hold, which, in his sleep, he did.

At Paddington Leah was heroic. She sorted out train times, rang Aza, arranged for him to meet her at Swindon. And all the while not asking Rachel why she was doing this. Rachel understood. 'This is how she's wanted me to be with her,' she thought.

Leah waited with her until the train left. They shared a coffee and an over-long, over-stuffed baguette. Amazingly Theo slept.

'What do I tell Brendan?' Leah asked after settling Rachel, Theo and her baggage on the train.

'Tell him to go to Hell.'

'The operation—?'

'Yes?'

'You'll be back.'

'I don't know.'

If Leah was shocked she didn't show it. 'It wasn't a question.' She folded up the buggy and took it to the luggage rack. She came back to say goodbye.

Rachel gave her a kiss on her cheek. 'Thanks Leah. I really appreciate it. You've been so helpful with Theo. And I'm really proud of you.'

'I know. That's why I did it.' She left the train and stood on the platform, winding her finger round and round one of her longer tufts of hair.

Rachel watched her as the train pulled out. No longer a forlorn figure but glowing with purpose. It was like children and their dolls; they're always mothering them, nursing them, they always need something. Leah just needed to look after someone in a worse state than her. And now Theo had gone she would probably transfer her attentions to Brendan.

Theo opened his eyes, blinking curiously at the harsh lighting. He gazed up at his mother, full of love and need. The knot in Rachel's heart loosened slightly. Poor Theo. It wasn't his fault. He just wanted, needed to be loved. And his little soul trying to learn how to ask for it. His experiences in all his lives hadn't yet taught him that you shouldn't have to. Rachel breathed in a sigh of despair that nearly choked her. Had she learned that herself? We demand love as if it were a right, she thought. And it's not a right, it's a privilege.

She thought about what Valerie had said; it was her own lives she had to deal with. She'd been so focused on Theo, she'd barely had time to digest, work on why her own soul was being given a second chance.

The steady rhythm of the train speeding westwards lulled Theo back to sleep and before long Rachel's own eyes closed.

Brendan swirls a large black cape. She fights inside it, tearing at it, making a hole just so that she can breathe. An arm holds out to her, pulling her, dragging her through the rip in the fabric. It's Jonno. Blue eyes radiating.

'Why don't you come round anymore?' he asks her. 'We miss you, Brendan and me.'

'The next station will be Reading. We will shortly be arriving at Reading. Please make sure you have all your belongings. Great Western thank you for travelling with us and hope you've had a pleasant journey.'

Eyes closed again.

Brendan sits reading by the fire. An aged spaniel at his feet dreams noisily.

Splash.

A girl with copper curls holds out a book to Rachel, but Brendan snatches it.

'And then he laughed to think that what seemed hard

Should be so simple—' he reads.

Dark. Blue eyes radiating beams of silver light. A worried angel – red snakes, Medusa-like, crawling out of his head. Blood.

'Has it never occurred to you that you might be wrong?' asks Jonno. 'Might be wrong . . . might be wrong . . . might be wrong—'

Rachel woke. She had Theo held tightly against her stomach. He hadn't noticed, seemed, even, to be enjoying the closeness. She could feel sweat on her chest. The bump on her head was throbbing. She looked at her watch. Thank God. Nearly there.

Sitting in the back seat of Aza's car. Still holding close a sleeping baby. She looked at either the headlights lighting up the cat's eyes or her father's hair. He was so proud of the small silver curls that sat tight against the back of his head. He leant slightly forward, tense arms uncomfortably bent as they gripped the steering wheel. She knew these weren't his favoured driving conditions.

'What's the official line?' he asked. 'What do we tell Ella?'

Rachel wanted to throw her arms around him and hug him. 'I've come to see you.'

'She's out tonight. It's Quiz Night. We'll get you settled before she returns.'

'Don't you go with her?'

Aza snorted. 'I don't know anything,' he said.

'Are the camellias out?'

'Bit slow this year. Lots of buds fit to burst, but no blooms yet. Been inundated with snowdrops though. Can't remember ever having seen so many.'

'How lovely.'

'Yes. Yes they are.'

Rachel flinched as a lorry going in the other direction lit up the car as it passed.

'I think your mother was planning to go up to town tomorrow. To see Louise. I expect she'll change her mind now.'

'I hope she doesn't.'

'I must say that Roger fellow is doing a grand job of caring for her.'

Rachel flinched again.

'You don't like him, do you?'

'I don't trust him.'

Aza expelled a small laugh. 'You've never liked any of Louise's boyfriends. Not since you were little.'

'That's not true.' Theo stirred as if reminding her that she was avoiding the truth. He used to do that in the womb. It was like having your own personal lie detector, Rachel thought. At those moments she loved him with all her heart; the times when he affirmed their closeness. But they were only moments.

She thought of Brendan.

The car slowed down and pulled into the gravel drive.

'That was quick.'

'Not much in the way of traffic this time of night.'

In the house. Warmth, familiarity, comfort.

'I'll set up a feed for Theo before we go to bed.'

'I'll make you a cup of tea. We haven't got many of your herbal concoctions.'

'That's all right, Dad. I'll have whatever you've got.'

Aza put her bags in the hallway. 'Oh look. The answer phone's flashing. I'll leave it for Ella.'

'And I don't suppose you can work the microwave either.'

'Terrible invention. Wouldn't go anywhere near it.'

Rachel laughed. This felt right. It was a good decision to come here.

Even Theo seemed happier. He giggled and smiled and snuggled against his grandfather and was totally relaxed while he was fed and changed. He was still awake when Ella came home, bringing a change of atmosphere with her.

Naturally, she wanted to know everything. Rachel wasn't sure what to tell her, except that she needed some distance from home and would appreciate being allowed some space to sort her thoughts out.

This wasn't good enough for Ella. It wasn't what you did. Well it wasn't what she did. You just got on with it, did what you had to do. It was a pastime Rachel's generation luxuriated in to the point of destruction. And it wasn't only their lives but the lives of everyone around them that were affected, causing unnecessary pain and suffering on innocent bystanders, like Theo for example. It was Rachel's duty to protect him at all costs, not expose him to this self-indulgent wallowing.

Rachel sat open mouthed as her mother spoke, too shocked and too tired to argue. She said goodnight to her mother coldly, accepted with gratitude a comforting squeeze on her arm from Aza and went upstairs to bed.

A soft knock on her bedroom door.

'Are you awake?'

'Dad! Come in.'

Aza crept in, closing the door quietly behind him. 'She won't hear me. She sleeps with earplugs. But I still tiptoe around, just in case. How much did she upset you?'

'Enough.' Rachel's voice choked. She hadn't realised how hard it had hit her.

'It was all about Leah, all that.'

Rachel sighed. 'Yes, I suppose it was.'

'It's always all about Leah.'

'Poor Dad.' Rachel put her hand out and took his.

'She looks after me well.'

'I know she does. She always has.'

'We all have to do that at some point, you know.'

'Do what?'

'Stop thinking about things. It's a survival instinct.'

'I haven't got to that point yet.'

'Do you want to tell me about it?'

'I'm not sure I can.' A small quick shriek from Theo's dream. Rachel turned to look at her sleeping son. 'Theo thinks I should,' she smiled.

'A very wise child.'

'He must take after his grandfather, then.'

So Rachel told him. Told him what was stopping her from loving her son. Why she couldn't even see as far as the operation. Aza was having trouble understanding.

'But it's like . . . it's as bad as if . . . suppose you were told that Leah, or me, had been, I don't know, one of the guards at the camp. Or worse, the one in charge of turning on the gas, the one that locked the chamber doors—'

Aza stiffened, letting her hand drop. 'I wouldn't accept it.'

Rachel was ashamed of herself; she'd gone too far. 'But it was because of me, because I couldn't love him. That's why he died.'

'You can't ever prove that.'

'I'm sorry, Dad. But it's just not that simple.' Why was she always telling people that?

'"And then he laughed to think that what seemed hard should be so simple."'

Rachel sat up. 'I just dreamt that.'

'It's from Yeats.'

'Yes. I used to think he had all the answers.'

'You always were a dreamy, romantic adolescent.'

'I can't just stop believing.'

'You're going to have to do something.' He kissed her on the cheek. 'Look, I know, believe me, how hard it is to accept that there are simply some people who are capable of causing great suffering.' Rachel looked at him questioningly. 'On a large or small scale,' he added. 'And how much harder to accept that you may have been one of those people. But none of this should stop you wanting the best chance of a future for your child. That's the part I don't get.'

But Rachel couldn't tell him; couldn't tell him that without love, without care, without hope, there was no future.

'Has it occurred to you that you, Louise, and what's her name, Valerie, may be wrong?'

Again.

'Will you be all right?'

'Maybe.'

He got up and tiptoed to the door. 'Night, love.'

'Night.'

The door closed.

Rachel lay sleepless, alert to the night.

Outside the window a bat circled, squeaking its disturbing cry.

Fifty-Five – December 1921

The taxi pulled up in front of the terraced townhouse. The black front door opened and Davis rushed as quickly as his position would allow to greet the returning travellers.

Rachael stepped out onto the pavement and gazed up at the house that she hadn't seen for six weeks. She breathed in the London air. But it didn't flow smoothly through her, it stumbled over a tiny, but growing knot in her stomach. Sydney stood next to her and put his arm around her.

'Pleased to be home?' he asked.

Rachael answered by shivering.

'Don't worry. You'll be all right now.'

Rachael briefly leant her head against her father's shoulder, then turned to hold out her hand to the third person to emerge from the back seat of the taxi.

'Now I know why we call it New England,' said the young man, smiling approvingly. He stretched himself up to his full six foot two and rolled his head around to ease the advancing cramp. 'New England,' he said. 'But with smaller cabs.'

Rachael laughed. 'You'll get used to it,' she said.

'Davis, this is Mr Bennett Sterling,' said Sydney.

'Good to meet you, Davis,' said Mr Bennett Sterling, enthusiastically taking Davis' hand and shaking it vigorously.

'And you, Sir,' replied Davies.

'Come along,' said Sydney. And they went into the house.

Rachael took off her gloves and placed them on the hall table.

'If you'll excuse me,' said Sydney disappearing into his study.

'Are you sure you don't want to go straight to your hotel?' asked Rachael.

'Lunch first,' said Bennett, standing in front of Rachael and taking both her hands in his. He leant forward to kiss her but she moved her head away.

'I don't know about you but I'm exhausted. I think I'll freshen up. Here,' she said, opening the door of the library for him. 'Make yourself comfortable. I'll call for some tea.'

Bennett grinned. Rachael could not help but smile back. The way he crinkled his eyes, tilted his head slightly and seemed to relax his whole body was completely infectious and totally endearing.

'Tea?!' he said.

'Come on. Don't be such a tourist. They have tea in New York.'

'My first real English cup of tea!'

'Sit here.' Rachael pushed him towards a leather armchair and handed him a copy of *Country Life*. 'Read that. You can't get much more English than that. I'm going upstairs for a bath. I'll see you shortly.'

'Oh, I doubt that. But that's something else I guess I'll have to get used to.'

Warmth teemed through Rachael's blood. 'They were all madly jealous, you know.'

'Well, you did bag New York's most eligible bachelor. no wonder you couldn't make any friends.'

'Oh! And I thought it was the perfume I was using.'

Bennett pulled her to him and held her in a tight grip on his lap, nuzzling his lips against her neck.

Rachael pulled away. 'Bennett! You're very sweet and I adore you, but—'

Breaking glass – a rock on the floor in the middle of the

Persian rug surrounded by tiny shards of window pane.

Bennett leapt up and ran to the window. Rachael sank back into the armchair he had vacated and buried her head in her hands.

Sounds in the hall. Doors opening and banging. Loud knocking at the front door. Shouting.

Bennett turned to Rachael. 'Is this something to do with your militant political activities?'

She looked up. He was grinning. The house fell silent. Rachael relaxed. 'I don't indulge in any military political activities,' she said.

'Well,' said Bennett going to her, lifting her to him and settling her into a comforting hug. 'You should do.'

Sydney opened the door. 'Rachael? Are you all right?'

'Yes,' she answered from somewhere in Bennett's chest.

'I've called the police.'

Rachael sighed. 'That will only start it all up again.'

'He needs to be locked up.'

'Did anything happen while we were away?'

Sydney held out his hand. He was holding half a dozen envelopes all addressed to Rachael, all in the same tiny handwriting. 'There's over a hundred of these.'

'Wow!' said Bennett. 'This guy's pretty keen on you, huh?'

'And a parcel.'

'Can I see it?'

'I'm not sure if that's a good idea.'

'Daddy, I want to.'

Sydney shrugged and left the room.

Rachael went back to the armchair and perched on the edge. 'I'm sorry, Bennett. I should have mentioned it.'

'You certainly should have.' He pulled the footstool over to her and sat at her feet. 'I've come a long way. I'd have had to think more carefully about it if I'd known what I was letting myself in for.' He took her hand. He was all seriousness.

'It was so good to be away from it all. I didn't want to think about it.'

He started to tickle her palm. 'I mean, I've left my family, my friends. I'm starting a new job in a place far from home—' His fingers strolled up the inside of her lower arm. 'Given everything up to maybe spend the rest of my life with someone who—' He took a deep breath. Round and round the hollow of her elbow, slowly upwards. Then ferocious tickling of her underarm, '—attracts crazies!'

'Bennett! It's not funny.'

He stopped. 'No. I know. You'll tell me when you want to. I knew there was something.' He took both her hands. 'But it doesn't matter.'

Rachael leant forward and kissed his nose. 'Mmm. Maybe I will fall in love with you after all.'

Sydney re-entered. He held out a flat, square box. It stated: *Not to be opened until Christmas Day*. Rachael tore at the brown paper. Inside, a box was wrapped in a gold tissue paper secured with gold ribbon.

'I'm not sure about this,' said Sydney.

'I'm all right,' said Rachael.

She pulled off the ribbon and undid the paper, took the lid off the box – more tissue paper – then lifted out a dress made from a gloriously rich, deep red fabric, the colour of fine wine, shot with a silver that reflected tiny sparks of light. Instantly she dropped it as if it had burnt her fingers. A note fell with it. Bennett picked it up.

'Let's see,' said Rachael. She took it from him, opened it, read it, closed it again.

'What does it say?' asked Sydney.

Rachael handed it to him.

'"*The only thing I have that belonged to my mother. Now it is yours. That's how much I love you.*"' read Sydney.

Bennett was tapping his hand against thigh. Rachael knew that he was anxious to know what all this was about, how long it had been going on and, more importantly, how they were going to make it stop. It was a relief to her, somehow made it a little easier, that she could now think about, worry about, how it was affecting someone else – Bennett, the sweetest, kindest, funniest man she had ever met. It wasn't fair on him. Bennett didn't deserve this.

'May I talk to you, Sir?'

Sydney looked up from pondering the note. 'Yes, yes of course.'

Bennett looked over to Rachael. 'You go and have your bath. I'll talk to your father. We'll see what we can do about this.'

Despite the broken window, despite the hideous present, despite the relentlessness of Robin's campaign, Rachael felt an overwhelming safety. She lightly squeezed Bennett's arm as she passed him; a tiny gesture filled with care, gratitude and promise.

As she lay on her bed waiting for her bath to fill she allowed herself to believe that this *was* going to be over. She didn't know how, she didn't know when. There will be a time when Robin will no longer be scratching at her soul, demanding to be let in. She will be free of him. He will become, like Saul, little more than an unpleasant episode in her past.

Rachael knew she could look forward to a safe future. A future with Bennett. A future filled with love, care and hope.

that she could never think about you [illegible] [illegible] [illegible]
[illegible] [illegible] the [illegible] [illegible] [illegible]
[illegible] [illegible] [illegible] [illegible] [illegible]

[illegible] looked [illegible] [illegible] [illegible] [illegible] [illegible]
[illegible]

Benton looked over at Rachel [illegible] [illegible] [illegible] both
[illegible] [illegible] [illegible] [illegible] [illegible] [illegible]
[illegible] [illegible] [illegible] [illegible] [illegible] [illegible]
despite the [illegible] of [illegible] [illegible] Rachel [illegible]
overwhelming [illegible]. She [illegible] [illegible] [illegible] [illegible]
[illegible] [illegible] [illegible] [illegible] [illegible] [illegible]
As she lay on her back [illegible] [illegible] [illegible] [illegible]
[illegible] [illegible] [illegible] [illegible] [illegible] [illegible]
[illegible] [illegible] [illegible] [illegible] [illegible] [illegible]
no longer [illegible] [illegible] [illegible] [illegible] [illegible]
[illegible] [illegible] [illegible] [illegible] [illegible] [illegible]
[illegible] [illegible] [illegible] [illegible]
[illegible] [illegible] [illegible] [illegible] [illegible] [illegible]
[illegible] [illegible] [illegible] [illegible] [illegible]

[illegible]

Fifty-Six

From the tip of The Horse, Rachel can see the house. This always confuses her because you can't see The Horse from the house. It's all about perspective. She knows this from Brendan – how things get smaller the further you are away from them. 'Critical distance,' he calls it. Damn him.

She looks down at the model house and imagines she hears a baby crying. Her baby crying. She puts her hands over her ears. It can't get to her up here. No one can get to her up here. Not the hospital, not her mother, not Brendan and not Theo. Unfortunately the visions she carries around in her head are not quite so easy to leave behind.

March winds propel bi-coloured clouds. Up here the sun shines. Down there it is dark and grey. In another minute it will be the other way around. She remembers somebody saying something about England being the only place where you get all four seasons on the same day. Rachel loves that. She loves the surprise of the changes in the weather. She loves not knowing. It's that bit of her that rejects presignification; the weather is too trivial a thing to waste psychic energy on.

Is it possible that she sees Brendan's car – their car – pull up in front of the house? Two people get out. Leah and . . . is that tiny figure the giant she married? The miniature front door opens and closes. For a millisecond the cry gets louder.

She came up here to be alone. She came to Uffington to be alone. It's intrusion, at best, invasion, at worst. She hasn't reached the point of critical distance yet. It's all still too near. But she's at the top. She looks up behind her. No. She's only at the head of The Horse. The hill goes higher. She gets up and turns skywards. She's never had to go that far before, that high. But then things have never been this bad before.

There's a fence. A gate. She goes through. Uffington Camp. A strategic location dating back to the Neolithic. Bronze Age Spiritualists, Celtic Warriors, Saxon Traders. They all used it. An unparalleled vantage point.

She stands there. Arming herself. Six thousand years of history. All those souls. And now Rachel. She breathes deeply. Clouds race. She calls for the strength of heroes. Her fingertips tingle. Her heart feels both full and light. Full of lightness. She opens her eyes. She can't see the house so well from up here. But she believes the car has gone.

Too much reality too soon. She closes her eyes and tries to fill her lungs. But no. Knowing the car has gone, knowing Brendan is on his way, she can't let go.

Rachel feels uncomfortable. Strange, foreign, alien. There are enough old souls inside her fighting to get their presence felt, their voices heard, their needs met; she can't handle any more. She runs down the hill carried by the wind, through the gate, back to where she feels safe.

She tries to work it out. Five-minute drive to the car park. Fifteen-minute walk. In about ten minutes Brendan will emerge from the woods. Then for another ten minutes she will watch him coming closer. Slowly growing. Getting bigger. A constantly shifting perspective. A moveable object rearranging her view of the landscape.

She's not had long enough to work out what to say. What to tell him. Because she's not had long enough to work out what she thinks. Why has she not learned that Brendan would always do this to her? Nothing goes unchallenged. She uses up immense energy justifying and explaining herself. He is like a child who has just discovered curiosity. All questions begin why. They, and he, demand explanation for things that have no explanation. There is no simple acceptance.

Except when it suits him.

She is facing the house, the wind blowing up the hill against her face suddenly changes direction and whips cold into her right ear. She turns her face to the left and sees him striding towards her.

Rachel pulls her legs up against her chest and hugs herself, protecting herself. She puts her arms over her head and her head down on her knees. Tucks her head under her wing. She waits for his voice, knowing that it will begin before he reaches her, knowing that it will be angry and knowing that she hasn't the energy to fight.

She stays like that for five minutes. She hears nothing. She moves her head to the side and peeks an eye out. No Brendan. She puts her head up and looks around. Then she sees him. He is standing below her on Dragon Hill. On the flat. Where the dragon's blood spilled and no grass will grow.

Rachel stands up. Brendan turns to face her. Rachel is confused. He is smiling and waving. Beckoning to her to join him. Holding his arms open for her. She blinks. That's better. That's the Brendan she was expecting. Still, staring, challenging and angry.

'RACHEL!'

The wind carries her name to her. But what is he doing down there?

He has come this far to her. Now he wants her to make some effort to come to him. If she does then she will show willing. But it will be a compromise because she doesn't want to see him at all. Should she refuse? Make him walk up the hill to her?

Something makes her turn back in the direction of the car park. Struggling to get the buggy over the style, a baby balanced over her shoulder, is Leah.

Rachel looks from Leah and Brendan and back again. Three points of a triangle.

Is it possible that Brendan has arranged this? Is this some kind of a test? To see where her true loyalties lie? No. She's making this up, creating a conflict that doesn't exist. Presenting him with a reason for giving up on her.

He calls her name again. He hasn't given up. Brendan calling her name. She loves the sound of her name. There's something so comforting, so reassuring about people you love using it. She knows what it feels like. She tries to use other people's names as much as she can.

She looks at him again. He's moved closer. Left the flat and is on the steep slope now. Getting nearer. He is not as angry as she first thought. She looks over to Leah, who is momentarily hidden from view by the hill. Rachel kneels up to try and find her. Leah is rushing, trying to dodge the rasta sheep. But one of them practically has its nose in the buggy. Rachel jumps up. There it is again. That instinct to protect. The same one that allowed her to not even question, when she ran from Brendan, whether she should take her baby with her, or not.

She is glad to be reminded of those moments. They are the bricks she needs to lay the path that takes Theo to the hospital for the four hour surgery. To have a Dacron Patch stitched to the edges of his heart, over the hole. The bit that won't close. As Theo grows, the heart tissue will mesh, eventually dissolving the Dacron. Growing a healthy heart.

But it isn't that which worries her. It is the idea of her baby lost inside the equipment. He will be in Intensive Care. There will be a chest drain, a heart drain, catheters, wires connected to a heart monitor, more wires to test his blood pressure, and he will be breathing with the help of a ventilator. There is the worry of the drain not working, sacks of fluid building up around the heart. There is the risk of the movement of the heart tearing the stitching. The heart pumping, doing what it's supposed to do. Yet every beat slowly, efficiently working the patch loose. Not mending.

Rachel shakes her head. She knows too much. This is more information than she needs. There are too many things that can go wrong.

The triangle is getting smaller. They are closing in on her.

Bump. Bump. The buggy shakes and rocks over the uneven path. Rachel flinches. Another brick.

An opening of unclouded sky. Fierce sunshine. For a moment she feels warmth on her face. She lies back on the rough grass. The face comes to her. She sees him clearly now. This is his true face. Not the blue, bloated, dead one. There is something about him. A look. A blondness. What is it? No use. It won't come to her. She tries to concentrate by screwing up her closed eyes, but as she does, the image fades. So she relaxes her eyelids. She examines his face. In slow motion he lifts his head, throwing his fringe from his eyes. Long, well-manicured fingers run through his hair.

Suddenly she pities him. Before, he disturbed her. There is a vacancy in his eyes. Something is missing from his soul. She'd not noticed that before. He parts his lips to speak. But there is no sound. Rachel moves her head slightly, trying to tune into his frequency. '. . . song's . . . not over . . . yet.' is what she catches.

His face changes.

She sees him for who he really is.

Now she knows why those eyes, that smile, that blondness are so familiar to her.

And knows that this is the first time that she is seeing him as herself, not her past self. Rachel. Here and Now. That past life. Getting in the way. Blocking, evading, distracting. She must let it go.

She needs to concentrate on what she sees and remove *herself* from it.

This was what she hadn't done. And this is what may have cost her baby his life.

The face goes, evaporates into a white light. Rachel has to put her hands over her eyes to shield them from the brightness.

'RACHEL!'

She sits up. Brendan has got to her first.

Jumping up she grabs Brendan's hand. 'We've got to get back. We must go to Jonno—'

'Oh, no you don't,' he says. 'You're not pulling that one on me. Not now.'

'It's all right,' she says. 'It's over. I'm fine. Oh, Brendan.' She flings herself at him. She wants to comfort him. He'll need it. One son fighting for his life and the other . . .

Leah, puffing and panting. Tries to speak. Theo sleeping.

Rachel bends down to him. Gently lifts him out. Holds him against her. Rocking back and forth. 'I'm sorry,' she says. Her tears are wetting the fine dark hairs on his tiny head. She holds him close, closer still. 'I'm so so sorry.' She looks over to Brendan. 'I now know who he is.'

Brendan looks at her. He closes his eyes and bites his lip to stop the flow of words bursting to come out. The ones he allows out are: 'I've always known who he is. He's our son.'

'Yes,' she says. 'That's what I wanted to tell you.'

In relief, Brendan breathes out the unsaid.

Leah is still trying to catch her breath. She's come a long way. 'Mum . . . and Dad . . . out. I was going . . . to . . . stay with Theo . . . while Brendan . . . came up here. The phone—'

Brendan goes to her. Holds her up while she refills her lungs. 'What is it?'

'Iris.'

'Oh God,' says Rachel. 'Is the baby all right?' But she knows. She knows what Leah has climbed the hill to tell them.

'. . . not the baby—'

Brendan looks at Rachel.

But Rachel can only see Jonno's blue, bloated face and pendant tongue.

And hopes to heaven that she is wrong.

Epilogue

Robin fastens his belt, pulling it tight, making it uncomfortable. Reaching for his jacket he checks the pockets. Wallet. Keys. He decides to leave them behind; he won't be needing them.

Jonno lets himself into his father's house and calls out. No answer. He checks the rooms just in case. But no. The house is empty. There is no one home. Now. Where to do it?

Standing in front of the full-length mirror on the wardrobe door, Robin becomes slightly giddy. He's been staring too hard; focusing too intently on one point. His eyes. He's trying to see if it's there. If it's visible. If anyone that he passes in the street on the way will know, just by looking at him, what he is going to do.

He's been avoiding mirrors lately. He doesn't want to see the distortion of his former self. His real self. This is one thing he can never forgive her for. Changing him. Changing everything about him. How he thinks, how he feels, how he sees the world. But worst of all, how the world sees him.

And this is what has made being in his skin intolerable.

*

Jonno looks around the room. Panicked eyes darting. Searching. The door. He knows it's possible to do it from a door. How though? He think it's some kind of pulley system. Banging the door shut. Belt attached to the outside door knob. Not sure. Can't risk getting it wrong.

Looking up he sees the light hanging from the ceiling rose. Light flex. Yes. That's a possibility. An antique glass shade hangs from a hook. He's momentarily distracted by a memory that makes him smile. Rachel spending an exorbitant amount of money on that shade. Rachel spending exorbitant amounts of money on all sorts of things. Brendan complaining, Jonno defending.

But stopping to remember has allowed doubts in. Doubts don't make things better, he tells himself. They don't change anything. They won't change his life. They won't take away his knowledge. It's the knowledge he can't live with.

Once you know that it can be like this, how can it ever get better? And he knows. Because he sees it on a daily basis. There are all sorts of ways of denying it. He's been amazed at the lengths people go to in order to deny their pain. But he knows. He's made a lifetime study of it. There is no way it can ever truly go away.

Lying coiled, asleep, among Robin's socks, is six feet of thin, soft rope. He pulls it out from the centre, winding it round and round his fingers, pushing away his thumb until it hurts. He then starts to wind it around his other hand, pulling it tightly. Twelve taut inches separate his hands.

He brings the rope up under his chin bringing his arms up behind his head. Pulling. Pulling hard on the rope. It's going to feel something like this.

His arms drop. The rope slackens.

He rubs his neck where it hurts. But it's inside on the windpipe where he has done the most damage. He doesn't like how his tongue feels either. Pushed out of place. Moved forward. Bruised. Swollen.

Round the room. Out of the window. Eyes searching. The garden. Trees. The tree house. When did he last see it? He has a vague memory of a summer party. Wedding anniversary. That was it. Brendan and Rachel's first wedding anniversary. Jonno had wandered down the garden because he had wanted to get away from her. Because he was feeling it particularly badly that day. He'd looked up and seen a few rotten timbers. But the ladder. The rope ladder still swinging from a branch.

He closes his eyes with relief. He has discovered his escape route.

Robin sits on the edge of the bed, lifting one end of the rope high, then letting it drop. He does it again. Higher and higher. Until his arm is fully stretched.

A different game. He makes a small loop and puts his wrist through it. With his other hand he extends the rope. Pulling. He watches his fingers straighten as the knot tightens. Is this what is going to happen to his body? As he releases the knot his hand goes limp, relaxes. His fingers curl with relief.

He shouldn't be doing this. He's beginning to prefer feeling rope free. But then he thinks of her and what his life has become. He neatly coils the rope and puts it in his pocket.

It's time to go.

Two belts. That gives him about seven foot to play with.

Jonno sits on the branch dangling his feet over the edge. There isn't much left of the tree house. It was supposed to have been built to last. Nothing lasts. Except pain. And love. Two sides of the same coin.

He joins the belts together, buckling one to the other, then tries to buckle it to the branch. It won't because when he tries to pull it tight the two buckles meet and won't pass over each other. He'll have to only use one. He sidles along a few inches to where the branch thins and fastens the belt around it.

But he hasn't got enough length to make a loop big enough for his head, tie the knot and jump. He can only manage this if he does it lying down. Then he'll have to roll over the edge.

He spreads himself along the branch.

The spot was chosen a while ago. It has to be as near to her as he can get. He has to provide maximum opportunity for her to be the one to find him. Robin wishes he could guarantee this. Ideally he would like her to find him in the house. The home that should have been theirs. But now it was never left unattended. He's been humiliated enough times already trying to see her, enter their home.

It isn't exactly how he wants it, but he's determined, as always, to make the best he can out of a bad situation.

It's after midnight.

He crosses the Heath without even a moon to guide him. It has to be this way. He can't risk being seen from the road. One field in total darkness. Negotiate the ditch. Maybe there'll be a late lamp burning on the other side. Something to steer him towards his destination. But no. Nothing. He has to feel his way among the trees. Make sure that he was found the right one.

And none of this is easy carrying a small wooden ladder under his arm.

Everything is in place. Jonno takes a deep breath and rolls off the branch. In the time that it takes – an immeasurable time somewhere between a millisecond and eternity – everything changes. The last thing he sees is not the house where he grew up. The last thing he feels is not the impossibility of a life with no refuge.